What people are saying about

The Taking

Dona Masi's debut novel, *The Taking,* finds a most interesting way to bridge two very different worlds: the quaint New England village of Pangea New Hampshire, and a place of uncertain location, light years away from the planet John Diparma and his daughter, Vera, call home. Add to this plateful of literary intrigue generous helpings of anger, disappointment, disillusionment, jealousy, and friendships slowly ripening to romance, and Masi's novel becomes both an emotional tale of Old New England values and a gently woven paean to life both here at home and in corners of the universe so distant, so vast, and so mysterious that we know we've only just begun to understand them.

Ross Alan Bachelder, author of *Revenge: Tales Best Read in the Twilight Hours*

T0282057

The Taking

A Novel

The Taking

A Novel

Dona Masi

ROUNDFIRE
BOOKS

London, UK
Washington, DC, USA

CollectiveInk

First published by Roundfire Books, 2024
Roundfire Books is an imprint of Collective Ink Ltd.,
Unit 11, Shepperton House, 89 Shepperton Road, London, N1 3DF
office@collectiveinkbooks.com
www.collectiveinkbooks.com
www.roundfire-books.com

For distributor details and how to order please visit the 'Ordering' section on our website.

Text copyright: Dona Masi 2023

ISBN: 978 1 80341 550 5
978 1 80341 643 4 (ebook)
Library of Congress Control Number: 2023944137

A CIP catalogue record for this book is available from the British Library.

Design: Lapiz Digital Services

Cover art © 2023 by Patricia Haendler

UK: Printed and bound by CPI Group (UK) Ltd, Croydon, CR0 4YY
Printed in North America by CPI GPS partners

We operate a distinctive and ethical publishing philosophy in all areas of our business, from our global network of authors to production and worldwide distribution.

When people gazed at the sky at night in Pangea,
New Hampshire, they could see the galaxy from their
backyards. The dark nights of sparse streetlights brought the
universe to life and accentuated the starlight on the woods.
Sometimes, unexplained orbs were also seen hovering in the
patch of sky above the town.

Part 1

Chapter 1

Vera stood in the center of the living room with her hand resting on her dog's thankful brown head, the house empty except for them. Her father had promised to be back by the time the bus dropped her home from school, but it turned out to be another broken promise—when he said he'd be there, but she ended up alone, except for Spark. She scratched her dog behind the ears. He always made her feel almost as protected. She pressed her legs against his feathery, soft fur for warmth. Even with her coat on, she felt cold. The woodstove had long since gone out. She had to wait for her father to get home for it to be warm again.

Their house—the one her grandparents had lived in, her father had grown up in, and her mother had lived in once upon a time—was like other old New England homesteads, penetrable to the wind through little chinks even with insulation. On freezing mornings, the cold air and condensation on the windowpanes left murals of frost on the glass. According to Vera's dad, he was going to replace the old, leaky windows with airtight ones when warmer weather arrived.

Not only was she cold, her stomach was growling. She heard loudly the rolling-barrel-with-a-tiger-inside-it sound it made. She wanted to wait for her dad to come home so they could have a snack together like they did sometimes. But he'd broken his promise, so she thought he didn't deserve it. And she reminded herself that she didn't need him to make her a snack. She'd make one herself.

Still, she stayed and waited for him, hoping it'd be soon. She passed the time staring at the fireplace bricks around the woodstove, looking deeply into them, letting herself be hypnotized in order to see down to the minutest grains of sand. That was how she usually observed things: how she watched ants on hot days, her favorite pastime. She'd lie down in a sunny spot on the cement path to her house and watch the insects race off and then hurry back to their anthills with booty fifty times their size.

It seemed a little strange to her the connection she felt with them, as she stared into their tiny world, but she liked it.

And all the while, it never occurred to her how colossal and invasive she must seem to them. She was only seven. She was too young for philosophical questions. But she had an instinct for the truth. The truth was something that went beyond the surface of things.

Staring at the bricks induced a dreamlike feeling that carried her imagination away. Spark nudged her hand with his nose. He had just licked it, and it was slimy. "Yuck," she said, pulling away her hand. He whined and then uttered an impatient bark, and she realized that he was begging to be let outside to pee. She bent and kissed him on his head. "Okay, Spark," she whispered and kissed him again.

He ran ahead to the front door and scrambled outside when Vera opened it. Then he loped down the stairs and around to the backyard. She saw him start to lift his leg on a tree as she closed the door. She walked through the hallway toward the kitchen, hearing her shoes squeak with every step on the wood floor. The sound cut sharply through the empty house and triggered a shock of fear, and again she wished, but harder than ever, that her dad would come home. The shadowy light coming through the kitchen windows spilled at her feet. It glowed on the walls and floor in indefinite shapes, like ghosts, but she closed her eyes and made herself walk past them.

She felt like she could breathe again when she entered the kitchen. It was the brightest room in the house, with its large windows with crisscrossing panes of wood that made it easy for her to imagine that she lived in a castle. The walls were painted a bright lemony yellow that made it seem like the sun was shining even on the darkest days. She went directly into the pantry, which was to the right as you came in. She strolled between the shelves that lined the walls, admiring the jars of canned tomatoes, string beans, pickles, jellies, and jams that she had helped her Aunt Bonnie to make. Aunt Bonnie had grown all of the vegetables and fruits herself, which Vera thought was fantastic. She lifted up each jar to the light and examined its colorful contents with pride, and she felt more than satisfied with herself.

There was a slender window at the far end of the pantry, and sometimes, like now, she stood there and gazed outside at the apple trees. Since now it was winter, they were sleeping, but in the spring they had beautiful pinky-white blossoms that smelled unforgettably sweet and lovely. When she stood in this spot for long enough, sometimes she thought she could hear whispers, and then she'd imagine they were the voices of her grandparents and great-grandparents, who'd lived there a long time ago. She could almost see them picking apples off the trees. And then sometimes she'd take out their pictures to look at, and she'd almost feel like they were there.

It suddenly became darker in the kitchen. The sun had gone behind a cloud. Vera dragged a chair to the cabinet to get a glass. She shuffled the glasses around looking for her favorite Winnie the Pooh glass. Little pieces of glaze had worn off Pooh's red shirt from so much handling, but his friendly face was still vividly intact and smiling reassuringly at her. She went to the refrigerator for the milk and carried it to the table with both hands. When she started to pour, her hands shook with exertion. She doubted she'd be able to hold the bottle steady, and she thought she'd drop it, but her will was stronger than her muscles, and she persevered without spilling a drop. But pouring from the heavy bottle went slowly in splashes and trickles into the glass. When the glass was full, she slid the chair over to the next cabinet for the cookie jar. Reaching it, she dipped her arm in up to her elbow. Three cookies remained of the batch she and her Aunt Bonnie had baked, two for her dad and one for her, or two for her and one for her dad. She took them from the cookie jar and climbed down.

The glass of milk was heavy and slippery, and she was scared she'd drop it or the cookies, or both, carrying them to the table. Finally, she safely set them down on the table with a sigh of relief. It felt like a little victory that she'd managed to do it. At last, she could sit down and eat. She took a bite of cookie and drank a gulp of milk, and Spark barked to come in. She stood up and went to let him inside. He hurried into the house like he was late for something and sniffed the cookies as he passed them on the way to his water bowl. She watched and laughed at the way he drank the water in big, sloppy mouthfuls and chomped at it like it was a bone. Water sprayed sideways from the corners of his mouth and all over the floor.

"You're a really messy drinker, Spark," Vera said. She got a towel and wiped up the spills.

She went back to the table and picked up a second cookie, then dunked it in the milk and counted to five. A couple of soggy chunks fell off in the glass, and she chugged the lumps of cookie pieces and milk. This was her favorite way of eating cookies, and her dad's favorite way of eating them too. The last cookie lay on the paper towel, saved for her dad, though she felt tempted to eat it herself because she liked cookies, and, also, she didn't feel like sharing with him. Outside, the wind thrashed the branches of a tree against the house, and she jumped at the noise. Spark came over and sat at her side. His eyes flashed at the third cookie on the paper towel and then at her. At that moment, she decided that the cookie belonged to Spark, because he never let her down, and she picked it up and popped it into his mouth.

"Don't tell Dad. He doesn't like it when I give you people food."

Then she rose, took her dirty glass to the dishwasher, and left the kitchen. The hallway was much draftier, and she stopped at the closet for a warm hat to put on. Spark came around in front of her and sniffed her dad's old sneakers that were sprawled on the floor.

"Watch out, Spark," she said, as she closed the door.

With Spark following her, she walked to the living room, holding her arms across her chest and trying to pretend she wasn't cold. In the living room, the windows faced the driveway and the road, and she could watch for her dad. As she gazed out, she thought she should get the woodstove ready for him to light when he came home. She went and sat down on the hearth and picked out some kindling from a box that he always made sure was full, and she began to form a little pyre in the belly of the woodstove. She crumpled pieces of paper into balls and laid slender shards of wood on top of them. Then she stuck small pieces of wood inside the openings that would make it light right up. When it was done, she sat back and looked at it. Now it was built, but she wasn't supposed to light it.

"Where's Dad, Spark? It's cold," she said. He came over to her and sat. She shook her head. "We can't light it until Dad gets home."

Understanding, Spark trotted over to his bed and lay down and closed his eyes. Vera watched him fall asleep, and pretty soon he began to bark, making little muffled woofs as he slept.

"He must be dreaming again," she whispered. But she couldn't stop herself from laughing a little.

A few minutes later, the phone rang, startling her. It made her jump, and she accidentally knocked her head against the bricks. It hurt badly enough for her to feel like crying, but she didn't.

"Hello?"

"Hi, it's Louisa."

Vera brightened at the sound of her best friend's voice and stood up joyously on her tiptoes. "I know your voice. Hi, Louisa."

"What are you doing, Vera?"

"Nothing, just petting Spark."

"My mom and I are going shopping. Do you want to come?"

"I don't know if I can," Vera said.

"How come?"

"I have to ask my dad."

"Go ask him."

"He's busy."

"What's he doing?"

"He's working," Vera said, because this part was true. "He's out in his shop." This part was the lie.

"Well, go and ask him," Louisa insisted.

"I can't. He doesn't want to be disturbed."

In the background, Vera heard Louisa's mother Gwen talking. "Does Vera want to come with us?"

"She doesn't know if she can."

"Has she asked her dad yet?"

"She said she can't."

"What? Let me talk to her, honey." A second later Gwen took over the phone. "Hi, Vera."

She smiled at Gwen's voice on the other end of the line. "Hi, Gwen."

"What are you doing now, honey? Want to come shopping?"

"Yes, I want to go."

"What did you say? I didn't hear what you said."

"I said I want to go."

"Well, ask your dad. I'll wait."

Vera hesitated. She knew what Gwen would think if she told her the truth.

"Vera, is your dad home yet?"

"No, not yet, but Spark's here."

"You mean he didn't — never mind. Louisa and I are going to come over right now, okay? We'll be there real soon."

"Okay."

"See you in a little while."

Vera hung up the phone and shot a longing glance out the window. She thought she heard his truck coming down the road, but when it passed the driveway she saw that she was wrong. She moved away from the window and placed herself in the center of a puddle of sunshine on the rug. She stood there enjoying the warm light bathing her face. It relaxed her. A second beam of sunlight came through the other window and draped itself over the back of one of the overstuffed chairs. She sat down in the chair in the halo of light and snuggled against one of the chair's big arms, which was as plump and comfortable as the bosom of a matronly aunt. As she sat there, she thought she should do her homework. She had to study the list of words she had to learn for spelling. She closed her eyes and saw them in her head: *sail* and *sale, red* and *read, deer* and *dear* . . . but the warm sun made her too sleepy.

She tucked her hands between the cushions of the chair and closed her eyes and fell into a half-sleep, and dreamed that her dad would be home soon. She hardly noticed that time was passing and the sun was waning in the late afternoon sky, drawing its light away. She was watching a scene play out in her mind of his truck coming to the trees in front of the house and turning into the driveway. Then he got out of the truck and called her name as he came into the house.

She didn't know at first that what she was thinking was real, but the noise of the engine made her open her eyes. She looked out the window to see if she was right, and in the driveway, she saw her dad's black truck with the stenciled letters that spelled the name of his business, John Diparma Construction. She pressed her nose to the window and watched as the truck door opened and he stepped out with a bag of groceries in the crook of his arm and his tool belt slung over his shoulder. The urge to run and meet him was so strong that she could hardly resist it.

"Vera? Where are you?"

She didn't answer. She wanted to make him find her.

"Vera? There you are, sweetie. Hi."

"Hi."

He walked over to her and knelt down on one knee. "You're awfully quiet. What's the matter?"

"Nothing."

"Okay." He hugged her, and she deigned to hug him back, but loosely. "I'm sorry I'm late," he said. He turned to Spark and rubbed his bobbing head. "Hi, good boy."

Vera stepped away from him. "Where were you?" she said.

"I was at work, of course. But I couldn't get away on time. You've only been home a few minutes anyway, right?" he said, kissing her cheek.

No, it was longer than a few minutes, but Vera didn't say so.

***

John stared down at the top of his daughter's head; it was the only thing that was clearly visible of her, for she had turned her face away. He studied her coolness toward him with the eye of someone who'd experienced it many times. Obviously, she was pretty mad at him, and he felt guilty about it. He told himself not to be late the next time.

"Did you get yourself a snack?" he asked.

"Yes."

"Cookies and milk?"

"Yeah."

"Good. Are there any cookies left?"

"No, sorry."

She sounded smug to him, but he ignored it. "Oh, that's all right. It doesn't matter. You and Aunt Bonnie can make some more."

"What kind do you want next time?" Vera asked.

He was glad that she seemed to care. "Any kind is fine with me. They're all good." He noticed that she was shivering. "Are you cold? Of course, you are. It's cold in here. Come help me start a fire."

He let go of her gently and walked to the thermostat. "You could've turned up the furnace if you were cold. I've showed you how, remember?"

"Yeah."

"Why didn't you?"

"I don't know."

He sighed. *My little martyr*, he thought, and he rotated the dial until he heard the furnace kick on.

"I can't reach the thermostat," Vera said.

"You could've stood on the couch," John said.

"I thought we were going to have a fire anyway."

"Yeah, but in the meantime, the furnace will get it warm in here until the fire gets hot." He went to the woodstove, and Vera followed him.

"It's ready to light," she said into his ear as he knelt in front of it and opened the door.

"It sure is. Good job," he said, patting her on the back. He thought to himself how well she'd learned to do the things he'd taught her. It made him feel proud that she was so independent for a seven-year-old kid, but then there were some things she refused to do just because he wanted her to do them.

"Aren't you going to light it?"

"Hold on," he said. "I need a match, of course." He took a long matchstick from a tin box on the hearth and struck it on the bricks. He put the flame up to the paper between the kindling, and in a few seconds the fire ignited. "I'll fetch some logs from the porch."

"I'll get them," Vera said. She stood up before him and rushed to the door.

"Okay, don't hurt yourself," he said.

"I won't." When she came back, she was carrying two big logs in a bundle in her arms.

"Wow, thank you," he said, helping her to put them down. He squeezed her small bicep. "My, what a strong little thing you are."

"Thanks. Put a log on. The fire's going to burn out."

"Okay, okay, muscles. Keep your shirt on. I know what I'm doing," he said, shaking his head. He opened the door and threw in a log. "There we go. Thanks for all your hard work. I couldn't have done it without you, baby."

She picked up the other log and handed it to him. "Put this one on too."

"Okay."

The fire grew. They sat on the hearth staring at it through the glass panel on the door. They were quiet. The cast iron of the woodstove pinged and rang as it got hotter. John reached behind Vera and turned on the blower, and a warm stream of air poured out and began to fill the room. He put his hands into the flow of heat and rubbed them together to warm them, and Vera did the same. He reached for her hands and wrapped his big papa bear paws around her small baby bear ones. She scooted nearer to him, and without realizing it, she began to thaw.

"I'm sorry I wasn't here when you got home from school," John said, knowing that an apology probably wasn't good enough for her. "But the job I was doing was harder than I thought, so it took me longer than I expected."

"But you promised."

She is pissed at me, he thought. But she had a right to be. "I love you, Vera, more than anything in the world. I shouldn't have left you on your own. You're too young for that. You weren't scared, were you?"

"No."

"That's good," he said, feeling a little less guilty. Since she seemed to accept his apology, he felt free to act like her father again. "Do you have homework?"

"Spelling."

"Okay. Anything else?"

"No."

"Nothing else?"

"I'm not lying."

"I didn't say that you were lying. But when I was a kid, sometimes I fibbed to my parents about my homework, so as your dad, I wanted to be sure you weren't leaving anything out. I just want you to keep doing well in school, Vera."

"I didn't lie."

"Okay, okay. Anyway, you'd better get busy. I've got things to do too. I'll be in my workshop. Let's get our homework done now so we don't have to worry about it later."

"Can we play a video game tonight?"

"After we eat and do the dishes. So, where's your homework?" he said, looking around for Vera's books.

"In my backpack."

"Where's that?"

"On the stairs."

"Better fetch it."

John waited for Vera to take her sweet time to get her homework. "Are you coming?"

"Yeah," she said, as she stepped back into the living room.

"Make yourself comfortable and get to work," he said, before he turned to leave.

"Will you test me on my words later?"

"Yes," he called over his shoulder at her, and he went into the kitchen and then outside.

***

Vera settled down with her homework in the overstuffed chair and dumped the contents of her backpack on the floor. She fished the pile for her spelling workbook and opened it on her lap. It took several minutes to pick out the colored pencil that she preferred to write with this time. She barely got started when she remembered that Gwen and Louisa were on their way over. She threw the book down and ran out of the living room. Spark was roused from his nap by the commotion, and he lazily got up and trotted after her. They went outside and then down the short path to John's workshop and burst in on him.

John looked up from his workbench in surprise. "I thought you were doing your homework. What did you come out here for?"

"I forgot to tell you. Gwen and Louisa are coming over."

He stopped what he was doing and stared past where Vera was standing. There was a stunned and worried look on his face. "When are they coming over?"

"Pretty soon."

"Come on. We've got to pick up the house."

Vera ran to keep up with him. "Wait, Dad. Can I go shopping with them?" she said.

"Shopping? When do they want to go?"

"Right now."

"You have to do your homework."

"I'll do it when I get home."

"You'll be too tired," John said, shaking his head. "Tell them another time. Okay?"

"Please, Dad? They're coming to pick me up."

"Why didn't you ask me first?"

"You weren't home yet when they called."

"So it sounds like I don't have a choice. All right. But you'd better do as you promised and finish your homework when you get home. It'll keep you up past your bedtime, though. And frankly, I don't like that."

"I don't break promises," Vera said.

After a few seconds, John said quietly, "They'll be here anytime. This place is a mess. Help me clean it up."

Vera turned around three hundred and sixty degrees to check the room. "I don't think it's messy."

"Yes, it is. And we're wasting time."

She didn't jump in to help right away when he began to pick up the clutter. He put some things away where they belonged and found places to hide the other stuff. "Why don't you put those pillows back and fold up the throw blanket," he suggested.

She picked them up and tossed them uncaringly onto the couch.

"Take it easy, Vera. You're so rough on things."

She folded the blanket with exaggerated neatness and set it smoothly on the back of the couch.

"Better. Now please pick up your shoes and take them up to your room."

Vera stared at her shoes, which lay side by side tucked under a chair. Then she looked at his shoes, which were splayed apart, one by the woodstove and the other one under the couch. It hardly seemed fair. He hadn't picked up his shoes. She knew a hypocrite when she saw one.

"Your shoes, Vera?"

"You should pick up your shoes," she said.

"Yes, and I will. But I told you to put yours away."

She didn't budge.

"Vera?"

Vera whisked up her shoes and threw them one after the other at the door of the woodstove, like dual grenades. When they hit their target, they ricocheted and came halfway back across the floor. "You're mean. I hate you," she screamed.

"What are you doing? You're going to break the goddamn glass."

Tears streamed from her eyes. She could barely see through them. She ran away upstairs to her bedroom and slammed the door. Her explosion of outrage reverberated through the house.

***

John stood at the bottom of the stairs, looking up after her. *What the hell just happened?* he thought. He went back to the living room to pick up his shoes and put them away. When they were in his hands, he squeezed them like rubber stress balls, and it took the edge off his frustration. He set them in the closet, and while he was in there, he brought out his guitar. He took it out of its case and walked to the windows in the living room, strumming a few deliberately connected chords—the beginning of a song he was writing. He'd been working on it for a long time and hadn't quite figured it out to his satisfaction. For a while, he'd lost interest in it, but lately he'd returned to it. For the last few nights, he'd started pecking at it again after Vera had gone to bed, and he felt at last that he had the tune now, but it needed words. He walked around playing and singing phrases that came to him to try them out.

He saw that the moon had come out, and he sauntered to the window and played the fledgling song to the newly risen lunar disk. The music also traveled upstairs and into the wide-open hallway on the second floor. The acoustical echo made John think about when he and his friends would play their guitars together in college in the voluminous stairwells of their dorm.

***

Chapter 1

Vera lifted her face off the pillow when she heard him singing. The words were hard to hear through the closed door, so she got up and opened it a crack. She sat on her bed and listened for a little while, but the music was drawing her to him. And so she rose and left her room. She crept halfway down the stairs and sat down and tried to be very still and quiet.

His back was turned to her, and she knew he wouldn't be able to see her in the spot where she was on the stairs. It was a brand-new song for her, and she liked it. She liked how he sang it. His voice was full and raspy, and it sounded fantastic to her. She felt a strong urge to start dancing, but she made her shoulders rigid to stop herself from swaying and bouncing around. She pointed her eyes straight ahead at the octagonal window for a focal point to keep still. Like that she sat without moving a muscle and watched the sky as she listened to him play.

Outside, the sky grew darker, and while this happened her imagination took on a life of its own. She saw long columns of shadows across the lawn. Many other times like this she had stared into the dark, trying to see inside it or through it, because she thought it was hiding something.

It seemed to her now that something moved in the dark front yard. It was only a little movement that attracted her attention, just a tiny flicker, but seconds after, there was more movement. She tiptoed down to the next landing and looked out more closely at the yard. There were multiple circles of shiny red lights floating together in a line. Then the headlights of a passing car swept across the yard and illuminated it so that she could see six white flashes and faces, and she realized that she was looking at a small herd of deer that'd come to eat the shriveled crabapples off the tree. She was delighted to see the does. She looked around to see if there might be a buck around. Her dad said that when you saw a herd of does there might be a buck that was following them.

17

The deer gathered in a pool of moonlight that shone down on them. The light was becoming brighter, and the deer stood frozen, as if they were trapped by it. Vera thought the moon was unusually big and bright. It was hanging very low above the tops of the trees, almost teetering on them. Then it started to fly horizontally in the sky, and she was shocked because the moon was not supposed to move that way. A second later, the moon started to fade before her eyes. It faded and faded until it was swallowed by the dark, and then it was gone.

She screamed, and John put down his guitar and hurried to her. "What's the matter?" he said, pulling her toward him to hug. "Are you hurt? Did you fall down the stairs?"

"No," she said, shaking her head emphatically. "I saw something scary." She pointed outside.

He looked out the window and among the trees for the strange person or animal that might've startled her. "Wait here," he said. He stepped outside and walked around, but he didn't see or hear anything. All was empty and quiet, and he went back in. "There's nothing out there, Vera. What did you think you saw?"

"The moon."

"The moon? What's so scary about the moon?"

She didn't know how to answer him. It had just acted strange. The memory was already disappearing from her mind, and it'd just happened. She didn't want him to ask her questions. At the moment she thought he was going to, the doorbell rang.

***

John noticed a pair of his socks on the floor and picked them up and shoved them in his pocket. As he crossed to get the door, he remembered that he hadn't seen Gwen in couple of weeks, but it felt much longer than that to him. He turned the knob and opened the door wide, and Gwen and Louisa came in. When he looked at Gwen, he had to stop himself from gawking. His eyes were bedazzled by her silver earrings. They glistened against her neck. He felt like a crow obsessed by a beautiful, luminescent object that it'd found and didn't want to let go.

"Welcome," he said.

"Hello, John."

"Hi," Louisa said, as she hurried to the stairs where Vera was.

"Hi there, Louisa," he said.

Now, he and Gwen were alone and facing each other. He noticed her hair, which she wore piled on top of her head in a messy bun. He liked the look a lot. Then it occurred to him that she might be able to tell what he was thinking, so he stopped.

"So how are you, Gwen?" he said casually.

"Fine. So when did you get home?"

He knew he was being criticized. "A little while ago." He stepped away, feeling the need to distance himself from her. "So Vera said you asked her to go shopping with you."

"Yes, we won't be out that long. Did she ask you?"

"Can Vera come?" Louisa said, piping in enthusiastically.

"Yes, I told her she could," John said.

"But that's not why we rushed over, though," Gwen said. She tossed her head back and looked him in the eye.

It was plain to him that she was mad at him and was dying to tell him that. Before either said anything, they heard Louisa talking worriedly to Vera and trying to comfort her.

"Don't cry, Vera. Why are you crying? Vera's crying, Mom."

"What's the matter, Vera?" Gwen said, going to her.

"She said she was scared when she looked outside," John said.

"Scared of what?"

"I'm not sure. It just happened a few minutes ago. I was talking to her when you and Louisa got here."

Gwen put her arm around Vera. "I'm sorry we couldn't get here sooner, Vera. At first my car wouldn't start."

"Your battery again?" John said.

"Yes. My next-door neighbor came over with his jumper cables to get it started."

"That was neighborly of him. I'd be happy to change your battery for you, Gwen. I'll even go and pick a new one up for you, if you want."

"No, thanks. I'll bring the car to my mechanic," she said.

"Great. Then I'm off the hook," he said. And he decided he'd never mention it again. Gwen gave Vera a Kleenex to blow her nose. "Do you still want to come with us, honey?"

"Yes," Vera said, in a voice weak from crying.

Gwen stood up to talk to John. "You still don't mind, do you?"

"No. Can you have her home fairly early, though? She still has homework to do."

"Yes, of course. Vera, are you ready to go now?"

"I have to put on my sweater. It's upstairs."

"Okay, well you guys go do that," Gwen said.

The girls climbed the stairs together to go to Vera's room. Louisa whispered something to Vera that made her laugh. Their giggles echoed in the stairwell. Gwen and John listened to their footsteps treading across the hardwood floor.

"Is it okay to put this here?" Gwen asked, indicating a sack of books to set on the bookcase.

"Yeah."

"We just got these at the library," she said, unpacking them. "I don't think Vera's read them yet."

John touched one of the books and opened the front cover. "Thanks, Gwen. I think it's really nice that you're always thinking of her. She appreciates the books you bring her."

"I know she does."

"And I appreciate it too."

Gwen stepped forward. Her eyes seemed to be saying something to him. He couldn't tell if she was going to kiss him or hit him. Standing next to him, the top of her head was aligned with his jaw, and her hair tickled his chin.

"I guess I'll take this opportunity to say it. I'm a little worried about Vera, John."

"You shouldn't be. She seems okay now," he said. He wasn't being honest with himself. His concern for Vera was more heightened than the ordinary anxiety of a parent. His fears were different than most, more perplexing, stranger. But Gwen didn't have to know that. "She's okay."

"Then why was she crying?"

He breathed deeply and exhaled to remain patient. "She said she saw something in the yard. I think it was just her imagination."

"Well, she does have a great imagination. It's one of the best things about her. But she was so scared."

"You're right, she's very imaginative. So you shouldn't worry anymore."

"I'd like to say something else, John."

"Okay."

"When we called Vera earlier, she was alone."

"Yes, for just a little while. I couldn't get away from work."

"She's only seven years old. Don't you think it's irresponsible to leave her alone at home for any length of time?"

"Irresponsible? Well, I don't think it's a good idea. Today was kind of unusual. Normally, the babysitter is here, or I am," he said. He struggled not to react defensively. He walked away from her and went over to the window to escape. "It was a lot crazier day than I expected it to be."

"It happens more than you realize. I know Vera's a sensible kid and mature for her age, but still, she's only seven."

"I know how old she is," he said. "It's the second time you've told me. Look, getting home late from work once in a while doesn't make me a terrible father."

"I'd be happy to pick Vera up after school and take her to the library with me if you're going to be late," she said. Her shoulders relaxed, and she moved closer to him. "I don't mean to be judgmental. I'm sorry it sounds that way. It concerns me that you don't have a problem with leaving Vera alone."

He crossed his arms against his chest protectively. "How long has your car battery been giving you trouble, Gwen?" It was his turn to say something about responsibility.

"A couple of weeks."

"One of these times, you're going to get stranded somewhere, maybe with Louisa. It could happen in the middle of nowhere too. That seems a little irresponsible to me."

"Come on, you can't compare that to your daughter arriving home to an empty house and a broken promise."

"I don't care what you think about this, Gwen. I'm not an irresponsible parent."

"I didn't say that exactly. I didn't say that. But, whatever, I'm sorry."

"I know I'm not perfect. Neither are you. And you know as well as I do that it's harder when you have to do it alone. So cut me some slack."

"I know, John. But what if there was a fire or a weirdo showed up at the door?"

"You don't need to tell me about the bad things that happen in the world."

There were sounds of laughter and bouncing from Vera's room.

"They're jumping on the bed," John said. "Vera sounds happy enough now."

"Can we go outside and talk?" Gwen said.

"Why?"

She looked up the stairs and then back at him. "Please."

"All right, and we'll check out the stars at the same time."

Gwen paused at the threshold. "Don't you want your coat?"

"I'll be fine."

Gwen pulled her jacket collar higher around her neck as they walked away from the house. When they stopped, they saw the bright light in Vera's room, and they could see the girls jumping on the bed. It was a dark night with a large moon, and there were a few wispy clouds.

"It's cold tonight," John said, zipping up his fleece pullover.

"Go get your coat."

"I'm fine."

They walked a few steps more, and it took them out of the perimeter of the porch light, and they could no longer see each other distinctly.

John put his cold hands inside his pockets. "We won't be out here all night, right?"

"No," she said, grinning at him. She squeezed his arm and drew away again just as quickly.

For a second, he thought about holding her hand — but only for a second, because there was no purpose in it. It'd send the wrong message, and he wasn't sure that he meant it or that she would want to know about it.

"I got you to come outside so the girls wouldn't overhear this. I should've told you about it before now, John."

"What is it?"

"I didn't think it meant anything at the time."

"What happened?"

"About a month ago when Vera was at our house, they were playing in the yard, and at one point, Louisa came in to go to the bathroom. Vera stayed outside on the swing. I looked outside to check on her. I saw her swinging back and forth, and she seemed perfectly fine."

"Then what?"

"Then she started screaming, and I ran outside. She was in tears for no apparent reason. I looked and she wasn't hurt. I took her in the house and we sat down and I tried to get her to say what was the matter, but she was upset and incoherent. All she said was something scared her, but she couldn't tell me what it was."

"I don't have any idea," he said.

"Neither did I. So I tried to take her mind off of being scared. I took them on a bike ride. She enjoyed it, and it seemed to make her forget."

"She scared herself with her imagination again," he said. "Like she always does."

"Maybe there's more to it, whether it's something she's imagining or not. One time I heard her tell Louisa there were strange people who came to take her. Could these be hallucinations?"

"I think it was just her imagination."

"You're not worried at all?"

"I told you. I think she's fine."

"She told Louisa that she calls the strange people the little men."

"The little men?"

"It's not a joke."

"I'd never joke about the welfare of my kid, Gwen."

"I wasn't trying to insult you. Just bringing your attention to something. Do what you think is best."

"I will."

"Of course."

"Do you hear them?" he said, pointing at Vera's window. "Listen to them laughing. Vera's happy and laughing like a normal kid."

"Yes. But don't you think she must feel lonely sometimes, though?"

"We all feel lonely sometimes. Of course, she does. She hasn't got a mother. But thank God she has my sister and you."

"She does, but you're the most important person in the world to her, and she's very proud of you."

"Oh, really?"

"She tells me so all the time."

"Not to me. Not often. Thanks for mentioning it. That's nice to hear."

"I don't know if she realizes you're proud of her, though."

"I am proud of her."

"I don't think she knows that actually."

It mattered to him what Gwen thought of him, and she thought he was a terrible father. "Man, you're on a tear tonight."

"I don't mean to be critical. But I care about Vera. How could I not care about her?"

To hear her express her feelings about Vera softened the rock in his heart. *Thank you for loving Vera and watching out for her.*

Spark barked inside the house a few times and stopped.

"He's probably feeling left behind," John said. "Hey, look up. The stars are coming out."

"Oh yeah, they are. They're gorgeous."

"It's a pretty night."

"It is. John, Vera never talks about her mother. Is that because she doesn't really remember her?"

"Vera was still a baby when her mom went away. She was two."

"Oh, that's so sad. She hasn't seen her since then?"

"Neither of us has seen her. The older Vera gets, the more she looks like her mother."

"Oh, really?"

"Yeah. But as far as her personality goes, she's more like me. Unfortunately for her, right?"

"Don't say that, John."

"Sorry. For a second, I was feeling a little sorry for myself. I'm done."

"So, how long were you and her mom together?"

"We would've been married ten years, and before that we were together for a few others."

"What happened to her?"

"She didn't die. Not as far as I know. I don't know if she's alive or not. I don't know anything about her other than what I knew before she left. So I don't know."

"That's all right. Thank you for sharing that with me."

"You're welcome," he said, grinning at her. He'd kept the subject pent up for a long time. It felt good to say something to someone about it. "She walked out on us."

"That must've been really hard. I'm sorry," Gwen said.

His armor was chinked when he looked into Gwen's eyes. They showed her concern and empathy. He caught himself looking for something else in them too. "Yes, but it's worked out all right. Vera and I are happy most of the time. That's what matters," he said. But he couldn't stop wondering what could've been if Suzy hadn't left.

"What was her name?" Gwen asked as if her mind had penetrated his thoughts.

"Suzanne," he said, picturing her. "Suzy."

Gwen paused. "And you could never find her?"

"No. I looked for her for a long time, and I never found her. So did the cops. For a while, I thought they were going to charge me with her murder. Fortunately for me, they never found a body. Ha, ha. Yeah, and then I finally gave up looking. I gave up on ever finding her so I could get on with what I had to do."

Gwen fell quiet. John knew the question she was going to ask next.

"Why did she leave? I mean, it's disturbing that she never came back to see Vera," she said. "That's probably too private.

You don't have to tell me, not if you're uncomfortable." Her voice trailed off on her last syllables.

He laughed. It was such an understatement to say he felt uncomfortable talking about it. "Well, no, it's not a comfortable subject. That's why I never talk about it. Actually, I try not to think about it too much."

"I understand. Why would you?" she said. "But Vera is Louisa's closest friend, and you and me, we're friends. I think of us as friends."

John pulled his hands out of his pockets and rested his arms against his sides. "Me too."

"I love her."

"I appreciate that, Gwen. You and my sister do everything for her. But my sister's a bit of a pain in the butt. I love her, but she can be hard to take. Too bossy," he said not unkindly.

"I won't tell her you said that."

"She already knows," he said. "I tell her. And she calls me an asshole."

They laughed. It felt like an opening—a glimmer of a moment to grab hold of and test the waters again, like he'd been doing for years but had never taken any farther. But just as he felt that urge, he thought of Suzy again. Why after so long did he feel he had to be loyal to her? She was the one who left them without even leaving a note. That was a long time ago, but it hurt when he thought about it.

"Suzy was a beautiful person. But she had emotional problems and depression that got worse after Vera was born. She would hear voices and see things. I thought they were delusions. That's what her doctor thought."

"What kind of delusions?"

"I don't know," he said. He shut his eyes to think. "She said she saw strange people coming to take her away—demons, ghosts, I don't remember what she called them."

"She sounds so troubled. It must've been difficult to know what to believe," Gwen said.

"That what she saw was real? Yes."

"Maybe those things really do exist."

"Maybe so."

"Did you ever consider the possibility she was telling the truth?"

"No. I didn't believe any of it."

"Oh," she said. "What about Vera?"

"What about her?"

"Could she be prone to the same delusions?"

No, enough, he thought. "It's too cold now. Let's go back in."

He started toward the porch, and Gwen walked alongside him. He opened the front door, and a funnel of cold wind shot into the house and whistled down the corridor.

On the second floor, Vera opened her bedroom window and leaned out and let herself be captivated by the stars. Louisa's squeaky voice chattered at her in the background. Vera tilted her head as far as she could to one side for a fuller view of the sky, so that she was almost sitting on the windowsill, and she seemed to hear the universe faintly call her by her name.

Chapter 2

Vera shoved her way through a bobbing bottleneck of her second-grade classmates waiting to be let outside for recess. "Everyone in a straight line," the teacher commanded.

Vera ignored her, turned her body sideways, and cut a path through the mass of other children. The teacher opened the door and the bright noontime light burst into the school. Vera rushed ahead of everyone into the sunshine and the fresh spring air. She found a lonely place to stop and closed her eyes and envisioned the sun and giant fireballs shooting out from it into space. She saw a well of infrared colors spilling from the sun's center. She opened her eyes and ran to the hill above the playground and started climbing it.

A few kids caught up with her, and Vera thought that she would make a race of it. She bolted ahead of them and ran at her top speed. All the while, she felt the sun shining on her like a blessing. She was the first to get to the top, and she looked out over the playing field and the schoolyard, the woods and the skyline. The hill where she stood had been the unofficial playground since her dad's time, and Vera thought that he must've looked down from there like this too. The hill was an area separate from the school, where the students went to play at recess even though it was supposed to be off limits to them.

Her dad had said the hill was actually manmade. The earth that had been dug up to build the school was heaped and piled there in giant mound. Then somebody had flattened it and made a plateau. Since then, the topside had been pounded flat into a playing field by thousands of small feet. Grass and wildflowers had propagated down its curvy sides, except on the well-trodden path that kids used to ascend it, and it'd become a little micro-environment of its own.

A boy named RJ sprinted to the top and halted next to her, and Vera took off running. He chased her, and they ran neck and neck toward an imaginary finish line at the edge of a tick-infested spread of high grass.

"We both won," Vera said, out of breath. She sat on the ground to rest.

RJ flopped down beside her. "It's called a tie."

"It's the same thing. Your hair's all messy like a nest," she teased.

"I don't care," he said, feeling his hair. There were clumps sticking straight up, and he tried to smooth them. "I was running."

"I can fix it."

"Quit it, Vera."

"Don't be scared."

"I'm not scared," he said, pushing her hand away.

But Vera had already finished. "There. It's fixed," she said, looking at him. "You have nice hair, RJ."

RJ touched his hair but put his hand right back down. "You should've stopped when I told you," he said. But he was smiling.

So she knew that he was not mad at her. But she did like his hair. It was hard to take her eyes off it. RJ leaned back on his elbows in the grass and stretched his legs out. She wished he had a camera so that she could take a beautiful picture of him with the sunny blue sky behind him.

"Do you remember the first day of kindergarten?" she asked him.

"I guess. Why?"

"That was the first day we met," she said.

"I remember."

"Louisa and I both liked you. We sat with you all the time. I sat on one side and Louisa sat on the other."

"Yeah," he said, as if it was too embarrassing for him to think about it. "My friends used to make fun of me for that."

A group of crows in a stand of trees started to squawk, and then they launched themselves and soared away to another set of trees. The branches bounced down and up when they landed on them.

"The crows sound like they're mad about something," RJ said.

"No, I think they were scared," Vera said.

Suddenly, the crows lifted up again and this time they flew far away beyond the power lines. Vera watched them until they became just tiny specks in the distance. Staring at the horizon, she thought dreamily about what it must be like to be a bird and how they must feel so free. She closed her eyes and tried to visualize beyond the blue to the stars. Then she heard the pound of fast footsteps come up behind her, and she opened her eyes and saw Louisa running toward them.

"It's so hot," Louisa said. She dropped down like a rag doll between them. She tugged her pullover sweater over her head and threw it on her lap.

"You just ran up the hill," Vera said in her sensible voice to contrast Louisa's blithe lilt.

She admired Louisa's yellow shirt that Gwen had gotten for her. Gwen was always buying things for Louisa, but also for her too. The shirt looked nice on Louisa, but Vera could not bring herself to tell her that in front of RJ.

"Let's go play soccer," Vera ordered her friends. "The game started."

She hopped to her feet and started running. She made a quick sprint and then glanced over her shoulder, but they were far behind her laughing and walking slowly. It hurt her because she felt excluded. The hurt was instinctive. She felt that they were ignoring her on purpose, and she was mad. She took off and rushed into the middle of the soccer game that'd already started.

"What team am I on?" she yelled.

"We need you," someone called.

Vera took her spot on the field with her team. She quickly gained control of the ball and moved it toward the net and maneuvered it to make a shot. She kicked and it went in, and the players on her team erupted in cheers. Also cheering were Louisa and RJ as they galloped up to her.

"Good job," Louisa said.

"Yeah, good job," RJ said.

Vera ignored them to focus on the game. She intercepted the ball again and kicked it at the goal, just as a girl from the other team was barreling toward her and neither one of them were looking where they were going. They smashed into each other and collapsed on the ground on top of each other, with the wind knocked out of them.

Vera lay there stunned as Louisa and RJ ran to her.

"Are you okay, Vera?" RJ said.

"Should we get the teacher?" Louisa said.

"No," Vera said. She got up slowly, and when she got to her feet she felt dizzy. The other girl was still on the ground recovering from the collision. Vera stared down at her. "You hit me."

"It was an accident," the girl said timidly. She scrambled to stand up.

Vera pushed her and she stumbled. The girl lost her temper and lunged at Vera vengefully. Vera blocked her swings and shoved her again, sending her flying backward, and her legs crumpled like paper lanterns. The girl started crying, but Vera was amazed at how easily she had knocked her down.

"I hate you." the girl grumbled.

"I don't care," Vera yelled.

"I feel sorry for you, because you don't have a mom."

"I have a mom. I couldn't be born without a mom."

The girl kept beating up Vera with words. "You used to have one. You don't anymore. She's dead."

"You shut up." Vera squared off opposite the girl and put her face only two inches away from hers. "My mom's not dead." "Then she ran away. She ran away because she hates you." "Shut up." The girl shook her head furiously. "She hates you." Waves of emotional pain washed through Vera's body, and then tears began to flow down her cheeks. She didn't want anyone to see them. She longed to get away by herself, because here she was barely breathing and she was blind from crying. She walked off the field past her team and her friends and struck out in the general direction of the woods to find somewhere where she'd be alone.

After only a few minutes, she didn't see the school anymore, but she could hear Louisa and RJ still calling to her. The sunlight poured lavishly on the field where she was walking. It washed the brown grass in gold all the way to the edge of the woods where the field ended. The woods still looked far away to her. But she wasn't tired. She'd never gone this way before, and so the journey felt like an adventure.

Finally, she came to the edge of the woods, to a little clearing with a stump set in the center of it. Walking on the wet, uneven ground had exhausted her, and she sat down on the stump and faced the field she'd just traversed. For many minutes, she sat and paid close attention to everything around her. Everything she saw made her think that she liked the spot. It felt so peaceful being alone there with only the company of the animals. She loved watching two little chipmunks chase each other around her stump. They darted this way and that way going past her feet in a blur, and she only caught glimpses of them.

It stayed pleasant like that for a long while, and during that time she didn't think about school or even Louisa or RJ. It was easy for her not to think about the things that bothered her. But then she began to notice the weather was changing. The temperature of the air changed from warm to cool. The sun had slipped away, and gray clouds had taken over the sky. Now there was a strong wind. It thrashed at the trees around her and forced their bottom branches to the ground. It filled up her shirt like a parachute and blew her hair across her face, and it swept up dirt off the ground and spat it at her.

She covered her head with her hands and curled into herself. She wanted to get out of there, but if she tried to run the wind might blow her away. She wanted more than anything to be back at school with her friends. She wished she hadn't left. Then without warning, the wind stopped, and deep silence drenched the woods. There were no signs or noises of any animals living there. There was a grave stillness over everything, as if everything was dead or didn't exist, and she felt like she was the only person in the world.

She rose to leave, but there was a strange pressure like a big hand on her chest. It pinned her down when she tried to stand. As she struggled, she grew panicky. The sound of her frantically beating heart drummed in her ears. The harder she tried to get away, the more hopeless it all seemed. She felt like she was bound with ropes wrapped around her entire body. Then in the east there was a bright flash of light in the opening between two dark clouds. She thought it was lightning and braced for a terrible storm. But then she realized that it wasn't lightning but the reflection of an object, a long, oblong-shaped object. The surface had a shiny, milky glow. The ends of it on both sides were stuck behind the cover of the two clouds. She didn't know what it was, but it sort of looked like a plane to her, except it didn't have any wings. It seemed to be watching her.

Then it moved. In an instant it hovered over her, and she realized that it'd come for her. A bluish light cascaded from it and shined with great force on her and squeezed out the space and the air around her. She felt as if she was hopelessly trapped — packed in with her feet frozen to the ground. It was the last thing that she remembered.

***

First, she became aware of two blurry images. But when her eyes were able to focus on them, she realized they were chipmunks. She watched them running around chasing each other. They stopped a few times to fight, and then one or the other of them turned and fled. They came so near her that she needed to lift her feet out of their way. As she watched them, she felt that she was being watched, and she also felt a sensation of weight above her head, as if a big, heavy thing was suspended over her.

She looked up to see if there was anything there, and she was petrified by what she saw in the sky. A big silver thing was poised in the wide gap between two clouds. The surface of it gleamed like a piece of quartz, giving off light that hurt her eyes. The worst feeling of dread came over her, and she started to tremble. If she couldn't see it, that meant it wasn't real. She shut her eyes for a millisecond, and when she opened them the thing was gone.

She jumped up and ran out of the woods, running for her life. She ran faster over the soggy, rutted ground than she thought was possible for her. She never slowed down or looked back. Eventually, the school was in sight. She'd no idea how long it'd taken her to go that far. From that point, it was only a few hundred yards to the playground. When she got there, the playground was empty and quiet. It seemed as desolate as the moon.

Her feet pounded on the pavement as she ran toward the school entrance, and she kept running until she was inside the school. She crept past the school secretary working at her desk in the principal's office, and then turned left to go down the corridor where her classroom was. It seemed strange not to hear children's voices, and she wondered why that was. She paused in front of the door of her classroom. She put her hand on the doorknob, but she was afraid to go in because the teacher would want her to explain why she was late, and she wouldn't be able to answer, and then the teacher would tell her dad, and he'd ask her the same question again, and she still wouldn't know what to say. She got up her nerve to turn the handle, but when she tried to push the door open, it was stuck. She shoved it with her shoulder and then with the full weight of her body, and it launched open, knocking her off her feet and dragging her over the threshold with it.

At the back of the room, the students were seated together in a circle with the teacher, who was reading a story aloud. She held her breath, waiting for the teacher and the kids to react to her arrival, but no one, not even the teacher, seemed to notice her. So Vera went to her desk and dragged her chair over to join the circle. She cringed at the noise of the chair legs screeching on the floor, but no one else even flinched at it. There was a small space open within the reading circle across from RJ, and she manipulated her chair so that it fit in it.

RJ was listening as intently to the story as the other students, but when Vera sat down, he looked toward her. They stared at each other. "Where were you?" he whispered.

Vera turned away, ignoring his question. Suddenly, she was very tired. Her mind felt especially weary, and now she could barely recollect anything about the strange atmosphere in the forest or the object she thought she'd seen. She didn't want to forget them, but there was nothing she could do to keep them from slipping away. In a minute or two she could only remember opaque fragments, and then the instant came when the last pieces were extinguished, and time reset to the moment before as if none of it had ever happened.

Chapter 3

Vera walked through the kitchen with Spark at her heels.

"Where are you going?" John said.

"Outside with Spark."

"You could help me with the supper dishes, you know."

"I will when I come back."

"Wait a minute, Vera," he said, as she steamed past him. She went out and slammed the back door behind her. "Hey, take it easy on the door."

The door opened, and Vera stuck her head around it. "I didn't mean to."

"If it breaks, I'm the one who's going to have to fix it or replace it and pay for it. You're old enough to know better. You're ten now, not two."

He was always telling her "You're ten now" or "You're only ten." It confused her. Which was it? Was being ten old enough to know better about everything? What things was it too young for? Now she really felt like going outside just to get away from him. It was a lot less frustrating being with Spark.

She ran down the steps after the dog. He patrolled the perimeter of the backyard, while she stopped inside the vegetable garden, leaned her head back, and took a long drink of the starry night. In the center of the garden was a telescope that John had set up years ago for stargazing. Vera kicked aside the old stalks of a tomato plant that'd grown up the telescope's legs. Its dried-up vines clung in tangles to the tripod. When Vera was much younger, she was too short to stand up to look through the telescope, so she used to kneel on a stool. But when she turned ten, she was finally tall enough. Ten was a magic number. It put her in the double-digits of her life.

Her shoulders almost touched the lower branches of the old apple tree. The tree had outgrown its space, and the branches now spread along the fence of the vegetable garden and between the chain links. She turned her critical eye to the rest of the backyard, which was in the same messy shape. Since it was late winter, everything looked shabbier, including the house. The trim around the windows needed to be painted. Her dad said he hoped to paint the entire house in the summer with her help.

She frowned when she looked at the weather-worn porch with its slightly crumpled foundation. But even with these flaws, their property didn't look neglected. The gardens yielded healthy vegetables and pretty flowers. The roof was new and waterproof. The front door had a new coat of dark green paint. To her, the house, yard, and forested surroundings were all beautiful.

Their home was on a rural road that ran from the center of downtown Pangea into the countryside. The road had tall, dipping hills along it for several miles. Driving on them felt like riding a roller coaster. John called them "grandfather hills." The house was one of a dozen farmhouses on properties that were farms years ago, until one by one the land was sold off to build subdivisions. Sometimes, Vera worried that would happen to their land. Her dad promised to put it into conservation so it never would. Past them a few miles lay a nature preserve with hundreds of acres of forests, rivers, and a small mountain called Blue Jobe.

It was March now, and the sunsets that Vera saw around her home were pink and blue and strikingly perceptible through the undressed trees. Soon spring would come. Spring was like a miracle to her. It took you by surprise and amazed you. It made her happy to think that in a couple of months the bare branches would be bursting with green leaves and blossoms.

The stars were high and bright tonight, and every direction of the sky was perfect for stargazing. In the vegetable garden, Vera pointed the telescope to the north, and she was about to peer through it when she saw Spark digging in the garden.

"Spark, no! Stop it! You're making big holes," Vera yelled. He stopped and lifted his head.

"Come here, boy." He sauntered over to her wagging his tail. "You know you're not supposed to do that, right? Yes, yes, you're a good boy. But don't dig in the garden." She kissed him on his head, and he wandered off again. Vera thought of another thing to tell him. "No skunks!"

He paused and looked back at her and then climbed to the peak of the compost pile and down the other side. She turned back to the telescope. There was a meteor shower that was visible that week, and she wanted to see it. The moon was up, but it was only a little silver sliver of a moon. She liked looking at the sky, but not as a hobby or for any reason like that. Sometimes adults asked her if she wanted to be an astronomer when she grew up, and she always shrugged and told them that she never thought about it. But sometimes when she looked up, it was because she hoped she'd see her mother's face in the starlight.

Spark was back, and he was sitting at her feet. He whined, and that got her to notice him. She peered down at his tilted head and perked ears. He was listening to the sounds that she couldn't hear coming from the darkness. Sometimes she wished she was a dog. She wanted to be able to hear and smell as well as Spark. The night seemed very quiet and empty to her compared to how he experienced it. An urge to hug him came over her. She wanted to do it so badly because he was so smart and she loved him so much.

She touched his neck, and it felt tense. He barked once under his breath and extended his nose out rigidly in the direction of the woods. Something had gotten his attention. She felt something too. Then she saw a blinking light in the woods.

She heard a loud bang behind her, and she gasped and put her hand up to her heart. When she realized that her dad had let the door slam, she wanted to yell at him. She turned around and looked up again. The light was gone.

Her dad walked toward her carrying her jacket. He seemed shy with her watching him. She didn't like that she made him uneasy, so she looked away.

He held out her coat for her to put on. "It's freezing. Quick, let's do this." He helped her into it and tugged it snugly around her shoulders. "You zip it."

Vera carefully hitched the zipper at the bottom of her coat and slid it up under her throat. He smiled at her, and she wanted to hug him, but more importantly, she wanted him to hug her.

He laughed, and she gave him an indignant look.

"What's so funny?"

"Nothing."

"Are you laughing at me?"

"No way." He put his arm around her shoulder. "Can't I feel happy when I look at my daughter?"

She said nothing. She still believed he was laughing at her.

He pointed at the telescope. "Is there anything unusual in the sky tonight?"

"There's a meteor shower," she said. She stuck her hands in her pockets. "You can look through the telescope, if you want."

"For a minute, honey. I still have calls to customers to make."

John knelt like a baseball catcher to look through the telescope. Vera stood behind him and tucked her head into the crook of his shoulder. The spicy smell of shaving cream lingered on him. She was not sure what handsome was, or if there was a special description of it, but in her opinion her dad was a handsome man. He had nice wavy hair that was a little long, and he was fit and strong. He was a musician and wrote music, and he used to be in a band.

They even had videos of his band playing at concerts. He wore leather pants and did splits in the air and danced around the stage with his guitar. She thought it was funny the way the girls in the audiences screamed at him. Some girls even threw their underwear at him, which Vera thought was gross.

Sometimes, she thought about playing guitar in a band too, and she daydreamed about being a rock star. She didn't know if she was as talented as her father, but what mattered more was getting him to teach her to play.

"I think I just saw a meteor," John said.

Vera lifted her head up groggily. She could have fallen asleep thinking on his shoulder.

He moved away from the telescope. "Come take a look," he said. "Do you see anything?"

"Not yet."

"Keep looking." He patted her shoulder. "I've got to go back in."

It shocked her that he was leaving. "Do you have to work tomorrow, Dad?"

"Of course, I do. Tomorrow's Friday. And you have to go to school."

"We only have a half-day tomorrow." Because he didn't say anything right away, she assumed he didn't remember. "Did you forget?"

He breathed deeply. "I'm afraid I did. We'll ask Aunt Bonnie to pick you up."

"But I hoped we could do something fun."

"I'm sorry, honey," he said, not sounding it. "But it's still a workday for me. And it's going to be a busy one."

She wanted to say she didn't care if he was busy. She was lonely. She just wanted to spend the afternoon with him. She'd hoped they'd go to the movies or on a hike. She felt as if he hardly ever thought about her when they weren't together — at least most of the time.

"I thought you liked going to Aunt Bonnie's."

He made her angry. "Yeah. Of course, I do."

"Then what's the problem?"

"The other day you said we'd do something on Friday afternoon."

"We'll do something together at night. We'll get fried clam dinners and go skating or see a movie. Would that make you happy?"

"Okay."

"You don't want to?"

"I do."

"You don't sound like it." He picked up a strand of her hair and shook it gently. "It'll be fun."

"I know."

"It'll be fun."

***

John studied his daughter, trying to understand what she wanted. He noticed how closely she'd grown to resemble her mother. She had Suzy's facial expressions, her cheeks, and her eyes. But she'd inherited her moody and stubborn traits from him. She was restless and anxious to change the world, like him, but he hoped she'd never be as frustrated.

He pointed at her legs. "Where did you get those leggings?"

"I got them from Gwen," she said.

"Boy, that's really nice of her."

"It is. She knows my style," Vera said.

"Yes, she does. They're cute. And they're very bright pink."

"They match my jacket."

"Your jacket's blue."

"Pink and blue go together," she said.

"And that necklace you have on looks new. Is that from Gwen also?"

"Yes," she said, and she showed it to him.

John touched the charm at her throat. "I'm glad Gwen picks out nice things for you that are your style." He knew nothing about little girls' fashion, and so he really appreciated that

Gwen catered to the girlie side of his daughter, because he knew he wasn't up to the job.

"Gwen knows what you like. It looks pretty on you," Vera beamed at his compliment. "Thanks, Dad."

He was glad he'd made her happy, but when he left her to make phone calls, she might feel that he was letting her down. But the calls were for work, and he thought she was old enough that she should understand.

He squeezed her shoulder. "I can't stay any longer, Vera. I have to call some customers. Come in soon, all right?"

"Okay."

Before he left, he took a last deep breath of outdoor air. "It's a very nice night. Isn't it, sweetie?"

She tilted her head and gazed at the sky, trying to see into its depths. She slipped her hand into his and squeezed it, and he squeezed hers back. "Can I ask you a question, Dad?"

"Yeah."

"Do you think Gwen's pretty?"

He felt that he couldn't lie. "Yes."

Vera smiled a little. "I thought so." She seemed even more emboldened. "Then why don't you ask her out for a date?"

He looked at her in astonishment. "What?"

"Why don't you ask Gwen out for a date? I think she'd go out with you."

"I decide who I date, Vera. It's none of your business." He'd wanted to sound firm, but he'd ended up sounding mean. After he said it, he asked himself what about her question should've made him so mad. "It's just that you can't decide for somebody who they like. You understand what I mean, honey?"

"Gwen thinks you're good looking too, Dad."

Despite himself he was interested in what Gwen had said about him. "How do you know?"

"I asked her if she thought you were handsome, and she said yes. And then I asked her if she liked you, and she said yes."

He wasn't a yeller except for an occasional quick outburst, but he wanted to yell at her now. He breathed in and out to control himself. "Well, what did you expect her to say, Vera?"

"I think she really meant it," she said.

For him, the conversation had run its course. "Let's drop the subject," he said. Then he bent over and kissed her on the head. "Come inside soon."

"Hey, Dad."

"What?"

"What are we going to do this weekend?"

"I don't know. What do you want to do?"

She looked at him shyly. "Will you give me a guitar lesson?"

"I don't know if I'll have time."

"Can we on Sunday?"

He didn't have a quick and credible excuse to give her to put her off. "I'll think about it. I don't know if I'm going to have time, though." Then he braced for the stormy reaction he knew was coming.

"You're so infuriating. Every time I ask you, you say no."

"How about this? Tomorrow we'll go by the music store and sign you up for guitar lessons. Ralph's a good teacher."

"But you said you'd teach me."

"That's not exactly true."

"But I've always wanted you to teach me."

"I'm not a good teacher, Vera."

"You haven't even tried."

"Yes, I did. And let's say I'm not a good teacher for you."

"But I hoped."

He winced. "Don't you remember, Vera? The couple of times I tried to teach you things didn't go very well. We just get too frustrated with each other. You'd be better off learning from someone else."

She stomped her foot on the ground, kicking up clods of dirt. "No."

"Okay, you don't like my offer? Forget it then. Obviously, you're not that interested in learning."

"I want to. But I want lessons from you."

He envisioned what it'd be like—a battle of wills just like it'd been before. "We tried that, Vera. And you didn't listen to me."

"I tried to, but the chords were hard, and you—"

"You didn't practice enough. And when I tried to make you practice, you gave me a hard time. You don't learn to play an instrument overnight or all at once. You've got to study and practice for years. I think you'd be more motivated if somebody else was teaching you."

He waited to hear if she had anything to say. "Anyway, make sure you come in soon," he said, and he turned and walked back to the house and went in.

Vera had a clear view of him through the kitchen window, and she saw him pour a glass of water from the faucet. On his way out, he flicked the light switch and the kitchen went dark. Staring into that black space she suddenly felt very lonely — even though she was with Spark standing underneath the magnificent starlight. She wasn't over being mad at him, but it didn't stop her from noticing that something was bothering him. He seemed restless, even sad, and she could feel what he was feeling in her own heart.

From the forest, an owl that hooted startled her. Another owl returned the call. Spark stood up and growled.

"Why are you growling at an owl?" she said, scratching the dog's ears.

There was a flash of light from something in the forest. She caught the light in the corner of her eye and turned toward it. It was a blinking light, a white light like the one she'd seen a short time ago. But after a second, she saw that it had different pale colors that faded in and out—white, silver, blue, red. It was hard to tell how far away the light was. It looked so close, but it could be far away. Spark made burly, threatening growls at the light under his breath. Then it just vanished again as swiftly as it'd appeared.

The two owls hooted at each other again, and then one took off from a tree. She caught a glimpse of its wings pounding in flight and then the silhouette of its body landing on the limb of another tree. Spark walked quickly to the path at the edge of the woods and started to go down it.

"Spark, wait." She turned her head and looked at the house and then back at him. "Okay, we'll go see." She spun the telescope around as she went past it and followed his silhouette into the woods.

He walked at her side for a while, but eventually, he went ahead. The path they were on was wavy and marred with ruts. The earth was still half-frozen and icy. Vera tried to walk without making a sound or falling. She tripped a few times jogging after Spark, and she had to slow down. In a show of understanding, he clipped his pace so she could keep up with him. The walking was hard, but she was proud of herself that she wasn't scared to be in the woods at night alone. She heard noises that sounded like breaking twigs, like several deer were on the move somewhere in the dark. Spark went on point to indicate the direction of the sounds. After a minute or two, the deer were too far away for her to hear them.

As she walked on, she didn't think about the distance she'd gone, until she started to get tired, and then she yawned so hard there were tears in her eyes and her legs felt like rubber bands. And she also felt uneasy about being so far away from her house. Her uneasy feeling evolved into fear when a coyote howled and she spotted it behind some trees. It was close, so close that she could see the moonlight reflected in its red eyes. Then she heard more howling and yelping, and she realized there were several other coyotes, a hunting party. She was immediately aware of the danger, and her fear intensified.

Then she heard the sounds of bodies thrashing in the brush, and something large went down fighting for its life, and she knew that it must be one of the deer she'd heard. She heard it scramble up on its feet, and then its hooves beat the ground, as it struggled to escape from the coyotes. She heard its last moments of screams and terror, when it finally succumbed and fell down dead. The coyotes yipped and howled, celebrating hysterically over their kill. Vera hadn't ever witnessed death. Her first confrontation with it made her heart pound loudly enough to fill the woods.

The image of the poor, dying deer was branded in her mind forever. She turned and started running, as the deer had tried to do. The wind kicked up and blew hard at her face, and so she tucked her neck into her chest, like a turtle, to protect herself from the gusts. The trees rocked and groaned in the wind, swaying so forcefully that she was afraid they'd fall on top of her.

Through the rumble of the wind, she heard the coyotes screaming. She looked around for Spark, but she couldn't find him. Under the cacophony of the wind, she heard him barking frantically. He sounded outraged and scared, and she knew in that moment that the coyotes had trapped him. She started to panic, thinking that he could die. It was too dark to find him with her eyes, so she followed his barking. Just then the moon appeared for the first time that night, big and orange, and at first, she was lovingly grateful to it for coming out to light her way.

It started to rise higher and to float toward her, growing brighter as it moved, until it was a fiery circle that set the sky on fire. The glow from it flooded the woods, and she was able to gather rocks off the ground as she ran toward Spark. She finally came upon him, and she breathed a sigh of relief that he wasn't hurt, but the coyotes had him surrounded. They trotted around him in a circle with slinked stances and open mouths.

Their utter wildness terrified her, but she had to save Spark. He kept barking and snapping to show them that he wouldn't go down without a fight, but she saw he was exhausted and growing panicky. The coyotes would spring on him at once when he weakened, and she couldn't stand it if he died.

"Don't give up, Spark."

He turned his head and looked at her pleadingly. The coyotes looked at her, and she charged them, yelling at the top of her lungs and heaving rocks at them like grenades. She aimed for their heads, snouts, ribs, and backsides, the parts of their bodies where the blows would really hurt them. The coyotes snapped angrily at their wounds and at her. A dizzying wave of fear came over her, but she bombed them until they broke their formation around Spark and ran howling into the woods.

"Spark!" she cried as she ran toward him.

She dropped to her knees and grabbed hold of Spark. He panted under the weight of her body, recovering from his brush with death. She wanted to melt into him and make the two of them one. She sobbed "I love you" into his shoulder and buried her face in his fur. "I'm so glad you're okay." He was the only one that she'd ever cried so hard in front of and the only one that had ever seen her as upset.

Her mom came into her mind, and she felt the pain of longing for her. Vera had a picture that she kept by her bed of her mom and dad looking beautiful and very much in love. She rarely saw pictures of her mom where she was smiling. She usually looked like she was thinking about something that made her sad. Vera wanted to know her, but she'd never been comfortable asking her dad about her. He hardly ever talked about her mom, and when she tried to ask questions, he only talked a little bit and then changed the subject.

A song that her mom had sung to her when she was a baby played in her head. It was one of the few things Vera remembered about her. When she thought about the song, she imagined her mom as an angel in heaven swinging on a star. She lifted her face from Spark's fur and looked at the sky, hoping her mom would be there, but there was nothing to see. She tightened her arms around Spark's neck and laid her head on his shoulder again, setting him off balance. But he adjusted to her weight and bore it kindly. Her chest heaved up and down with uncontrollable sobs. She cried past the point of being exhausted and until she almost collapsed on top of Spark.

After a while, she was so worn out from crying that she fell asleep, despite being so cold, and for a while she dreamed in peace. Her soft snores sounded similar to the flutter of a bat's wings. The little wisps of air that came from her nostrils tickled Spark's ear. Her body slid down his side inch by inch as she slept, until she fell off completely and slumped on the ground. She rolled onto her back with her arms and legs outstretched in her sleep. Spark shook himself and stretched his stiff spine, and then he lay down beside her so their bodies touched.

The peculiar red moon floated above them. Sensing its presence, Spark woke up excited and scared from a deep sleep to a blinding light that rained down on them. He began to whimper and pressed closer to Vera. He blinked several times at the light and covered his eyes with his paws and pushed himself against her as hard as he could, awakening her with his commotion. She woke up from the middle of a terrible dream, and it took her a few seconds to realize that the oppressive light around her and Spark wasn't part of the dream.

"Oh, no." She recoiled from the light. Her heart sank.

She tried to roll away from it, but she couldn't move. Utter silence and a feeling like she was inside of a bubble. She knew that if she yelled she wouldn't hear it. There'd be no vibration or sound. Then it happened. The light slipped under her body and lifted her in the air. Spark barked manically, as it drew her up to the moon-like craft and suspended her beneath it with her head and feet hanging down. In her agony, she was full of regrets. If she'd only listened to her dad, none of this would be happening.

She sobbed, but no one heard her, not even herself. "Oh, Dad."

And then she was sucked up into the belly of the craft, and in an instant, she was gone.

Spark ran around in a circle barking and growling, and in the middle of it he stopped and sat. He tilted his head and howled mournfully, wolf-like; an owl hooted. Then he collapsed from stress and exhaustion and dropped into a comatose sleep.

The red moon receded toward the tree line and shot into the sky like a bolt of lightning, leaving the woods pitch black. It moved faster and faster until it reached a great height, and from there it was just a pale pinpoint of light.

Chapter 4

Sometime in the middle of the night the fire in the woodstove had burned out. John stirred in the recliner and put his arms across his chest in a hug, then he quieted again. The light of the television screen blazed in the pallid living room with its sound turned down. His face was relaxed, and his sleep was soothing, until he began to dream. This dream was similar to other dreams, from which he'd wake up panicked but also knowing and feeling grateful that they weren't real.

He was always a prisoner in these dreams — but didn't know this at first — of a large group of people who he thought were insidiously evil, like in *Rosemary's Baby*, but he never realized they were evil until it was too late. He knew they were evil by their smell, a horrible sulfur smell that he associated with hell. Resisting them and their temptations was the hardest thing he ever had to do. Once he knew about them, he tried to escape. They made him think he had, and just as he thought he was free, they came out of the shadows and circled him. He was captive. In the dream, the loss of his liberty was unbearable for him.

The light of dawn slipped through the windows into the living room, falling on John's face. He was still dreaming; he was standing in a downpour trying to yell, and he felt as if he was fighting for his soul. Finally, his voice broke through, and he screamed at the evil people to free him.

He heard himself yelling loudly outside his dream, and he woke up. His heart was pounding, and when he stood he felt fragile, like he was made of glass. He walked stiffly up the stairs to the bathroom. A shower would snap him out of it and wash away the hangover he had from the dream.

When he got to the second floor, he noticed that the door to Vera's bedroom was wide open, even though she always kept it closed. The room was dark because the curtains were drawn. He said her name and listened for the sound of her breathing as his eyes adjusted. Her bed came into focus, and it was empty, the covers undisturbed. Then he remembered that the last time he saw her he was walking away from her toward the house, leaving her alone in the backyard.

"Vera!" he yelled. He opened the window in her room and called her.

For Christ's sake, where is she?

He turned and ran from the room to the stairs. On the way down, he caught the ball of his foot on a tack in the runner, and it took off a chunk of his skin, but he ignored the pain. He rushed to get his boots by the front door and winced as he shoved his injured foot inside his right one, and he left the laces untied. His jacket was still in his hands as he hastened out of the house. He searched the yard but found no trace of her, and at that point, he stopped and thought about where he should begin to look for her. She'd probably wandered off into the woods with Spark, and he'd eventually find her there somewhere . . . unless.

Oh no, God.

He fled down the path that led into the woods, plunging through a channel of smoky fog and gnarled limbs. Up ahead, he saw a cylinder of early morning sunlight shining through an open patch of the forest ceiling. At its hem lay a one-hundred-foot pine tree with its giant roots unearthed sideways, and he paid his silent respects to it as he passed by. It was a landmark of the forest, and he knew it well. It stirred up memories of skiing out toward pink sunsets, when he was a teenager and would wander in the woods in search of himself. This morning, the woods weren't idyllic, far from it. He entered the thickest part, where he knew it'd be harder to see her.

He clenched his fists and cursed himself for being a shitty father. He'd let her disappear from under his nose, and he knew he'd never forgive himself if anything happened to her. He'd been an idiot, but he'd apologize to her when he found her, and the thought of that consoled him some. A woodpecker was pecking in a tree, and the noise echoed through the forest. He looked around for it reflexively, but it faded in the distance as he moved on.

"Where the hell is she if she's not out here?" he said.

A crow flew away crazily from a tree. John turned his head in time to see it flap across the washed-out sky to another tree. In taking flight, the crow shook free a pink piece of cloth that was tangled in a branch. Now it was on the ground being skipped around by the wind. He knew the moment he saw it that it was Vera's headband, and he ran to get it before the wind seized it and carried it away. He took it from the branch and turned it around in his hands. *Thank God. No blood on it,* he thought. He put it inside his pocket and kept going.

After about a hundred yards, he came to a large circle of coyote tracks in the snow. There were three sets of tracks that led to a circle, and they followed each other around the circumference. In the middle was a set of dog tracks that belonged to Spark. He saw more coyote tracks rushing off into the woods, and then he spotted dog tracks and little boot tracks stumbling off in the opposite direction. Now he was euphoric because he knew he was close to finding them.

He followed their tracks, and eventually they brought him to a clearing of trees in the shape of a triangle. As he approached it, he glimpsed something blue on the ground, and he knew he'd found her. She lay stretched out on her back with Spark rolled up beside her. The trees around them had been severely damaged by something. The branches were torn asunder and left to swivel from their broken elbows until they withered.

He kept his eyes locked on her as he ran toward her. The thud of his footsteps didn't stir her, and even Spark didn't move a muscle at first. John dropped to his knees in front of his daughter and wrapped his arms around her and sat her up. Her head fell backward, and he cupped it in his hand as support. She moaned but didn't wake up. Spark, however, came to life growling and baring his teeth at him, and John was shocked to realize that his dog didn't recognize him. Then Spark lunged at him. John raised his arm to block the sharp teeth that were straining to bite him. While he had Spark by the throat, he struck him in the head with his elbow. Spark cried out in pain and crashed to the ground.

"I'm sorry, Spark," John said. His heart pounded from the violent contact and tears welled in his eyes. "I'm so sorry." By now the dog seemed to know who he was and was looking back at him with eyes full of fear and shame.

Vera had stayed in place on his lap throughout it all, barely breathing and still as a stone. He checked her pulse; it was soft and slow but there. She was holding something in her hand, and he opened her fingers to see what it was — a piece of bark from a white birch tree, coiled in loose concentric circles and singed black. He took it away from her gently and examined it closely, and he wondered how the bark could've been burned. But when he compared it to the trees in the triangle, he saw places where the bark was peeling off and charred like the one he'd found.

There was also an outline of an oval scorched in the earth. They were in the middle of it. Everything felt very strange and dangerous, and his instincts told him he should leave immediately, so he picked up Vera and hurried away from there, with Spark chasing after him.

He walked quickly with long strides, and Vera never felt heavy for him to carry the long distance.

"Dad?"

Her voice, though weak, startled him. "What, honey?"

"I saved Spark."

He smiled and kissed her forehead. "Good girl." He cradled her tighter and continued feverishly toward home.

Chapter 5

John carried Vera into the house and locked the front door behind them. It was contrary to his habit of leaving the door unlocked when he was home during the day, but normally, he didn't feel threatened. He brought her upstairs to her room right away and sat her down on the bed, and she fell back droopily onto the pillows. He left her to rest in that position while he went to call the school to report that she'd be absent that day. He walked to the windows in the hall and stared out at the oak trees as he dialed.

"Good morning, Pangea Elementary School."

"Hi. This is John Diparma. My daughter Vera has a cold, so I've decided to keep her home today."

"Oh, I'm sorry to hear that. I'll let her teacher know. I hope Vera feels better soon, Mr Diparma."

"Thank you. I'll make sure she gets plenty of rest. Goodbye."

Next he had to make a call to a client who was expecting him to tell him that he couldn't make it.

"Hello?" the voice on the other end of his phone said.

"Hey, Steve, it's John. Listen, my daughter's sick, and I have her home from school. So I've got to reschedule our appointment. Would tomorrow morning be okay with you? Sorry for the inconvenience."

"No, problem. I understand. Your kid's got to come first."

"Right."

"I'll see you tomorrow. I hope she feels better."

"Thank you. Bye, Steve."

Having settled those things, he put his phone in his pocket and climbed the stairs two at a time back up to Vera's room. She was sleeping just as she was when he left her. He opened the top drawer of her dresser and got out a nightgown. When he went to wake her up to put it on her, her skin was soaked with sweat and hot, like she had a fever. Her clothes were filthy and drenched. He swept away the debris from the forest floor that was stuck in her hair.

"Vera, come on, you've got to get changed. Your clothes are all wet." He took them and threw them in the hamper. "Here's your nightgown. Put your arms up so you can slip it on."

She sleepily obeyed and lifted her arms. The nightgown fell loosely around her shoulders, baring a small mark on the back of her shoulder. It was triangular in shape and bulged slightly under her flesh. At first, he wondered if it was a mole he wasn't aware that she had, but it looked too symmetrical and unnatural for that. He touched it with his fingertip. It was hard like rock or a piece of metal under her smooth skin. She moaned and rolled away from him suddenly, scaring the hell out of him.

"Vera, Vera—move a little, honey, so I can turn the covers down and you can get into bed."

Half-conscious, she slid to the foot of the bed and lay there with her arm under her head. When he was done, he coaxed her toward the covers and tucked her in tightly, and she fell asleep within seconds after her head touched the pillow. He leaned over her looking at her. Her nose sounded stuffy as she breathed, but other than that, she appeared to be sleeping blissfully, like nothing abnormal and weird had happened. He had to ask himself if there really was something ominous to fear, or if he was just being paranoid. Maybe the things he'd seen meant nothing, and what really happened was that Vera got mad at him and decided to go and get lost in the forest.

But then he remembered the bumpy mark on her shoulder, and he had to look at it again. He pushed her hair out of the way to see it. Yes, there it was: a tiny, pebble-like slab. He put pressure on it with his finger, and it sprung back to position when he let it go.

"Mom," Vera whispered hoarsely.

He was stunned to hear her call out for Suzy after all this time. The last time he remembered her doing that was in the immediate aftermath of her leaving them. "It's Dad, honey. I'm right here."

She opened her eyes and stared him in the face. "I saw Mom. We were together."

"You were dreaming. Go back to sleep, sweetie."

"No."

"No what?"

"It wasn't a dream. We were together."

He didn't know what to say, but it didn't matter. She drifted back to sleep before he had to decide. The blanket had come off her, and he tucked the covers up around her again. Before he left the room to let her sleep, he made sure he left her door open halfway.

The gleaming sunlight when he went into the hallway startled his eyes. He'd almost forgotten that it was morning. He paced the hallway restlessly, thinking whether he should call Vera's doctor. In the end, he decided it wasn't necessary because she seemed okay physically. She showed no signs of hypothermia from exposure or of any cuts or injuries. But what about the bump he'd discovered under her skin? He'd keep an eye on it himself for now and take her to the doctor, if needed.

He walked down the stairs and his footsteps squeaked on the floorboards, making the only sound in the house except for the furnace. He went into the living room, where he found Spark sound asleep on his bed. He was lying on his side, pedaling his legs in his sleep, as if he was chasing something or being chased — reliving the coyote experience, John thought. His growls and barks were faint and distant sounding, like they originated from an alternate reality. John petted the dog's back soothingly until he calmed down, and then he wandered over to the window and pulled back the curtains. He stood there for several minutes, staring at the road, but not a single car went by. It felt abnormally lonely and quiet to him, or maybe his mood made it seem that way to him.

Soon it hit him that he needed a cup of coffee and something to eat, and he went to the kitchen. He made a cup of coffee and looked through the cabinets and the refrigerator for food. He didn't want to cook anything, and nothing seemed appetizing to him, anyway. Still, he was starving, so he talked himself into having a bowl of cereal. Later, when Vera woke up, he'd make a big breakfast for them to share together—waffles. That was his plan, and it didn't matter what time it was.

He finished his cereal and made another cup of coffee, and the hot mug felt pleasant in his hands. He leaned over the counter and pressed the mug against the ache in his lower back and also worked the spot with his knuckles. He thought about lying down, but he wasn't sure if he deserved to rest and relax, because he'd already slept the previous night away, and during that time he'd forgotten all about Vera and allowed her to wander off alone in the woods. No, he didn't think he deserved to be comfortable. Vera could've been killed by those coyotes. All of it was his fault.

Then he thought back to the scene where he'd found her, and he saw it as clearly as if he was still there: the ring of broken tree limbs, the burns on the birch bark, and the oval of burned earth where Vera and Spark were sprawled in the center. A weather event, such as a mini wind vortex, a natural phenomenon, could've caused some of the damage, but he knew very well that it couldn't explain all of the physical evidence. Outside the kitchen window, the branches of a tree swayed in a strong breeze and struck the glass. It startled him, and it wasn't until then that he realized it was such a windy day. For a moment, his attention was diverted as he listened to the wind howling through the woods that surrounded his house with the same bullying force.

Across his property, there were thousands of trees, a forest with a mass of deciduous and evergreen trees—a forest in every direction. He'd grown up with these woods, and he loved them like an old friend, but at that moment he wondered if he could still trust them. He was confused and sorrowful, as if they'd betrayed him somehow. Looking at them made him feel claustrophobic and like he lived inside of a box. A box that anyone could see into through the bare glass.

Something told him to go around and close the shades. He started in the kitchen and went on to the other rooms, and while he was doing it, he wondered whether he was just being cautious or paranoid. In the end, he felt better, so it didn't matter. By then, he wanted to check on Vera again. Before he did, he looked at his phone to see if he had new messages, and he was glad that he had none. He put his phone in his pocket and climbed the stairs two at a time.

Her bedroom door was propped halfway open, just as he'd left it. He quietly entered and went over to her bed. She was sleeping soundly, curled up with her knees pushed against her chest and her arms wrapped around them. He thought of a fiddlehead fern as he looked at her, and the vision of baby fiddleheads growing in the swampy ground in spring was something nice to imagine.

He leaned over the bed and touched her cheek. There was a mist of fine sweat on her face, but her skin was cool. She stirred a little and yawned. He took that as a good sign that things were beginning to return to normal. Since she seemed all right, he left her alone to rest, thinking he'd come back to check again in half an hour. But as soon as he went out of the room, he felt adrift without Vera to watch over, and he didn't know what to do next.

He started to go to his shop, since he had work to do, and he thought if he did some of it now that he wouldn't have to scramble the rest of the week to finish everything on time. One of his failings that he knew of was overbooking his time, which was pretty much what every other construction contractor did to guarantee they had work. He felt compelled to do it, because he rarely found himself in the enviable position of being able to turn down a job. He was a working man, and he needed to work. But as he thought more about going to his shop, he decided that work had to wait for now, because Vera needed him more. He wasn't comfortable leaving her alone in the house, even though he'd just be right outside.

He wandered around the rooms downstairs, trying to think of something useful to do, but he struggled to muster the drive to focus on anything. His mind raced with different thoughts going back years. A little while ago, Vera had asked for Suzy, and now he said his lost wife's name out loud, which he rarely ever did, and he thought about their marriage. There was one night in particular when they'd stood over Vera's crib together holding hands. Black-eyed Suzy. The good memories had dimmed with time, but now he remembered what a lovely person she was, when she was happy in her mind and soul.

He leaned over and put his head in his hands. "Maybe I should've believed her. If I had, then maybe . . ." He hadn't thought of Suzy for a long time, but he'd always truly regretted that he'd doubted her. He stopped before he made himself feel worse. There was no use in reliving the past or dwelling on the mistakes he'd made.

He went back to the living room, and the shades were pulled down. He started to pull them up, and then he remembered that he'd just gone around and pulled every one of them down for the sake of privacy. His body felt too heavy for him to carry around, and the overstuffed chair by the window looked tempting and comfortable. He knew he had too much nervous energy and that he should settle in one place for a while. He stood in front of the chair, swaying from side to side, like he was about to lose his balance, and then he dropped into it, landing with a thud, like a bag of cement falling from the sky.

He leaned his head on the plush upholstery and tried to get comfortable. The cushion in the chair sagged, which hurt his lower back. He shifted around to find a better position, and after he was settled in the seat, he grew uneasy with the quietness of the house and longed to talk with somebody. Before he thought it through, he decided to call his sister. He knew it would please her, since she always complained that she never heard from him. He reached inside his pocket for his phone, but it'd fallen in the crevice between the cushion and the chair. By the time he fished it out, he didn't want to call her anymore. He loved his sister, but he couldn't stand the idea of being on the phone with her for three hours.

After ruling out Bonnie, he wondered who else he should call, and in those minutes, he admitted to himself that he'd wanted to talk to Gwen all along. It happened sometimes, when he felt the desire to hear her voice and to have a laugh with her. On some level he was always thinking about her. A couple of weeks had passed since he'd seen her, ever since the evening he'd dropped Vera off to spend the night with Louisa, and the girls had a rare but terrible argument that had kept them apart. The main thing that brought him close to Gwen was the friendship between their daughters, and they hardly ever crossed paths aside from that.

The cause of the fight between Vera and Louisa was still a mystery to him. When he'd tried to get Vera to tell him, she'd refused. Even though she was still angry and held a grudge, she missed Louisa, and he felt sorry for her. On the night before, there'd been an opportunity for him to spend time with her, but instead, he'd argued with her and gone back to the house, leaving things sour between them. But in his own defense, he felt like he'd had a good reason to get aggravated at her, because she'd embarrassed him by pumping Gwen with questions about him. But as upset as he was about that, he knew Vera was just a child, and he regretted everything about the way he'd reacted. She'd run away because of it.

There was always another chance to make things right. He lived by that motto, especially when it came to Vera, so he decided he'd ask her again about her fight with Louisa and hope she opened up to him. No doubt in his mind Louisa had told Gwen all about it right away, because unlike Vera, she blurted things out of her mouth, dramatically, as if she were an actress in a play. But Vera tended to be private and tight-lipped, and further complicating everything was that he and Vera both had short tempers. Except the difference was that he was the adult and she was his child, and it was up to him to know better. He accepted that it'd been necessary to be blunt with himself, but his berating had gotten too much for him. He began to feel that Gwen was right that he was a bad parent.

The chair he was sitting in suddenly felt like a trap. "Enough," he said, springing to his feet.

He looked down at his knuckles and realized that he was choking the hell out of his innocent phone.

"All right, take a breath. God, what's the matter with me? Am I going to call her or not?"

He dialed Gwen's number. Since she was at work, he thought she might not answer, but on the third ring she picked up.

"Gwen Effingham."

"Hi, Gwen."

His spirits lifted when he heard her voice, and he wanted to tell her that he missed her, but he managed to stop himself from saying it.

"Yes. Hello. Who's calling?"

He was stunned that she didn't recognize his voice. It was something he always took for granted. "It's John."

"Oh, hi. Sorry. I can't hear you very well."

He coughed slightly. "I was talking too low. Is this better?"

"Yes. How are you?"

"I'm glad I caught you," he said, bypassing the question.

"What's up?"

"Well—"

"I'm eating my lunch, in case. Sorry, I just took a bite."

He waited quietly listening to her chew.

"John?" she said, when he didn't say anything.

"I'm here. I'm just listening to you eat."

"That's embarrassing."

"No problem. So I guess I'm not interrupting your work then."

"No. How's Vera? I should've called, but Louisa didn't want me to."

He glanced upstairs. "She's all right," he said, while he pictured himself carrying her unconscious body home from the woods that morning. "She misses Louisa."

"We miss her."

"I don't know what happened, but I guess it must've been pretty serious for them to stop talking to each other."

"Vera didn't tell you?"

"No. You know her."

"I'm so sorry she didn't tell you."

He didn't like it that she felt sorry for him. "It's okay. Just tell me what happened."

"I should've told you right away, but I never thought the hard feelings between them would last this long."

"Was it Vera's fault?"

"No. It was neither one of their faults. Vera had a nightmare the last time she slept over at our house. She was moaning and crying in her sleep. Louisa woke up, and when Vera woke up she was very upset. She tried to tell Louisa about the dream, but Louisa didn't want to hear about it, because she was scared too. But Vera didn't stop, and Louisa screamed at her, and then they were both screaming at each other. I ran into the room, and

Louisa was crying, and she didn't want to stay there with Vera. So I brought them both to my room and they slept there with me."

"What was the dream?" He thought about other times when Vera had woken up from a terrible dream.

"When I asked her about it, she said that she was three years old in the dream, and there were people who came into her room and took her away with them. They made her float in a light in the sky up to a big dark shadow, but she couldn't see what it was."

"Did she say anything else?"

"No, that's all. But try asking her yourself."

"Are you being sarcastic, Gwen?"

"No, John."

"I don't think I need to ask her."

"Why not?"

"I just don't."

"What do you mean?"

He heard light footsteps creaking across the floor upstairs. "I can't talk about it now, Gwen."

Vera's shadow appeared on the staircase. "Hey, Dad?"

"I'm coming, honey," he said. "Gwen, I've got to go. Vera didn't feel well today, so I kept her home from school. She needs something."

"What's the matter with her?"

"She's got a cold."

"Oh."

"Yeah, just a small cold, but thanks for your help."

"I don't feel like I helped you."

"You did. One way or another, you always do."

"Dad?" Vera hailed him again.

"I've got to go. It was good talking with you."

"Tell her I hope she feels better. Let me know if there's anything I can do."

"Jesus," John said, glancing at Vera's reflection in the mirror in front of him.

She was standing at the bottom of the stairs, holding her hand over her nose and swaying feebly, like a reed in the wind. Her hands were bloody, and her nightgown was heavily splotched with blood. He rushed over to her.

"I have a bloody nose," she said, blood running down her throat as she talked.

"It's all right, honey."

"Am I going to die?"

"No, no, of course not. A bloody nose is messy and scary, but its harmless. Sit down here." He made her sit down on the stair. "I'm going to get a warm, wet towel."

He picked up his phone on his way to the kitchen. "I'm sorry, Gwen."

"Is Vera all right?"

He turned on the faucet and ran warm water over a soft towel. "She's got a bloody nose."

"Oh, no."

"She'll be okay."

He returned to Vera and placed the towel gently over her nose.

"Is that Gwen?" Vera asked, tapping his arm.

"Yes, honey."

"Tell her I can't wait to see her."

"Vera said to say—"

"I heard her. Tell her we miss her. John, don't let her lean her head backward. Have her lean forward slightly over her knees."

"I know what to do."

"Is she upset?"

"No, not really."

"Good. It's common for kids to get bloody noses, but I'm surprised that Vera got one. I thought she would've been past the age."

"I don't know."

"I'll let you go so you can take care of her, John."

"Before you go, Gwen. Maybe we should take the girls hiking soon, as a way of getting them back together."

"Good idea. I agree. Where would we go?"

"Blue Jobe."

"I've never been up there."

"It's beautiful."

"I'm sure. Get back to me about it. Bye, John."

"I will. Take care."

He kneeled next to the chair where Vera was sitting and holding the towel over her nose, and he was relieved that the bleeding had almost stopped. He rubbed her back softly, making little circles with his hand, the way he'd done when she was a baby.

"How do you feel?"

"Okay. Can I sit up?"

He helped her.

"My back hurts. Have I ever had a nosebleed before?"

"Probably, but I don't remember exactly."

"I don't either. I wonder why I got one now."

"It just happens sometimes. Don't worry about it."

"It's just that—"

"What?"

"It felt like there was something stuck in my nose, like there was a pin up there or something. But I can tell it's not there anymore."

"Jesus."

"What's the matter, Dad?"

"Does it hurt?"

"No, just a little sore and strange feeling. It's annoying."

"Maybe I should take you to the doctor—"

"No, Dad, I don't want to. I feel okay. I do. See, no more blood."

"I'll be keeping a close eye on you."

"I don't feel sick."

"Good."

"But I'm so tired. Did something happen to me? I feel like something did, but I don't remember."

"You got lost in the woods last night, and I found you this morning there."

"Spark was there too."

"Yes, he was with you."

"I remember that, but we weren't lost. Did I fall asleep in the woods?"

"Yes."

"And you found me?"

"Yes."

"Why can't I remember very much?"

"You look so tired, Vera. Go back to bed and have a longer nap."

"Will you come up with me?"

"Sure, of course. Go ahead. I'll be right there."

He took the bloody towel from her and put it in the sink to soak and went upstairs to her room. The door was closed three quarters of the way, and inside she was changing her pajamas. He waited outside until she was finished.

"You can come in now," she said.

He gently pushed the door open and went in. "Climb into bed and I'll cover you up."

She obeyed, and he spread the thick comforter up to her chin and patted it close to her body.

"Dad, you're tucking me in like I'm a baby," she said.

"Oh, I'm sorry."

She took his hand. Her eyes were dark and frightened. "It's nice."

It'd been years since he'd cried, but he almost did now. "I love you. Go to sleep," he said.

She closed her eyes and pushed her head deeply into the pillow. "It's light outside. How come I'm sleeping during the day? I'm supposed to be in school."

He touched her hair. "Shh. Go to sleep. I'll sit here with you for a little while." But he planned to stay for the hours to come for as long as she was asleep.

"Okay," she said, nodding groggily.

It surprised him how fast she fell asleep, like a much younger child, and he was grateful for that. He bent over and kissed her cheek and wished her sweet dreams. He hoped that wish would come true. Then he walked to the armchair and sat down in it. While she slept, he'd try to figure things out. It was necessary that he think, whether he wanted to or not.

He thought about the questions she'd asked about what had happened to her. She didn't remember much, and he wanted it to stay that way. He wished that he could be as oblivious too. He tried to talk himself into thinking rationally and to stop imagining things. But the broken branches, the peeling birch bark, the charred earth, what did they have to do with Vera? *Nothing. They don't have anything to do with her. They don't mean anything,* he thought.

He leaned back and rested his head against the back of the chair, and he began to feel his body relaxing, and he reached over and pushed the curtains apart to let sunshine in. He checked his messages, but this action didn't serve as a diversion from his difficult thoughts as he'd hoped it would. He kept thinking about the mark on Vera's shoulder and her bloody nose. He made a vow to himself that he'd never let anything like that happen to her again and said it over and over to himself, like a prayer. The hours passed, and the time came when sleep finally caught up with him.

***

68

Later in the afternoon, at five o'clock, RJ passed Vera's house with his mother as they drove home from his hockey practice. He stared out of the side window at the house and then out of the rear windshield after they had gone by it.

"Vera didn't go to school today. She was sick," he said.

"Oh," his mother said. "I hope she feels better tomorrow."

***

At five o'clock, John woke up and looked over at Vera. She'd rolled from one side of the bed to the other, but she was still in a deep sleep. Only because he absolutely had to, he got up and crossed the hall to the bathroom but left the door open behind him so he could hear the slightest stir she made. Impatiently, he hurried to finish what he was doing so he could get back to her.

Nothing had changed. She hadn't moved. He crossed to the window and looked down at the crabapple tree in the yard. The boughs of the old tree were heavy with robins. The birds bounced around from branch to branch devouring the shriveled crabapples from the past fall. Watching them gave a breath of life to the world and a suggestion of spring.

Feeling a little better, he sat down in the chair, and he was surprised at how tired he still felt and at how easy it was to fall asleep again in Vera's chair, which was not exactly built for a full-grown man. He fell asleep, and as he was sleeping darkness fell and the night wore on. Then at ten o'clock, a red-tinged moon that had the radiance of a star appeared in the sky above their house. The moon shone through Vera's window with a wash of light that fell directly on her and lit up her room.

Chapter 6

The little men piloted Vera along a corridor of their spacecraft, swinging their arms mechanically, like toy soldiers, for what and to where was impossible for her to know. There were four of them guarding her, forming a tight blockade that kept her from escaping, one on each side, one in front, and one behind her. Her head was dizzy, and her mind was disoriented. She felt nauseous. Everything looked as if it was underwater. There were bright lights coming from every direction and pinpointing on her. They obstructed her ability to see anything except her alien captors and their spindly shadows at the edge of the sickening lights.

They stopped and turned her so she faced one of the walls, and as she watched, the wall transformed into a screen that projected images of planets and stars. One of them was a glowing blue and white ball, and she thought how beautiful it was. She wanted to ask the little guards if it was Earth, but she was afraid to talk to them and to have her hopes crushed that what was happening wasn't real. She didn't want it to be true that she was far from home.

More images of countless suns, immense black holes, sparkling galaxies, and ethereal streaks of color more spectacular than a rainbow flashed before her eyes. But she was also shown things that she couldn't stand to watch, horrible destruction and suffering, and she had to look away from these visions. She sensed that her captors, or those who controlled them, were showing her these things for a reason, But being only ten years old, she didn't know what it could be, and she didn't care. All she wanted was for them to let her go. She tried to scream and run away, but there was an invisible force that prevented her from speaking or moving of her own free will.

Her guards turned around simultaneously, taking little box steps of uniform length to form four perfect, individual squares. They faced her. She felt instinctively this was a sign that they were aware she was struggling. They extended their scrawny arms out to her. They were barely taller than she was but were a thousand times stronger and able to control her without touching her. Now she couldn't avoid seeing their faces, even though she tried not to look. She'd never seen anything as repulsive as their bulged heads and huge, soulless eyes as black and dense as coal.

More terrifying than their physical presence was the memory that made her think that she had seen them before. They kept her moving—floating—down the corridor until they came to another corridor and turned down it, and Vera sensed that they were getting closer to wherever they were taking her.

She knew she was right when they abruptly stopped and went inside a room. She saw other small beings like her captors. Several worked together to undress her and laid her on a metal table. There were sharp edges around the table, and her finger grazed across one and cut her when they put her down. They saw what happened, and briefly paused to look at the blood that was squirting out of her finger, like they were studying it, and then turned to do something else. She wasn't used to being treated with brutal indifference, and it made her cry.

The metal surface was cold and hard, and she was naked and freezing, but she realized she could move around for the first time, so she rolled onto her side and curled up into a ball. This didn't make her warmer but it made it easier to believe that she was dreaming. There was a light bearing down from above her. She wondered whether the light had ever been used before to look at the bodies of young girls, like her.

She heard movement. It sounded like there were many of them running around in the background getting ready to do something to her. She closed her eyes to block them out. She could hear their weird shuffling noise getting closer. Then they slipped out of the shadows and into the light.

The one she thought of as the little doctor came up and touched the back of her neck and walked his long fingers across her skin. His fingers were clammy and nimble like the tentacles of a squid, squirming down her back. The little doctor uncurled her from her fetal position and rolled her over. He untwisted her arms and placed them at forty-five-degree angles at her sides, and she began to tremble because she knew that she could not stop him from doing anything he wanted to her. He straightened her knees and spread her legs apart, and she kept her eyes nailed shut in self-defense while he examined her.

The doctor put his fingers on her eyelids and forced them open. His eyes were waiting for her. They were as dark as wells. He made her stare straight into them, and her body began to feel tingly and numb. Her heart was racing like a bird's heart, but it began to slow, and her body became less rigid. She heard the little doctor talking to her in her head, telling her that she shouldn't be scared.

There were other small people around the table. She thought they must be the nurses who helped the doctor. When they talked to each other, they made buzzing noises. They looked like ants with their light bulb—shaped heads and pointy chins. One of the nurses held a tray for the doctor with objects on it for him to pick. He selected a long needle and raised it up to the light above her. It glinted in the light. As she watched, the nurses moved closer and extended their hands, and without touching her, they held her down while the doctor inserted the needle into her ear. He pushed it slowly deeper and deeper into the cavity of her ear, and it wasn't painful at first. She only felt a steady pressure, but the doctor kept pushing the needle forward into her skull. He was trying to push it all the way through her head, and the pain made her wish she was dead.

Her suffocated voice suddenly came back in her suffering, and she screamed. "It hurts, it hurts."

Immediately after she spoke, the pain went away. It was such a grateful relief that it seemed like magic. She was gasping for breath, and the doctor continued his examination of the rest of her body, in all the places that belonged to her. He scraped off little pieces of her skin and gave them to the little nurses, and they put them in what looked like little pieces of aluminum foil and took them away. The doctor towered over the others, though he was small too, but his giant black eyes were the same. By forcing her to look into their eyes, they could make her do whatever they wanted, and they didn't seem to know or care that they were terrifying to her. She thought of her father and told him that she loved him. She cried when she said it. The captors became very animated with interest over her tears. She thought that they were laughing at them.

The doctor finished his examination, and the nurses converged on her and took over for him. They tried to dress her, but they put her shirt on backward and her shoes on the wrong feet. Before the doctor left, he said something to her in her mind, but she didn't understand it. She wondered if he was being mean or just saying goodbye to her. But it didn't make any difference to her, because she prayed she'd never see him again.

After the nurses were done with her, they handed her over to a different group of little guards to escort her from the room. Exhausted, Vera teetered in the middle of them as they led her into a passageway and then another passageway. She stumbled several times, but on the last time her left foot caved underneath her, and the beings moved in swiftly to lift her. They used their power to levitate her, and she floated the rest of the way in a state of semi-consciousness, devoid of her sense of herself but aware of the universe being everywhere, including inside of her.

They went into a big room, where there was a strong smell like ammonia, and the smell awakened her. When she opened her eyes, there was someone directly in front of her staring at her. She looked away from the creature and put her hands over her head to hide. *Go away. Leave me alone,* she thought. But she had to see it. Its eyes were the fixed points of its phantomlike face and made her tremble.

Then it blinked at her, which she didn't think it could do, and it tilted its head, and she noticed that it had a graceful neck and movements that were different from the others she'd seen so far. It had an air of calmness that made her feel calmer too. Even though she hated this being, she felt awed in its presence. By looking at it, she could see how intelligent it was. It also seemed gentle, unlike the others who were cruel to her. When they'd done those terrible things to her, they hadn't cared if she was afraid. This individual seemed kind. She wondered if the creature would allow her to go home.

It gave her the feeling that it was reading her mind. If it was, then it knew she was confused and disoriented about how and when she got there. At first, she didn't remember much about what happened, but the memories grew clearer the more she thought about them, until she remembered everything that'd happened. Outside in their backyard, her dad had gotten mad at her, they'd had a fight, and he'd walked away from her and gone back in the house. Then she'd marched off by herself with Spark into the woods and hiked for a long time. There, Spark had been trapped by coyotes, and she'd saved him from being killed. She had other vivid memories of that event, so vivid that she could feel the weight of the rocks she'd thrown at the coyotes in her hands. The revelations came with sorrow and regret about what she'd done.

Let me go, she thought, and the creature heard her. It seemed disturbed that she was upset, and it raised its hand above her shoulder, and she felt a light pelting sensation on her skin, like rain was falling on her, which made her calm again. The being left briefly to get something from a table and brought it back to her. She wasn't interested when it tried to show her what it was, and she kept her eyes shut. She felt something soft and fuzzy on her cheek and ticklish on her nose. Then the being sat the object down in her lap. Cautiously, she touched the object and brushed it with her hand. She found that it had a nose and she could squeeze it, and it had ears that were round. It felt like a teddy bear, and she opened her eyes and saw that was what it was.

She wanted to hug it and wrap its fuzzy arms around her neck in a hug, but she didn't. It was tempting to cuddle its soft little body, except that it wasn't her teddy bear, and Vera didn't trust that this being was really her friend, just pretending to be. Giving her a stuffed animal was just a way to make her do what they wanted.

The being came closer. "The toy is for you."

She heard its message. She yelled her answer and flung the bear away, scaring herself with her outburst. "No!" Then she waited for what the being would do.

It blinked at her, and then it turned its head in the direction of noises that came from another part of the room. A group of the beings were huddled together in an obscure area. They stared at her too and made their buzzing sounds to communicate, and she thought they were talking about her, and not pleasantly. Her watcher went and joined them, and she watched, wondering what they would do next. She wanted the teddy bear back to comfort her. She wished she hadn't thrown it away. She looked around the room for it, and, finally, she spotted it across the floor about ten feet from where she was. She jumped down and crawled to it, picked it up, and climbed back on the table as quietly as she could.

The one she thought of as her watcher was arguing with the others about something. A few of them glared at her, making it clear they didn't like her. She felt more than ever that she had to escape from them. They looked exactly like the monsters she'd drawn with her crayons all her life. But there was no way to get out, and when she realized it was impossible, she started to cry. Her tears drew even more unwanted attention from the group of beings. Her crying got louder, and she was so upset that she shrieked like a baby animal in mortal danger. She looked into the watcher's eyes and pleaded for help. It returned and fixed its gaze on her, and that made her feel better.

Vera thought that this being might be female, which surprised her, because she didn't know if this species had genders. But this thought made her feel safe, and braver, brave enough to ask it if she could go home.

It spoke to her telepathically. "When we're done."

"When's that?"

The being ignored her. Vera's question was left to blend with the white noise of space. Then the being made her follow it out of the room, and they traveled for a long time without stopping. After a while, she couldn't tell if they were still moving, because she was lost remembering a day she'd spent looking at an anthill one summer, when she'd stretched out on the walkway in front of her house, with her cheek pressed against the sun-baked pavement, and watched the ants come and go from the anthill in never-ending shifts for their food. But the happy memory turned terrible when it struck her that the beings' faces looked like ants.

The being brought her into a looming, open area with green light like a mist that emanated throughout it. It took a moment for her eyes to adjust to the scale of the room. When her vision returned, she saw that all four walls shot straight up like cliffs to a great height, and there were tall towers with stacks and stacks of containers. She thought the containers looked like aquariums. She tipped her head back and looked up, but she couldn't see where the towers and aquariums ended. There was only a dark chasm that didn't seem to have a beginning or an end.

The containers were see-through with windows on all sides, and they had something in them. She strained to see what they held. Babies—hundreds of deformed babies—or tiny monsters—floating in bright green water. They weren't like any babies she'd seen, and she even knew what babies looked like before they were born. It made her sick to look at them, and she covered her eyes.

She heard the alien's words in her mind. "You're an intelligent child. Where do you think they come from?"

"I don't know."

"We go this way," it told her, as it led her away.

Ahead of them, she heard a cacophony of shrill and rowdy voices, like little kids yelling. The room they entered reminded her of the daycare center she had once gone to when she was very young. There were children there, but they didn't look like human children. They were strangely wild looking, skinny, and pale. They had almond eyes and round heads with pointy chins, and wisps of long thin hair on their skulls. The being took her over to some of the older children, who sat in a circle and played a game with a milky-white ball. One of the children tossed it in the air, and it took flight and flew off under its own power. Another child tried to snatch it, but it veered out of reach and flew in the opposite direction. The game didn't have any rules. The children were harsh and brutal when they tried to steal the ball from each other. They didn't seem to care if someone got hurt.

Vera saw enough to know that she didn't want to have anything to do with them or their game. The being indicated that she should sit down with them, but she refused. What she wanted didn't matter. It made her sit anyway. Two of the elfish children slid aside to give her a place in the circle. She squeezed her shoulders and knees close to her body to avoid her skin brushing against theirs.

The milky-white ball drifted to her, and a couple of the children reached in front of her face and tried to grab it, but it took off and hovered above her shoulder, and when they tried to catch it again, it flew straight into her hands. She locked her fingers around it, and it changed colors, one fading slowly into the other. The other children looked mortified, as if she had stolen it from them, but she was as shocked as they were. She turned it around and around. Its smooth round surface was soothing to the touch. Thoughts of her home filled her mind. She could smell their Christmas tree. She could see a plume of smoke rising from their chimney and her father outside stacking wood in the yard.

A girl came up to her and glared at her with hostility. Vera reflexively leaned away from the girl, but she couldn't help staring at her. She was ugly. Her scalp glowed through her sparse stringy hair, and she had no eyebrows. Her body language showed that she was ready to fight, but she looked like a skinny weakling. Vera thought that she could beat her up. Then the girl shoved her, but instead of retaliating, Vera opened her hands to give her the ball.

"Here. You can have it back."

The girl lunged for it, but she couldn't touch it. It flew away from her, dropped on the ground, and rolled out of sight. Neither the girl nor Vera knew where it'd gone.

"Go get it," the girl said.

It was the first time since they'd captured her that Vera had heard another voice or spoken words, and it left her so stunned that she couldn't understand what the girl said. She just stared at her in astonishment with her mouth open. The girl grew angry at Vera for ignoring her and shoved her. Immediately Vera's temper flared up, and she felt nothing but hate for the girl. She squeezed her hand in a fist to punch her, but at the last second didn't do it and swallowed the mean words she was about to say, because she remembered that bad things happened when she didn't control her temper.

"Okay, I'll go find the ball."

Without a clue of where to go, she just wandered around without a plan, trying to make sense of the landscape. Soon she got lost and forgot how to get back to where she'd started. All the walls and rooms looked the same. She approached them suspiciously, dreading what might be there waiting for her. She was about to give up, when the ball suddenly appeared in front of her and rolled down an incline to her. She squatted to pick it up, but it rolled away from her, and she followed it. It played this game a few more times with her, and on the last time it rolled the furthest and stopped gently in front of a pair of bare feet. To her, they looked like ordinary feet with five toes instead of four. She raised her eyes to see whose feet they were, and she saw that they belonged to a woman and that the woman was a human person like her.

The woman held a strange baby in her lap without embracing it, holding it loosely by its arm, and when Vera saw them together, she knew the woman didn't love the baby. The woman had a pretty face, except you could tell by looking at it that she was sad. She reminded Vera of someone, but she didn't know who it was. She had hair that was long and thick, like Gwen, and eyes that belonged to somebody else. Vera wondered if she was a prisoner too, like her. It seemed that way. She was crying, even though she was asleep. The ugly baby wiggled around and tried to grasp her nipple with its little wormy fingers. In her sleep, the woman groaned and moved her arm so it could suckle.

Vera hoped the woman would wake up soon so she could talk to her, and then neither of them would feel lonely. The little people were watching them. The ball that she needed sat at the tips of the woman's toes. The woman stirred and woke up suddenly. Vera was startled too. She stared wide-eyed at the woman.

"Vera?" the woman said. Her voice was hoarse as if she hadn't talked in a long time.

"You know my name? How do you know it?"

The woman sat up, jostling the baby, and it nearly fell off her lap. She didn't seem to notice, but Vera did. "I just do."

"How?"

The woman looked down at the ball and flexed her foot and kicked it lightly toward Vera. Vera picked it up and stepped back. "Is that your baby?"

The woman shrugged and nodded.

"What's your name?"

"Breeder."

"That's a real name?"

"No."

"I think I remember seeing you before. Do you remember me?"

"Yes, I remember you."

Vera paused before her next question. Instinctively, she asked the woman, "Are you my mother?"

The woman put her finger to her lips. "Shhh, they're watching us."

"Are you?"

"They're coming." She touched Vera's face. "We have to say goodbye now. I think they're finished with you."

"Does that mean they'll let me go?"

"I hope so."

"What am I doing here? What are you doing here?"

"I can't. There's not enough time."

"Did the baby come from one of those boxes?"

The woman bowed her head and sighed. "I'm sorry. Here they are." She ran her hand down the length of Vera's hair. "I'm sorry. Goodbye, Vera."

Vera turned around, and the being who had brought her there was right behind her. It told her to come with it, and it made her glide under its power. She looked over her shoulder one last time at the woman. She wondered if she'd ever see her again.

"I want to go home," she said to the being. "Will you let me go?" It seemed shocked that she'd dared to ask. She got a powerful feeling of satisfaction from doing that.

"Yes," it said.

"When?'

"I will let you know."

Vera lost control of her temper at that point and yelled at it. "Why are you doing this to me?"

But the being didn't answer.

"Where do you come from?" she demanded.

The air changed into a diorama that showed a galaxy in the universe, with dissecting lines between the planets and the stars. The alien pointed at a constellation. "There," it said.

"How far away is that?"

"From your home?"

"Yeah."

"Very far."

"Tell me your name? You know mine, but I don't know yours."

"You can call me whatever you want."

"Gross would be a good name," she said.

"It doesn't matter. You won't remember us when we bring you back."

"No, I'll remember. I'll never forget this."

"No, we don't let you remember."

"You can't do that. I'll remember."

"No."

"Let me go. I want to go now."

"All right. It's time you go," it said.

A radiant beam of light appeared at Vera's feet. When she looked inside it, she saw a long golden chute that plunged down to a black depth. Then something happened that made her lose her footing. She slipped, or was pushed, and fell into the beam of light. She spun and tumbled wildly down through the corkscrew, yelling for her life. "It's too fast! It's too fast! It's too fast!"

She could see a swatch of blackness far down at the bottom of the chute of light. It looked like only a slit at first, but it got bigger and bigger the closer she came to it, and it opened like an envelope waiting to catch her, but she passed through it and popped out the other side into her world, where she saw Spark. Before she knew what was happening, she hit the ground with an enormous *thud*, and rolled and flopped around until her body ran out of momentum.

She slept the remainder of the night in the forest next to Spark, on a bed of pine needles surrounded by a circle of white birch trees with burn marks on their bark. Where early the next morning, John found her.

Chapter 7

Vera was awakened from a nightmare by a truck that passed the house in the middle of the night. When she awoke, she was sitting up in bed, and her back was rigidly straight, and her heart was pounding. The details of the dream were fresh, so she remembered that she was surrounded by bizarre little people and was forced to look at their big ant-like eyes. It scared her because it seemed so real, like she had dreamed about something that had really occurred. She was even afraid that they might be there right now in her room.

Her eyes scanned the different areas of the room. Near the window, she saw the outline of a person in her chair, and she froze. Right before she screamed, she realized that it was her father sitting in the chair. All of a sudden, she felt warm and content and relieved to feel safe again.

He looked terribly uncomfortable in her undersized armchair that was built to fit a kid, not a grown man. She wondered how long he'd been sleeping there, and she was surprised that he could sleep there at all. She tried to guess what time it was. She wasn't even sure what day it was. But she remembered that earlier that day her father had carried her from the woods.

The chair squeaked when he jerked in his sleep, and it made her jump. Then he mumbled something that she couldn't understand and started to snore, like he always did when he slept sitting up. His snoring didn't bother her, and it usually made her laugh, but not tonight. A shiver ran through her, and she pulled her blanket up to her chin, but she couldn't get warm. A long time ago, she could've climbed in his lap, and it would've made her forget her bad dream, but she wasn't a little child anymore. She was ten, and she was too old, which was too bad because she remembered more awful things about the dream. In the dream, she was alone in the woods and she saw a silver object in the sky, and there were people in the windows looking down at her, and she was sure that they were going to capture her.

"I'm just a kid, so leave me alone," she said. They could still be listening.

She lay down and buried her head under the blankets to wait for sleep to come that would make her oblivious. But the path to falling asleep was difficult, and she lay awake for a long time before she succumbed. When at last she was asleep, it was a deep and rhythmic sleep that would protect her until it was morning.

Part 2

Chapter 8

RJ's dream was interrupted each time the snowplow came during the night to clear a fresh dumping of snow from his street. When he fell back to sleep, he incorporated the seismic sounds and vibrations of the snowplow into his fantasy dream that starred him and Vera. He was sixteen, and she was turning sixteen in a couple of months. For a while, both night and day, he'd thought about her more than he'd ever had, and in a very different way. It was disconcerting to realize that he was in love with her, after being friends since they were six years old.

RJ's dream was like a bad science fiction movie, where the snowplows in his neighborhood became deadly mechanical monsters. They were lined up in a menacing row across the hill above the town. Their headlights flashed on and pierced the air, like the eyes of a demon. The engines rumbled and shook the earth as the trucks jerked forward, yard by yard, to the edge of the hill, and all together, they plunged and stormed the town. The streets buckled underneath their weight, and the buildings collapsed. The residents fled from their homes screaming and ran around looking for places to hide. Everyone knew they were doomed.

Amid all the chaos and destruction, RJ frantically searched for Vera. From a smoking pile of debris, he heard her scream, and he rushed there to find her. He called her name as he followed her screams, and found her trapped underground in a pit that used to be the first floor of the town hall. The only way he could get to her was by climbing over a heap of mangled cars, which if he breathed too hard would topple and crush him. He jumped and landed on the side of the heap, scrambled to the top and down the other side of it with his hands and feet, and then dropped down onto his stomach and crawled to where she was. A beam that had fallen had pinned her to the ground, but he was confident that he could get it off her.

"Are you hurt?" he asked, as he helped her to sit up.

"No, I don't think so."

"Thank God."

"Oh, RJ," she swooned. She fell into his arms, and he felt like James Bond.

They lay back and remained there a long time, waiting for the end of the violence. When at last it was over, they came out of hiding into the setting sun. RJ held Vera's hand and explained their predicament. Of all the people in Pangea, they were the only ones who were left to carry on the human genome. At the end of the dream, when they were about to kiss, he woke up suddenly, and when he realized that he was awake he hit his fist on the mattress.

"Damn it," he said.

It was barely light out, and there was still time to go back to sleep and finish the dream. He closed his eyes and tried to sleep, but the TV was blaring in his mother's bedroom, and he just couldn't relax. She'd fallen asleep all night with it on again. He wished she wouldn't do that, because he'd read that it wasn't good for you. His mom and he were close. It'd always been just the two of them, and he was protective of her. His mom and now Vera were the people he cared about most in the world.

A snowplow went past his house to clear the street after the snowstorm, and it made his bed shake. He pulled the covers up to his chin and stared at the skylight above his bed. He couldn't see the sky because of the deep snow piled on top of the glass. To watch the day dawn, he turned his head and looked out one of the other windows. A pale sun was rising behind the snow and clouds. Since he couldn't sleep, he started thinking instead about his day and the work he had to do. He had an old lawn tractor that he'd rebuilt that he used to plow driveways to earn money.

The pretty meteorologist who gave the weather report had predicted the snow would begin to taper off about 7 a.m. What that meant to him was that he had lots of time. It'd only take thirty minutes for him to shower, get dressed, eat, and leave, and he'd be ready long before the snow had stopped. Even so, he thought he should get up. His body was itching for activity. It was comfortable lying in bed, but he was bored with just thinking. The idea of working all day didn't bother him, because he enjoyed the work. Plowing with his tractor was fun for him. He thought of himself as a fresh air freak, and he liked to be outside.

One concern he had was whether the tractor would start right away or if he'd have to do something to it first. Every time the engine turned over without a hitch, its rumblings and pops were music to his ears, and he felt proud of himself, especially considering that the tractor was old and he wasn't the best mechanic. He'd taught himself how to rebuild the engine — with a little help from John. He was very happy with the finished product. This was the second year he'd used it, so, so far so good.

The old tractor required constant maintenance. He didn't particularly like having to be a mechanic and work on it himself, but it was cheaper than paying someone else. He did feel a sense of accomplishment from fixing it and making it run as smoothly as he could, but this was just a happy consequence of doing a necessary job that didn't interest him very much. He didn't think of himself as being a natural at it, but he was glad he'd learned the skill. He liked his tractor. He approved of its rugged character. It was durable. It faithfully continued to make him money, and he planned to keep it running as long as he possibly could.

As he thought over the day ahead, he was struck with the cold reality that his first customer that morning was Mr Leblanc. By far his worst customer, Mr Leblanc was a cranky old man who complained if RJ wasn't there clearing his driveway before the last snowflake fell. RJ thought it was ridiculous that Mr Leblanc even cared about that, since he was retired. His other customers were nice, and they didn't treat him the way Mr Leblanc did. He liked them, but he couldn't like Mr Leblanc even though he'd tried. Mr Leblanc was always rude to him, and worse than that he always owed RJ money and made him feel like he was trying to swindle him when he asked him to pay.

For two years, he'd always been courteous to the sour old man no matter what, but now he was tired of kissing his ass, and he didn't care if he lost him as a customer. What he needed to do had become obvious to him, and he made up his mind that if Mr Leblanc didn't pay what he owed today, he was going to drop him as a customer. Having made that decision, he felt relieved.

There was a knock on his door. "Are you awake, RJ?" his mother said.

"Yeah, Mom. Hi, I'm awake."

"Good morning. Want some pancakes?"

"That sounds great. Thanks." He heard her shuffle in her slippers as she walked away on the wood floor.

He swung his legs over the edge of his loft bed and climbed down the ladder. The room was chilly, and for a second he considered going back to his warm bed, but he resisted the urge to do it. As soon as he was up, he went to the bathroom and took a shower. Then he got dressed in his long underwear, sweater, and snow pants, and went downstairs for breakfast.

The kitchen was empty. His mother had made the pancakes and gone back upstairs; he heard her in her bathroom above the kitchen, singing in the shower. He poured a cup of coffee and glasses of milk and juice, stacked eight pancakes on a plate and put a sliced banana, blueberries, butter, and maple syrup on top of it while he toasted a couple of bagels. When he was done eating, he put his dirty dishes in the dishwasher and called upstairs to his mom to say goodbye. With his coffee thermos in his hand, he stepped outside into the blustery aftermath of the big snowstorm.

When he went outside, the wind was blowing with a force that swept the snow into the air and into a cloud. It swirled around him like a sandstorm as he walked to the garage. On the way, it occurred to him that he might use the snowblower that day instead of the plow. It had gotten so there wasn't anywhere else to put the snow, but the blower would spread it all around. He bent down and felt under the snow for the garage door handle. He had to tug on it because the bottom of the garage door was frozen to the ground. He lifted the door, and when he looked at his tractor he grinned, and then got to work changing out the plow for the blower.

When he finished, he stepped back to admire the tractor. For him, it had turned out to be a real moneymaker because he could charge for plowing in the winter and mowing in the summer.

He climbed on the tractor. "Okay," he said and patted the steering wheel. "I hope you're ready this morning."

The engine started on the first try, and he rejoiced as he pulled out of the driveway. He turned right and drove down the sidewalk and blew away the drifts of snow with his machine. The cascade of snow that streamed from the chute of the snowblower attracted the attention of people on the street who were shoveling out their cars. Some people gave him the thumbs-up and smiled. He perked up because of their friendliness. The tractor had started, and people were nice, so the day had started out well.

Everything was good except for the fact that he was on his way to see Mr Leblanc. RJ's spirits sank the closer he came to his street. Before he turned down it, he heard tires screeching and spinning and an engine revving viciously.

"Crap. He's got himself stuck," RJ groaned.

A smokestack stream of smelly exhaust puffed from the tailpipe of Mr Leblanc's big, rusty-brown Buick LeSabre, or land yacht, as RJ referred to it. Mr Leblanc thought it was a classic, but RJ thought it was a piece of shit. As he pulled up to the end of Mr Leblanc's snow-socked driveway, he rehearsed what he'd say about the overdue payments. He hoped for the best but was prepared for the worst, and if it didn't work out, Mr Leblanc would never see him again. He believed it was time to stand up for himself, and that alone bolstered his confidence.

The big, heavy door of the LeSabre swung open, and Mr Leblanc got out of the car. He cursed in French under the fur-trimmed hood of his jacket and stomped through fresh snow to the back wheels. He picked up a snow shovel in his big wool mittens and shoveled furiously, wielding the shovel like a weapon of war around the LeSabre's fat tires. RJ had to duck out of the way to avoid being struck.

"Good morning, Mr Leblanc," he said. He put out his hand to shake mittens with him.

Mr Leblanc scowled at RJ's invitation to shake hands. "Where've you been?"

"You are my first stop of the day," RJ said, trying to be polite. "I was waiting for most of the snow to stop."

"You should think about your customers instead of what you want to do. Now go take care of my driveway so I can take my wife to church."

RJ couldn't help but wonder why Mr Leblanc wasn't a better person, if he spent so much time going to church. Mr Leblanc stared at him as if he had some idea of what RJ was thinking. He made RJ nervous, and his confidence level slipped a notch. He was nearly too rattled to bring up the thorny subject of Mr Leblanc's unpaid bill.

"Mr Leblanc. Mr Leblanc."

"What?"

"Can you shut off your car so I can talk to you a minute?"

"Why?"

"It's hard to talk over the noise. And the exhaust is polluting the air."

"What are you—some kind of an expert?"

"No. But aren't you just wasting gas?"

"Mind your own business, kid," Mr Leblanc said, wagging his finger in RJ's face. "My wife likes the inside nice and warm when she gets in."

Controlling his temper wasn't easy, but RJ gently repositioned Mr Leblanc's finger away from his nose and calmly stated, "You should shut your car off, because you won't be going anywhere for a while."

Mr Leblanc glared at him, clearly angry to be challenged, but at the same time, he looked bewildered and crestfallen, like he knew that he'd lost the argument and that RJ was right and he was wrong. In his petulant way, he stomped back to the car through his trail of bootprints and shut it off. He shook his car keys in the air and pointed at the house with them. "I'll be inside."

"Mr Leblanc, can I talk with you for a minute, please?"

"What now?"

"Before I snowblow your driveway, I'd appreciate it if you pay me first for the last two times I was here." *There*, he thought. He'd finally spat out the words, and he'd been blunter than he thought he'd be. He was almost as surprised as Mr Leblanc. "And for today too," he added.

"Just go ahead and get my car out. We'll talk about it later."

"I'm sorry, Mr Leblanc, but if you don't pay me today, or make arrangements to pay me in installments, I can't plow your driveway anymore."

Mr Leblanc clenched his mittens into fists. "I'll get somebody else to plow. You can keep mowing my lawn."

"No, Mr Leblanc, I won't mow your lawn either. I have your bill with the current amount you owe me. I'll take a check if you don't have cash, since you don't use technology."

Mr Leblanc frowned, his eyes flashed red at RJ, and he abruptly turned and walked away.

"Wait, Mr Leblanc. Where are you going?"

"To get your money!" he said, slamming both doors behind him.

RJ thought that sounded good, but he wasn't sure if he should believe it. It was a victory for him, but he had a sick feeling in the pit of his stomach that there'd be another argument and more delays, and also he felt guilty, like he'd done something wrong. Mr Leblanc thought he had. But without a doubt, Mr Leblanc had been taking advantage of him. RJ stood by that principle, and he didn't care what Mr Leblanc thought.

Ten long minutes passed while his disgruntled customer left him waiting in the cold.

Then the door opened, and Mr Leblanc's wife leaned her white head out and waved. "Good morning, RJ. Do you want to come in for a cup of hot cocoa?" she said in a sunny voice that was a million miles sweeter than her surly husband's.

"Oh, I can't, but thanks, Mrs Leblanc. Maybe another time?"

"Yes, anytime, RJ. Oh, it's a cold morning, isn't it? I keep trying to get George to move to Florida, but he won't budge."

"Yes, it's pretty cold. Do you think Mr Leblanc will come out soon?"

"I'll tell him to hurry up. When he came inside, he went into the bathroom with the sports page. George! I think he's finished. George!"

Mr Leblanc appeared behind his wife at the door.

"Here he is. I'll see you later, RJ. Have a good day."

"You too. Bye, Mrs Leblanc."

Her husband stepped aside to let her pass, and then he came out and plodded back down his snowy stairs. As he walked toward RJ, Mr Leblanc stared directly at him. RJ felt like it was the moment of truth for whether Mr Leblanc would pay him or not.

Mr Leblanc stuck out his hand and opened it to reveal a ball of crinkled money in his palm. "Here. This is for the last two times and today, and also in advance, to cover the next three snowstorms."

RJ stared at the wrinkled cash of ones and fives that Mr Leblanc clasped in his hand. The bills looked like Mr Leblanc had just gotten them out of his piggy bank, and RJ wondered for the first time ever if Mr Leblanc couldn't afford to pay him. "You can just pay me for the last two times, and I'll send you a bill for this time."

Mr Leblanc shook his head and thrust the money at him. "No, here, take it. A hundred and twenty for plowing, that's what I owe you, right? Including today?"

"Yes."

"And then a hundred and twenty for the next three storms."

"What? No, you don't have to pay me in advance."

Mr Leblanc slapped the money into RJ's hand. "I said take it. Nobody can say that George Leblanc is a cheat."

"Thank you," RJ said, putting the money in his wallet. "You'll be my first customer every morning."

"I better be." Without saying another word, Mr Leblanc went back in the house.

"Here comes the door slamming," RJ said, wearily.

A few seconds later, there was a big bang, as Mr Leblanc went onto the porch. He bent over to take his boots off and started to cough. RJ could see what Mr Leblanc was doing, and he had a glimpse of his skinny, weak-looking ankles when he took off his boots and socks and put on his slippers. RJ thought that for a small, frail man, Mr Leblanc had a lot of venom, and it made him wonder if he'd always been that way or if he'd changed, maybe because of things that'd happened.

Without any more delay, RJ began working on Mr Leblanc's driveway. There was a lot of snow on the ground, and it took him forty-five minutes, but when he was finished, the driveway was clean and smooth. After that, he shoveled the Leblancs' steps and walkway and spread deicer on them. He was sitting on his tractor, about to leave to go to his next customer, when he saw Mrs Leblanc wave to him from the window. He was surprised that Mr Leblanc was standing next to her, and he was even more surprised when he showed him the barest sign of friendliness by nodding at him. Then Mr Leblanc dropped the edge of the curtain and went into the house. RJ threw back his head and sighed with relief that he could move on from Mr Leblanc and that he'd finally gotten him to pay. Now the rest of the day and whatever else he had to do sounded easy.

He felt confident his tractor would start right away, since the engine was still warm. It growled like a tiger, which was exactly the way it was supposed to sound. The rest of the day was smooth and productive as he worked resolutely to get through every driveway on his list, stopping just once to eat the sandwich, cookies, and apple he'd packed for lunch. At about four o'clock, his work was done, and he spent a few minutes reflecting on the day. He felt he'd accomplished a lot and earned good money. The day had started out difficult, but it had turned out well.

He decided that he needed to try harder to develop a cordial relationship with Mr Leblanc, if he'd let him. Something about their relationship reminded him of Einstein's theory of relativity, which he was studying in school. If time and space were relative, it seemed to him it must be that he and Mr Leblanc had the ability to shape their destinies, meaning that their choices about how they interacted with each other mattered, because everything was relative, depending on how people approached things. He could see how the theory of relativity applied to him and Mr Leblanc. He derived hope from it that someday they'd be able to tolerate each other.

It was nice to get to the end of the day and to feel that it was successful. Now, at last, he'd go to Lily Pond to practice hockey before he headed home. The late afternoon sun languished on the horizon. Sitting on the lump of cash in his wallet, he drove along the side of the road. In the west, ribbons of pink and purple ran through the winter twilight, and the giant evergreens blew in the wind and stroked the pastel sky. But he couldn't look up for very long, because he had to watch the road. Several cars passed him, some of them going way too fast. He didn't feel safe, especially when going around corners. He kept an eagle eye out for cars and stayed ready to jump out of the way if a driver lost control.

Luckily, the traffic subsided as he got closer to the pond. A small parking lot sat just ahead on the right side of the road, and he turned in and kept driving all the way to the ice, where the snow that'd fallen the night before was piled up to the top of the tractor's wheel wells. He turned the snowblower on and cleared a large rectangular area on the ice for skating. When he was done with that, he stopped the tractor and shoveled out the hockey net. Then he shook the snow off it and stood it up on the ice. Now it was time for him to practice, and he felt excited, like he always did when he played hockey. He went back to put his skates on and to get his stick and a puck.

When he stood up on his skates, his legs felt strong and sturdy, and his whole body felt fit and relaxed. His muscles were wound and ready to explode with energy, but he took it easy and skated around in circles for a while for fun, and with every rotation he picked up a little more speed and power. At last, he skated to center ice and made a shot at the goal, and the puck went in. He kept making shots for a long time from different angles and from different distances from the net, and he practiced defense too. Shards of ice flew off his skates as he rushed up and down dozens of times, and when he took his first break it felt like his lungs were going to burst.

While he caught his breath, he slowly skated toward a small island, until the snow became too deep for him to continue and he stopped. When he was young, he went to the island a lot with his friends. They paddled to it in his canoe to camp, and when they were there, they practically lived on the blueberries that grew in thickets along the shore. In the summer, it had a dozen different kinds of songbirds that nested there in the trees. Around the shore, he saw leftover stalks of weeds encased like fossils under the ice. The island had changed since he was a kid. Each year, when the weather was warm the ring of vegetation around the island spread a little farther out into the water, and the pond got smaller.

It was now twilight, and RJ noticed that the tops of the trees had become smudgy silhouettes against the sky, and he thought it was time to go home. He skated back and removed his skates, and as he was about to leave, he saw a small light in the distance near the other shore. At first it was still, but then it began to move in a line above the snow-packed ice. It was so faint that he had to watch it for a few minutes to be sure it wasn't a reflection from a car headlight. It vanished a few times and then came back again.

After a short time, he realized the light was coming closer to the shore. He strained his eyes to see exactly what it was. Slowly, he realized that there was a person out there. He wondered what the person was doing hiking around in two feet of snow on the frozen pond in the dark. He was very curious, but cautious too. He thought about leaving, but he waited to make sure the person was all right.

As the figure moved toward the shore, he became certain that she was a girl. She stumbled and fell down on her knees. Even though she got up and kept walking, she continued to struggle, and he decided to go and help her. The moon rose and shone on the pond as he was going toward her, and it illuminated the girl and the white pom-pom on the top of her hat, which he had thought at first was a spot of light. He could also see the profile of her face, and at a glance, he realized it was Vera.

"What's she doing out here?" His breath steamed out in cold mouthfuls of air as he spoke.

He started running to her as fast as the snow would let him, but before he was halfway there, he had the thought that he might scare her if he came up on her abruptly, so he slowed down.

"Vera!" he yelled. His voice came back across the pond as an echo.

She stopped and looked around her, but then she started running awkwardly in the direction from where she came, and he knew he'd scared her and she didn't realize who he was.

"Vera, wait." He hoped this time she'd recognize his voice.

But she kept trying to run away, and she slipped and fell on her knees, and awkwardly managed to get up again. Walking was difficult for him too, but he chased her. She flinched when she saw him and kept looking behind her to see how far away he was.

His heart pounded. *Why is she running away from me?* he thought, because it didn't make any sense. How could she not know who he was? He was about to catch up, and it took only five more paces on his skates to get beside her, where he could grab her. When he did, she screamed. He was unaccustomed to making her panic, so it shocked him, and he dropped her arm.

Her eyes were full of fear. "Leave me alone."

"It's okay, Vera. It's RJ. It's me. Are you all right? What's the matter with you?"

"RJ?"

"Yeah, it's me. What are you doing out here?"

She looked at him as if she still didn't understand. "RJ? Just . . . just go away and leave me alone."

"What? No, I'm not going to do that. You seem so confused."

"I'm cold."

He took her hands and warmed them between his, and he thought she'd pull them away, but she accepted his gesture. Her body was shaking, and at the risk of startling her, he put his arm around her shoulder and pulled her close. "Are you going to tell me why you were walking around on the pond?"

"Do you know you just scared the crap out of me?" she said.

"I wanted to avoid doing that. I'm sorry."

"Don't you ever come up behind me and grab me like that again."

"I promise I won't."

She turned her face away from him, and then they both fell quiet. He listened to her uneven breathing, and it sounded as if she was gasping for air. Never had he seen her like this before.

"Come on, Vera. I'll take you home."

"No, wait."

"What's the matter? You're making me worried. I'm your friend, and you need me to help you."

"No, I don't."

"Vera, what's happened? You're acting so strange. Are you going to tell me what you're doing here?"

"You tell me what you're doing here," she snapped back.

He didn't appreciate her angry attitude at all. He thought she owed him an explanation, not the other way around. "So what do you want to do?" he said. "Do you want to stay out here all night?"

He got frustrated with her because she wouldn't answer his questions. At the same time, he was overwhelmed by the intense love he felt for her. "Well, I'm not, so I think I'll go now," he said. He walked a little way and turned around. "I'm serious."

"Then go, RJ. I told you to leave me alone."

"No, I can't," he said, as he came back to her. "I can't leave you alone out here. You look sick."

He stepped closer to her, where he could see her expression better and she could not ignore him. The moonlight washed across her face and lit the dark pupils of her eyes. He could feel the weight of the cold wind pressing against his back, but the air that filled the space between them was warm like a campfire.

"You knew it was me when I called you, didn't you? Or at least a couple seconds after. Why'd you run away?"

She placed her head on his shoulder. "I don't know. Let's just not fight, okay? It's such a waste of time."

He squeezed her hand. "No, I don't want to either." He dropped his hand at his side, and when he stopped touching her, he saw that she was looking at him in a way that he'd never seen, and he liked it, but it caught him off guard. By the time he stopped feeling surprised, it was gone.

"So, we should go now. I'll take you home," he said.

"I was walking home—from the library."

"Huh?"

"I was taking a shortcut. That's what I was doing out on the pond. I take it sometimes."

"That's kind of dangerous. Don't you think? I don't think you're telling me the truth."

"Why do you say that?"

"Different things. You could hurt yourself and freeze to death, or you could run into a weirdo. You never know. I don't think you should've been out there, especially not by yourself."

"That's kind of insulting."

"I don't mean it that way."

"Well, I can take care of myself. I know my way around here as well as you do. So don't worry."

He took a breath to cool his temper. It drove him crazy that she was being so difficult when he was just trying to help.

"You didn't say why you ran away? What were you scared of?"

"You! You looked like Bigfoot charging up on me. Of course I was scared."

"No, before that."

"I don't know what you're talking about. And I thought we weren't going to fight."

"It probably wouldn't be okay with your dad for you to be out here like this."

"Probably not," she said, as if she didn't care what her dad thought.

He sighed. "So you were taking a shortcut?"

"Yeah."

He shook his head. "I don't believe you, but I won't ask you anymore."

"I don't care if you believe me or not. No, I lied. I do care," she said, looking queasy. "I feel dizzy."

"Lean on me," he said.

"No, I think I can walk myself. Let's just get out of here. What time is it?"

"It's after seven o'clock."

"Oh, my God. My dad will kill me."

"Do you want to call him?"

"My phone is dead."

"You can use mine."

"No, he can yell at me when I get home."

"Whatever you think," he said, doubting her decision.

When they finally got to the makeshift ice rink, he got on the tractor and patted the seat. "Hop up."

"How has this been running?" she said, as she climbed on. She put her hands around his waist to hold herself steady.

She couldn't see him smile. He turned and looked at her, because he couldn't help it. "Pretty great," he said. He saw that she was gazing at the sky, her head tilted backward. "What is it?"

"This'll sound strange. But do you ever see into the spaces between things, RJ, like all the molecules and atoms in the air between the leaves and everything?"

"No, not really. Do you?"

"Yes, sometimes I can."

"Is it the spirit of nature, or something?"

"It's something like that, but even more."

"I can't picture what you mean."

"Sorry. Sometimes I think I'm crazy."

"I don't think you're crazy, Vera. You're you, and I think you're great."

"Thank you."

He put the tractor in gear and drove on a path of moonlight toward the shore. Hundreds of stars were visible and sparkling like gemstones. In the northern sky, he noticed a star that was moving, and he assumed at first that it was a shooting star. Then suddenly there were two shooting stars moving in tandem, side to side and up and down. They accelerated to an incredible speed and shot way up high in a staircase pattern, to his astonishment. He tried to watch them as much as he could, until he couldn't see them anymore. *Where did they go? What were they?* he thought. He wondered if Vera had seen what he'd seen. He wasn't sure whether he should trust his own eyes.

Vera slid closer to him and tightened her arms around his waist. To him, it felt so comfortable, and right that he almost turned around to kiss her, but he thought it might upset her. While they drove, she didn't say anything, and neither did he because he was trying to watch the sky to see if they came back, and once he almost drove the tractor into a snowbank.

They were almost at Vera's house when RJ saw two lights moving in the sky. The pair of otherworldly, sapphire eyes— that he'd seen before—and he felt like they were watching them.

Chapter 9

John stood up to his calves in the snow that blanketed his yard. The cold air had a severe bite to it, but he liked the tingling sensation that it produced on his skin. He always felt freer and breathed better in the cold. He was a New Englander, who lived by the seasons and the distinctions between them, such as a year that had a hard winter or the absence of one. As is true for everyone on the planet, the place he came from accounted for who he was. He'd gone outside for more refreshing air because the heat of the woodstove had made the house too hot and drained his energy. Now he felt invigorated by the cold air that was wrapped around his body. It was soothing, which was why he made a point every morning to go outside into the cool air to clear his foggy head and relieve the soreness in his joints.

He looked at the time on his phone to see how soon Vera would be home, and it was later than he thought. It was after six, and she usually got home from working at the library on Saturday at five thirty, but he wasn't worried, because she was with Gwen, who was giving her a ride. He looked up and admired the sky that evening, which was a deep purple with a silver moon for decoration. The temperature was about twenty degrees, but the wind chill made it feel more like zero.

Spark had rallied his old bones and left his bed to go outside with him. John put his hands in his pockets and walked around the yard to see where he'd gone. From a close distance away, an owl hooted in a tree, and the sound resonated within his body, like a chant. He loved hearing an owl hoot in the woods, and so did Vera. He thought about the times they had listened to it together.

He still hadn't found Spark. "He must be in the woods. Spark, come!" He heard rustling and he saw Spark trotting through the snow between some trees, looking like he was trying to find a good place to go to the bathroom.

The wind picked up and it got colder while John waited for Spark to do his business. When it was this cold, he didn't remember what the heat in the summer felt like. The wind blew underneath his shirt, sending a shiver through him. He tucked it in and zipped his hooded sweatshirt, and then he felt warm. He was thankful to have this cold, snowy winter.

Last year's winter had been a disappointment. It was eerily warm, and there was practically no snow. The ski industry had suffered, and a drought had followed in the summer. Sometimes he thought about moving to the northern part of the state to follow the cold as it waned in more parts of the northeast.

Spark, on the other hand, had become a wimp about the cold in his golden years. But he was fourteen, and he had arthritis in his hips and big white circles around his eyes. John couldn't blame him for being old. Most of the time now, all he wanted to do was to sleep in front of the fire. He was old, but he was still beautiful. Complete strangers still stopped them to say he was a beautiful dog.

"He's got a lot of life left in him," John said, thinking out loud. But he knew that Spark would never be the same athletic dog that he once was. He had a photograph of him from his younger days that captured him bounding through the snow, spraying his brown coat with snowflakes as he ran. He became nostalgic thinking about it. Just then, Spark walked up behind him and nudged his hand with his nose.

"Hey, old man," John said, petting him. "Where'd you go?"

He was glad to see him again because he'd heard coyotes howling in the woods recently, and God forbid if they came after Spark. With that thought, he suddenly remembered when Vera had saved Spark from a pack of coyotes. That was a long time ago, and he hardly ever thought about it anymore, but there were still times when he did. They were infrequent, but when they happened it was like groundhog day, where he'd suddenly relive and then forget the same event, only to repeat it again and again.

Spark looked up at him and wagged his tail. A clump of soggy, dead grass dangled from his jaws.

"Yuck, let me have that. You can't digest that, buddy," John said, pulling the wad of stringy vegetation out of his teeth. He tossed it on the ground. "Okay, time to go in."

He started walking, but after a couple of steps he stopped when he heard his name being called and looked around to see who it was. He saw no one. Then he heard it say to him loudly and clearly, "You need to paint the house."

He knew the voice. "Suzy," he said. He held his breath.

"The house needs to be painted," it said.

It was her voice just as he remembered it. The years between the past and present began melting away. "I plan to," he answered.

"Vera," Suzy's voice said.

"I try to take good care of her. But you shouldn't have left us." The first words he'd spoken to her in thirteen years were meant to make her feel guilty, but his pain over losing her was still raw, even after all that time.

He waited for her to answer him, as if she was really with him and they were having a conversation. He knew it was crazy, but he couldn't help himself. He listened, hoping she'd speak to him one more time, but after a while, he didn't sense her presence any longer, and he assumed she was gone.

Even though it was impossible, he wished he could go back in time so he could change the way things had turned out between them. Every problem and obstacle that he and Suzy had faced seemed easy to overcome, in retrospect, and he had certain knowledge that his life would've been better if she'd stayed. To him, it seemed like he hadn't moved forward with his life because she'd abandoned them, and he was stuck in the past somewhere between being fulfilled or alone.

Spark walked by his side to the porch and up the steps. There was a reflection of car headlights in the window, just as he was about to open the door. He turned around and saw a car stopped on the side of the road in front of his house. The shine of the headlights flashed off the tin roof of the shed. He wondered what it was doing there, and he decided to walk down the driveway to take a look.

He got to the end and slowly approached the car from the back. Another car went down the road in the opposite direction and lit the interior of the parked car with its headlights. It allowed him to see the silhouette of a man behind the wheel. He kept going toward the door, but before he got to it, the man in the car stepped on the gas, and John had to get out of the way. In an instant, all he could see of the car were its red taillights in the darkness getting farther away.

He had a queasy feeling in his stomach about what had just happened. It seemed as if the man in the car had taken off as soon as he realized John was there. The man could've been spying on them. But John told himself that was ridiculous, because why would anybody want to spy on them? Even though it couldn't be true, it made him furious. He took deep breaths of the cold air to feel calmer, and he was able to say to himself that he was being irrational. The man was probably parked there because he was lost or something as ordinary as that.

He walked back to the house, and within a few seconds another car came down the road. He stopped to watch it. Its blinker came on, and his tension rose again as the car pulled into his driveway. Then he realized it was Gwen's car, and Spark rushed to greet Gwen and Louisa as they got out.

They wore wool hats and mittens with snowflakes on them. Seeing Gwen wrapped up in cozy softness, he was filled with desire for her, and he wanted to say that she looked pretty, but he was afraid of sending the wrong message about his feelings.

He looked at the car, expecting to see Vera getting out, and he was surprised when he saw that she wasn't there. "Where's Vera?"

"You mean she's not home yet?" Gwen said.

"No, I thought you were bringing her home."

"We were going to, but she disappeared," Louisa said.

"She disappeared? What do you mean?" he said. He shoved his hand in his pocket for his phone. "I'll call her."

"I've called and texted her a bunch of times, but she didn't answer," Louisa said.

He looked at Gwen. "I don't understand this."

"I looked for her at five o'clock when the library closed, but she wasn't in the building, John," Gwen said. "And I asked everyone if they knew where she was, but no one had seen her for hours."

John checked his phone for a message from her. "Nothing yet."

"What should we do? I hope she's okay," Louisa said.

"I have to look for her."

"I'll help you, John."

"You don't have to."

"But I want to."

"She was with you all day, Gwen, and yet, at the end of the day when you were supposed to take her home, you couldn't find her." He knew he shouldn't have said it. Of course, it wasn't her fault.

"What about you, John? Did you even talk to her once today to check in?"

"She was with you, so I didn't think I had to."

"If you had, maybe you'd know where she is now."

"You're so critical, Mom," Louisa said.

"It doesn't matter, Louisa. I don't have time to fight with your mom."

"God, you two sound like you're married," Louisa said.

John felt his cheeks flush in embarrassment for being shamed by a fifteen-year-old kid.

"Louisa, don't interfere, okay?" Gwen said.

"You're being rude, Mom."

"I didn't mean to be. I'm worried."

"Maybe Vera went off somewhere with RJ. I wouldn't be surprised," Louisa said.

"No, she wouldn't do that without telling me," John said.

He heard a burring noise that made him think there was a small-engine vehicle coming down the road, and it was getting closer and louder. They looked down the driveway to see who was coming, and RJ drove in on the tractor with Vera sitting behind him. John looked at her with conflicted emotions, relief that she was all right and anger that she'd gone off somewhere and hadn't told him, and by doing that she'd frightened him.

"Thank God," he said, as he strode to them. "Where've you been, Vera?"

"I'm sorry."

"Where were you?" Louisa said.

"Why didn't you come back with Gwen?"

"I'm sorry, Dad. I'm sorry, Gwen."

"We were worried about you," Gwen said.

John came closer to her and looked her in the eye. "You were supposed to get a ride home with Gwen after work. The people at the library said they hadn't seen you when she asked them. Where were you? What did you do?"

"You're not even giving me a chance to say anything," Vera said.

"It's not Vera's fault," RJ said.

"What do you mean?"

"I went to the library this afternoon and talked her into leaving early to go out to Lily Pond with me."

"You did? That wasn't cool, RJ. To be honest, I'm pretty disappointed in you," John said. He turned away from him and looked at Vera. "And you did that without telling anyone? In the first place, cutting out of work was irresponsible."

"I know, Dad."

"Why didn't you say anything to me before you left, Vera?" Gwen said.

"Or answer the messages we all left for you?" John said.

"My phone was dead."

"I'm sorry about everything, Mr Diparma. If I hadn't made Vera come with me, this wouldn't have happened."

"RJ didn't do anything," Vera said, becoming emotional. "It wasn't his fault."

"You've got a lot of explaining to do," John said.

"But I . . . can't, Dad."

"You can't what?"

"I can't explain. I was at the library. Everyone said I wasn't there, but I was."

"But no one saw you after three o'clock, Vera," Gwen said.

"I don't know why they said that. I was there the whole time."

"But I couldn't find you when it was time to leave."

"I don't know, Gwen. I don't remember." Louisa put her arm around Vera's shoulder. "I'm okay, Lou."

"Go inside, Vera," John said.

"We should go, Louisa, so Vera and John can talk," Gwen said.

"Gwen, please let Louisa spend the night like we planned," Vera said.

"That's up to your dad."

"Yes, of course Louisa can stay."

"Are you sure, John?"

"Yes. There's no reason to change the plan."

"Okay, I guess it makes sense. Are you still going skiing in the morning. Is everyone still up for that?" Gwen said.

"Yes. First thing in the morning," John said.

RJ stepped forward. "I've got to get home. I've been gone all day."

"Be careful, RJ," John said.

"I will. I'll see everybody later."

"Good night."

Vera left with RJ to walk him to his tractor and stayed to say goodbye to him. John watched them, and he noticed for the first time that their lifelong friendship had blossomed into physical attraction for each other. He read it in their body language, from their flirty postures as they talked. In his eyes, they were suddenly nearly grown up. His mind tried to project into the future, when Vera and RJ were in their twenties, but Vera's future was indistinct. He asked himself why it was so hard to imagine it.

When RJ left, Vera slowly walked back to them. "Let's go in the house, Louisa," she said.

"Okay. First, I've got to get my stuff out of the car."

"I'll give you a hand," John said. He picked up Louisa's skis and ski bag from the backseat. Louisa got her knapsack out of the front.

Vera took the skis and bag from him. "Louisa and I'll take them inside, Dad."

"Okay," John said, giving them to her. He couldn't quell the feeling that she was hiding something. Nothing made sense. Why did he suddenly think he had to watch over her more carefully than ever? "I'll be in. I'm going to talk to Gwen for a minute."

"Bye, Mom. See you tomorrow night."

Gwen hugged her. "Goodnight, honey. Have fun tomorrow. Everybody, plan on dinner tomorrow at our house when you get back. Does that sound good, John?"

"Sure."

"You look exhausted, Vera. Get some rest."

"I'm going to, Gwen."

Vera and Louisa went inside. About that time, it started to snow again, and John's attention was drawn to the pear tree. Its gray bark glowed like silver against the landscape of the white sky and white snow. The snow fell from the sky in large, quiet flakes. The air was thick with it, like someone had turned a giant bucketful upside down and dumped it out. His hair was wet and weighed down with it. The melting snowflakes melted into cold water and dribbled down his neck. But it was all good.

"What are you looking at?"

"The pear tree. It's beautiful when it sparkles on nights like this," he said.

"How old is that tree?"

"Oh, it's got to be at least a hundred years old."

"Does it still produce pears?"

"Yeah, most years it does."

Gwen stepped away as if she was leaving. "I've got to go. Thanks for taking the girls tomorrow, John."

"Wait. Come in for some coffee."

"I can't."

"I've got tea."

"No, I'm sorry."

"Well, how about some hot chocolate with marshmallows?"

"Hot chocolate with marshmallows? Oh, wow."

"Okay, come on."

"No, I can't. Not tonight."

"Oh, why not?"

"I'm going out."

"Where to?"

"I'm seeing a friend."

"A friend?"

"Yes."

"So you have a date."

"Yes, John. I have a date. Jesus, you're awkward. I'll see you later," she said and started to her car.

"Yeah, you'd better get going, if you don't want to be late for your date."

She spun around and confronted him. "What's your problem?"

"I don't have a problem. Nothing. Good night and be careful driving."

"Hey! Where are you going?"

"I'm going back inside."

"Why?"

"You're leaving, right?"

"Wait a minute. Let's not go away mad at each other."

"I'm not mad."

"Well, then I guess I'm wrong. You're a shithead, you know that?"

"Stop a second, Gwen."

"Stop being a coward. Your sarcasm is just a shield to hide what you feel."

"Oh, yeah? What do you think I'm hiding?"

"I don't know. But if you've got something to say to me, then say it."

"Damn, you think I'm a shithead and a coward, and that's in addition to thinking I suck as a father."

"No, no, I don't think any of those things about you. Hardly, hardly. It's just that—never mind."

If he was feeling sorry for himself, he thought then so be it. "Well, you give me the exact opposite impression."

"You know this friction that we have? Sometimes I think it's because, well, it's a symptom of something else."

"Friction? What friction?"

She ignored his joke and stepped closer. "Before I leave, do you want to know my actual opinion, John?"

"Of what?"

"Of you."

"I'm not sure I want to."

"You're a noble man. That's what I think," she said.

"Noble? Nobody's ever applied that word to me before. Why do you think so?"

"Someone who is noble has integrity. You have integrity."

"I try."

"And someone who is noble has a beautiful soul. You have a beautiful soul."

He smiled at her. "Now that I didn't know."

"All right," she said. "Now it's time for me to go."

He walked with her to her car. "So, are you sure you should go out on your date in this weather?"

"Yes."

"Maybe you should tell the dude to stay home."

"I'll see you later, John."

It felt risky to say what he was thinking, but he did it anyway. "Gwen, I just want you to know it matters to me what you think of me." When he said it, it was like he'd hung his emotions out in the open air for her to see them.

She got into her car.

"Drive safe," he said.

"Thank you."

He watched her turn onto the road, and seconds later, she was gone. He stood there for a long time, with the snow descending around him from the sky, staring at the spot where her car had disappeared from his view.

***

"Aren't you going to turn on the light?" Louisa said, from the doorway.

Vera's mind was far away from the reality of her bedroom, her house, or Louisa. She heard Louisa's voice from the other end of a long tunnel of deeper thoughts.

"Turn on that lamp, Vera."

"Oh, yeah," Vera said, paying attention this time. But a part of her brain remained distant. She felt like she was carrying a heavy weight inside her, and she couldn't think about anything but that. It was barely noticeable, but when she flicked on the light switch her hand was shaking.

"It's still too dark," Louisa said. She walked around the room turning on lights.

Vera couldn't tolerate the sudden bright light. She wanted to run from it and crawl beneath the comforter on her bed and mash her face into her pillow to block it out.

"It's too bright, huh?" Louisa said.

Vera nodded. She was glad to have Louisa there. She understood her more than anyone.

Louisa turned off the overhead light and a lamp. This is good now, right?"

"Yes, it's perfect."

Louisa closed the door. "Why do you still have your coat on?"

"What time is it?" Vera said, undoing her coat.

"It's eight thirty."

"Eight thirty? I didn't think it was so late," Vera said.

"It's still early enough to watch a movie. Do you want to?"

"Yeah, I do, but I need to take a shower."

"Okay. You go do that first."

Vera gathered her pajamas and robe to take to the bathroom. "I can't believe it's eight thirty. I thought it was only about seven o'clock."

"No. How come you're so spacey about the time?"

"I don't know." She could feel Louisa watching her intently. She changed the subject to get her to stop. "I'm excited to go skiing tomorrow. Are you?"

"Yeah, what time are we leaving?" Louisa said.

"Around six, I think."

"Crap, that early? I'm just kidding. I'll be awake before you, Vera. You look like you're really tired."

"Yeah."

"But something else is wrong. I can tell."

"No, there isn't."

"I thought you'd tell me. I didn't think I'd have to drag it out of you."

"Will you frigging stop it, Lou?" She opened the door. On her way out, she turned around. "I'm sorry," she said, and she left.

In the shower, she let the hot water run on her for a long time, until the bathroom was foggy with steam. She didn't worry about wasting water or heat this time, because she needed the hot water to cleanse her. It made her feel drowsy to the point that she almost fell asleep when she stood under the showerhead so that the hot water ran down her spine. There was an area on her lower back that was sore, and she had several other sore areas on her stomach, neck, and thigh.

She took her time washing her hair, because even that was hard to do. "Why am I so . . ." she started to say aloud, but her voice trailed off because she couldn't wrap her mind around what was wrong. She kept thinking about what Gwen and Louisa had said about her—that she was nowhere to be found when they went to look for her, but she didn't understand how that could be true. And yet, she didn't remember anything that'd happened after the middle of the afternoon. She didn't remember saying goodbye to anyone, leaving the building, or walking down the stairs. She didn't remember how she'd ended up way out in the snow on Lily Pond.

She realized all this with a growing sense of panic. Even the nice sensation of the hot water lost its power to soothe. She stepped out of the shower and onto the mat with wobbly legs. Suddenly, she was convinced that something had happened to her. She felt afraid to be alone anymore, so she put on her pajamas and hurried back to her room.

When she went in, she saw Louisa stretched out on the couch, asleep in her bright pink pajamas. Vera got two blankets from the shelf in her closet and placed them over her gently. Then she stopped the movie, turned off the TV, shut off the lights except for the night-light by the door, and climbed into bed. She lay on her side and looked across the room at Louisa. She was snoring peacefully with her hair splashed across the pillow. Vera thought it was easy to see in her relaxed face how beautiful she was.

"I love you, Lou," she whispered. She felt so glad not to be alone.

Soon she fell asleep. During the night, she woke up several times from a distressing dream. At around 2:00 a.m., the dream finally stopped, and she dropped into oblivion until morning.

Chapter 10

As Gwen was kissing her date good night on her front porch, she was thinking that he might be the first man in a long time who might be right for her. Not only was he smart, interesting, and successful, he was extremely good looking. On paper, he sounded great. She liked him so much that she kept kissing him, even when she thought it'd be the last kiss and then he'd leave. They were up against the storm door making out, and she thought, *Thank goodness it's two o'clock in the morning and the bulb in the porch light is burned out, or everyone in the neighborhood would see us.*

It was cold and snowing out, but they lingered over their good night for half an hour, until Gwen decided she really needed to send him home. She gently pushed him away. "You'd better go before you can't get your car out. Thank you for tonight. I had a lovely time."

But then they kissed again, and she didn't want it to stop, and two more inches of snow fell while they continued saying goodnight. At one point, he said something about how cold it was, and of course she knew he was suggesting that she should invite him in. She mulled over the idea, because it was one of the rare nights when Louisa wasn't home. She was spending the night at Vera's, and in the morning, John was taking them skiing, and that left her free to sleep with this man if she chose. Except they'd only gone out on a few dates, and she didn't know him very well. She was cautious by nature and reluctant to take things too fast. She knew she was leading him on and making him think there was a possibility that she'd have sex with him tonight. The only thing she was sure of was that they couldn't stand outside all night necking like teenagers. It was actually an exciting dilemma to be in.

As she considered these things, she remembered a humiliating incident from her past, and just thinking about it caused her to feel ashamed all over again. It happened when she was in college and at a hockey game. She and her friend's boyfriend put on a very hot and heavy public display of affection in the stands in front of five thousand people. She found out later, to her horror, that there were more eyes watching her and her friend's boyfriend in the third period than the game.

Gwen had known her friend's boyfriend longer than her friend had, most of her life, in fact. They went to the same school from elementary through high, and he was one of her brother's best friends, and when they reached adolescence, a romantic spark developed, but they didn't act on it. She always felt like there was unfinished business between them. When their paths crossed again in college, she used their history to justify sneaking around with him behind her friend's back. She deceived herself into believing that it was destiny intervening to bring them together.

Worst of all, on the night of the hockey game, her friend's father was sitting just five rows behind them. After the game, as they were leaving, he rushed from the stands and confronted them, and he yelled at them and said things that shamed her. He told them that he was going to tell his daughter, and he did. After that, the girl cut Gwen off as a friend but continued to go out with her boyfriend for the rest of the year. Ironically, the boyfriend made a point to steer clear of Gwen, even acting as if they didn't share a history or have latent feelings for each other.

It was the only time she ever slept with a friend's boyfriend. It didn't make her feel proud, but at least she could say she never did it again.

"What are you thinking about?" her date asked.

She didn't like that he then kissed her on the nose. "I guess I'm getting tired," she said, as she stepped away from him. "You must be tired too."

"Hmm, yes and no," he said.

"Yes, but it's so late." The sloppy kiss on the nose finally gave her enough willpower to make him leave. "Thank you for a great night. I had a lot of fun." She honestly meant it.

Before he went, they made plans to see each other in a few days. "I'm looking forward to it. Be careful on the road."

"Oh. I've been meaning to ask you. Do you like to ski?" he said.

"Downhill? I'm not very good at it. I actually like cross-country skiing a lot more."

"I have a place in Stowe, and there are miles of trails around it for cross-country. I'd love to take you there. "Would you like to go up for a weekend?"

"It sounds nice."

"Great. I'll plan something. Good night," he said.

"Good night."

She waited on her steps for him to walk to his car. He turned it on and took his scraper and swept away the snow from the roof. They waved to each other, and Gwen went inside.

"I hope he's not stuck," she said, as she looked at him from the window. She thought if that happened there were two options, she'd either spend the night with him or make him sleep in his car, but neither was acceptable. He'd have to call for a ride.

She sat down in a chair. The room was very dark, except for a splatter of light that spilled over from the kitchen, and she liked it that way. She curled her legs underneath her and wiggled around in the chair in search of a comfortable position. The blanket on the back fell into her lap and she wrapped it around her body. Outside, he was still clearing off his car, and by the time he'd gone from one end to the other, he had to go back around and brush off the windshield again. She didn't know why his meticulousness annoyed her so much, but in her eyes, he was beginning to seem shallow.

She didn't think she should go to bed until he was gone. "Come on, hurry up."

Then he got in his car and tried to drive away, but the tires spun in the snow, and he was stuck. She held her breath and watched, waiting to see if she should go outside and push behind the car. He backed up and went forward, and backed up and went forward, trying to get traction under the tires, and he put his foot down hard on the gas pedal and the car lunged and came unstuck.

It was a relief to watch him driving away. She felt drowsy, and she leaned her head on the back of the chair. She didn't mean to go to sleep, but as soon as she closed her eyes she couldn't resist it. A little while later, she awoke from a dream about him. She sat up and pressed her hands against the cold window and stared out at the snow. In her dream, she'd spent the night with him, and now she wished that she had. From her dream, she also realized that one of the reasons she'd sent him home instead of sleeping with him was because of her feelings for John, and she was angry at herself. So she promised herself that from then on she'd set a different course and seize the moment the next time. She felt full of regret; tonight could've been a night to explore something new with someone who was willing.

"Oh, John," she murmured. And then she forced herself to stop thinking about him.

She felt like she lacked the energy to climb the stairs to go to bed. The idea of washing her face and brushing her teeth sounded much too hard. The word that she used to describe how she felt was *depressed*, but she knew the feeling would pass. She pulled the blanket tighter around her chin and went to sleep.

A few minutes later, while she was sleeping, she felt a pain in her stomach and woke up. The throbbing spot that hurt so much was red and hot to the touch, like she'd been poked hard by the end of a broom handle. For a moment, she thought she must be crazy for imagining that someone else was in the room, but the air felt charged with electricity, and she thought that she heard humming, and she nearly called out to ask who was there. She just watched instead for telltale movements in the dark. After a few minutes, she stood and walked very quietly, looking from room to room, until she was certain she was alone.

Satisfied with her search, she decided to go to bed. She still felt a little on edge, and she hoped it didn't keep her from going to sleep. She decided to sleep as late as she wanted in the morning, and even if she didn't get up until noon, she didn't care. Going to her bedroom, she saw through the window that it'd stopped snowing. There was a whitish-gray wall of clouds that almost made it seem like it was daylight out, even though it was still hours until dawn.

Then she saw a car pull to the side of the road across the street and park against a line of snowbanks. When no one got out of the car right away, the thought crossed her mind that it could be her neighbor's daughter getting home from a date with her boyfriend.

"What are they doing out there?" she muttered. "The girl's only sixteen. Oh, God, I should mind my own business. I'm not her mother." But she was also thinking about Louisa. So far, there wasn't a need to lay down the law about boyfriends and curfews, but that time was coming. In March, Louisa was turning sixteen.

As Gwen finished these thoughts, the driver's door opened and someone got out. It wasn't her neighbor's daughter, after all, but a tall man with broad shoulders. He stood in front of the driver-side door, looking massive as a statue beside the compact car. His face was smeared with shadows, the way the top of a big pine tree becomes at night. She thought there was something familiar about him, like the way he carried himself with his back straight and his shoulders a little bit slouched and also the way he stood with his hands in his pockets.

"It's Peter," she said, recognizing him. It was her friend Peter Cristopholos, the maintenance supervisor at the library where she worked. Her first thought was that something bad had happened at the library. She flung open the door.

"Peter," she called from the stoop.

He looked up and straightened his shoulders at the sound of her voice. He walked toward her, and with his large footprints he blazed a trail through the snow in her yard. His coat was unzipped, and it dropped off his shoulders.

"What's happened?" she said, running to meet him. "Was there a fire?"

"No, no. There wasn't a fire. The library's fine. Don't worry," Peter said.

"Oh, thank God. But is there another emergency?"

"No. Everything's just how you left it this afternoon."

"Oh, that's good. You scared me, Peter."

"I didn't mean to. I'm sorry."

"That's okay. It's okay." She was extremely relieved. A few seconds later, when she was no longer frightened, she looked at him in bewilderment. "Why are you here then? I mean, if you were coming to see me."

His face dropped and his half-smile disappeared. "Yeah, I bet you're surprised to see me."

"Well, yeah. I can't imagine why you're here. It must be important. But what is it?"

"Can I talk to you?"

"Are you all right?"

"Can I come in? Please, Gwen."

"Okay, yes, Peter. Come in."

"Thanks."

He practically filled the doorway when he stepped over the threshold. In the interior light, she had a sharper view of his face, and she was taken aback by the look of exhaustion it had and the deep dark circles under his eyes. She could tell he was nervous. His eyes were wide, as if he were aghast because he'd witnessed something terrible. She felt compassion for him, but also, she felt alarmed and guarded at his presence at her home in the middle of the night.

"Have you been drinking, Peter?"

"No, I haven't."

"Why don't you take off your coat?"

He pointed at the closet. "Should I hang it in here?"

"I'll get it," she said, and she took it from him and placed it on one of the hooks.

"Thank you," he said.

"Come in the kitchen," she said. The way he looked at her made her feel self-conscious. She pretended she didn't notice it, but she made sure that her skirt was pulled down to her knees where it was supposed to be. "Can I make you some coffee?"

"I haven't had a drink all night, but if you have something, I wouldn't mind one now."

"Well, I have beer, and I think I have a bottle of bourbon, believe it or not."

"Bourbon would be great."

She got the bottle and two glasses and poured them both generous drinks. Peter smiled and wrapped his large, muscular hands around the stocky glass. There was a stream of prying questions she wanted to ask him. It was three o'clock in the morning, and she had the right to ask them. Instead, she waited for him to talk.

They drank together at the same time. Peter finished his drink and poured another one without asking her, and she didn't mind that, but she was worried. Before he drank, he gazed at the amber bourbon in his glass, and he looked like whatever he was thinking was painful for him. His hands shook when he lifted his glass.

For the next few minutes, she sat across the table from him in silence, thinking this was a side of him that she hadn't seen before in the decade that she'd known him. Her friend Peter was a level-headed person and was always the one who took charge of things. There were times when he would get very quiet and seem withdrawn, but he was a nice person and always eager to help. He was good at his job as the town's building maintenance supervisor, and he was a good boss and respected by the people who worked for him. So what was he doing coming to her house in the middle of the night, and why was he so anxious?

The sense of desperation she felt coming from him transformed the familiar person she knew into an unsettling stranger. She wanted him to start talking, and if he wouldn't, she was going to ask him. But she let him sip his drink for a little while. Her heart jumped when he put down his glass on the table with a *whack*, because she wasn't expecting it. The glass was half-empty. He pushed it aside to make room to spread his arms. He leaned forward and held his head in his hands atop his columned forearms.

"Peter?"

"I hope you don't mind me saying this to you, but, well, I think John is a lucky man, and I hope he appreciates you."

Her heart sped up and her pulse was beating. She hurried to tell him that he was wrong. "Peter, John and I aren't involved. We never have been involved."

"Really? I thought you were."

"No. Never."

"Then who told me that?"

"I don't know, but it's not true."

"Apparently, I don't know what I'm talking about. I'm sorry. I should've kept my mouth shut."

"Someone else said that to me too. I don't know why."

"Well, it seems strange to me to find out you're not."

"Why?"

He smiled slightly. "You're in love with each other. Aren't you?"

"What? No."

"I think you're wrong about one thing. John is in love with you."

"That's ridiculous."

"Well, I guess you'd know best. But last year at the Halloween party at the fire station, when you, John, and the girls all came dressed as clowns, I remember thinking that you looked like you were a family."

"Our daughters are friends. That explains our acquaintance."

"Huh. So that dumbass has never told you how he feels about you?"

"Of course not. There's nothing to tell."

"He's a bigger dumbass than I thought he was. If I was him, I wouldn't let any more time go by to say how I felt about you." He emptied his glass, and he reached for the bottle to pour another drink.

She blocked his hand and moved it away from the bottle. "That's enough, Peter. I'm worried about you driving. The roads are slippery."

"This will be it. I promise," he said filling his glass. He raised it to his lips. "Thanks for your concern."

"You usually don't drink like this, do you?" She'd never seen it, but now she felt like she hadn't known him as well as she thought she had.

"I'm thirsty tonight. I was driving around for a long time without anything to drink."

"Why were you driving around?"

He shrugged and didn't say anything.

She put her hand on his arm, a mix of muscle and meat like the rest of him. "What's wrong?" she said.

He laughed and shook his head. "You won't believe what I've got to tell you."

His laugh was dark and sardonic, and it scared her. She got angry. "Well, what the hell is it? I was on my way to bed."

"Will you believe me?"

"I don't know. Look, please stop the riddles. Why'd you come here? Does your wife know where you are?"

"No, not at this exact moment. Actually, she hasn't seen me since last night."

"Last night? What happened? Did you have a fight?"

"No. It was nothing like that. We never fight. No, it doesn't really have anything to do with her."

"You're my friend, Peter, but you'd better tell me what you came here for, or I'm going to kick you out of my house."

He put down his glass and stood up. "I can't believe what an idiot I am to intrude on you like this, Gwen. I'll go."

"Wait a minute."

"No, you don't need to know this."

"Sit down."

"Gwen, we're friends, aren't we?" he said. His big voice sounded small. "I take care of the building and you take care of the books, right?"

"Yes."

"Tonight while I was driving around, Gwen, I stopped in front of John's place."

"Why?"

"I went there to speak to him about something, but I pulled over on the side of the road and sat there and tried to talk myself into knocking on the door. I saw John walking up behind the car, and I was afraid he'd recognize me, so I took off. He probably wondered what the hell was going on."

"Peter, I don't get it. Why were you so mysterious? Why are you being so mysterious now?"

"I know something about Vera that he should know."

"What about Vera?"

"I thought if I told him and he didn't believe me, I'd have done more harm than good. It doesn't even make any sense to me."

"Has something bad happened to Vera? Did someone hurt her? Tell me, so we can help her."

"You can't stop them."

"If somebody is hurting her, of course we can. You're starting to sound crazy to me, Peter."

He grinned at her strangely, darkly. "By now I feel like I am. But it's true. They come for you on their timetable, when they want, and all you can do is just try to get through it. If you can, you pretend you're somewhere else, and it's not really you strapped to the table, just your body, and you put your mind somewhere else. It's like going to the dentist or getting a colonoscopy," he said. He laughed, but it was deadly serious.

She thought there was something seriously wrong with how he was acting. *What's he saying?* she thought. The web of details he threw at her scared her and took away her ability to think. "Peter," she said gently. "Why don't you go lie down on my couch for a while, before you go home? You're drunk and you're tired."

"Yes, I'm both those things, but I'm also not making this stuff up." He put his hand on hers.

"Peter—"

"Wait a minute, Gwen. These beings that come for Vera come for me too. That's how I know."

"Vera? Who comes for Vera?"

"I don't know who they are or where they come from, and all I can tell you is they aren't human."

"I don't understand. What the hell are you talking about?"

"It's beyond my understanding too. All I know is that it's real," Peter said. "They come for you, and it's never a matter of if, but when. Sometimes it's just a few days, but sometimes months or years go by between their visits. After they bring you back, you can't remember what happened, because they take away your memories. But you're anxious all the time because you have minutes or hours of missing time that you don't remember, and other odd things that happen to you that you can't explain ... But five years ago," he continued, "I started to remember everything, and then it got so I couldn't forget it, and I knew about them and what they were doing to me. And ever since then, I've lived with the dread of when it's going to happen again, and whether the next time will be the one when they don't bring me back."

Gwen lost patience and stood up and shoved the chair under the table so it shook. "And Vera?" The chair buckled back and forth and crashed back into place. "What's this got to do with her?"

He stared at the chair with his sorrowful eyes and took her hand again. His fingers twitched, entwined with hers. Gwen stiffened and waited.

"They've been taking Vera since she was little, practically a baby."

"What? No. I'm sorry, but do you know how crazy that sounds?"

"I know, but I'm not making this up. I wish I were."

"John told me that Vera's mother had hallucinations, and what you're saying sounds exactly the same."

"They're not hallucinations."

"You think they're real?"

"How do you tell somebody about something like this?" he said. "It's so far from normal. People aren't equipped to believe it. I couldn't make myself tell John. And telling you is the hardest thing I've ever done. You don't think it's possible?"

He was so blunt that it felt cruel, but then there was a small chance that he was being honest. She clung to the idea that he was delusional. "Why would I?"

But even as she denied it, she thought how she'd always felt there was something inexplicable about Vera that made her different from other children, even Louisa, and there'd been some incidents that'd given her the strong feeling that Vera had been in contact with something outside of the material world.

"I thought you might've, because you've watched her grow up, and you're a sensitive person," he said.

She could see that he was in agony because she wouldn't accept what he said. His emotional pain showed on his face. It made her think. And just today, Vera had gone missing from the library for hours but remembered nothing about it, and she wouldn't or couldn't explain what she had done.

Oh, God, she thought. *I'm starting to believe him.* "Why are you so convinced that this is happening to her?"

"Because I've seen her on their ships. Like I said, they take me too."

If the phenomenon was real, then it could also be affecting Louisa. "What about my daughter?" she said, panicking.

"No, no they don't take Louisa. You don't have to feel afraid for her, Gwen."

She put her hands over her face and struggled to process all that she'd heard. Everything felt surreal. His story still sounded absurd, but she sensed the truth of it.

"Did it happen yesterday afternoon?" she said.

"Yes. They took me too. I saw her on their ship."

"She just seemed to vanish from the library yesterday. No one knew where she was." She had to stop because she was crying. All of a sudden, she believed him entirely. It took her a moment to be able to continue speaking. "But why? Why do they take her? What do they want with her?"

"I still don't understand why they take who they take, but I don't think it's coincidental either. They've probably got a lot of reasons, but I can only guess. They tell me certain things they want me to know up to a point, but they're always in control."

To her, he sounded like he'd given up. She promised herself not to ever give up on Vera. "You make it sound like there's no hope. Then why did you tell me all this terrible shit if there's nothing we can do?"

"I mean there's no hope in trying to stop them. If I could protect Vera that way, I'd do it. I've hoped and prayed for years that they'd leave me alone, but it hasn't happened yet. So now I only pray that I can accept it, live with it, and maybe be happy. It's the only thing I can control. There's a reason for what Vera and I go through, and it's up to us to figure out our purpose in all of this. Gwen, it's the only way, and you can help Vera with that. You can help her."

Peter still had the same square jaw and curly black hair flecked with gray, but since she'd found out his secret, he no longer looked like himself. He'd given her the biggest shock of her life, shattering the assumptions she had about creating your own destiny and having free will. It had changed everything. Nothing was the same and it never would be.

"They're ugly little bastards, you know? They're scary to look at, but you know they're a little scared of me, too, because I don't make it easy for them to capture me. I hurl them all over the place, like I used to do to tacklers when I played football in high school. I can't let them take me without a fight. It feels like I'm punching balloons. But they keep coming at me, and after a while, they always win."

Peter bent over and tucked his arms around his stomach as if it hurt. His voice sunk low. "I'm sorry I can't protect Vera. I can't even protect myself."

"What do they do to her?"

"They do tests."

"What kind of tests?"

"On her skin, on her organs, and her body cavities."

"How horrible."

"They get to know her. They have a way of expanding your mind. It's weird, but I feel a connection with them. I hate it, but I do. They do awesome things that you can't even imagine. They can lift you up in a beam of light and bring you to their ships. They can freeze time."

The way he talked about them made her sick. "You sound like you admire what they do. They're not helping Vera, they're hurting her. They're hurting you."

"I don't know exactly why they do it. Sometimes I think they're trying to change us. They taught me things. Maybe it's for the better, maybe not. They also torment me. I don't know if they mean to, but they're willing to … It's terrifying when they come for me. It gets deadly quiet, and nothing is moving. It's like you can't sense any life around you. It's as lonely as being on the moon. The air gets thick and electric, and reality is mixed up, like in *The Wizard of Oz*, a hellish Oz, and you realize they're coming for you."

Gwen shuddered. If what he was saying was true, it was unbearable.

"I can't live with what they put me through unless I think it has a purpose. That's what I hope," he said.

"There's no purpose in your suffering."

"After twenty-five years, I hope there is," he said.

"Twenty-five years?"

"That was the first time I was abducted. It was in October, and me and my wife were driving on Wentworth Road, and that's where it happened."

"That's near John and Vera's house," Gwen said.

"Yes, I know it is."

He began to tell her the story. His face was marked with suffering, and his air of defeat and fatalism broke her heart. On that night, he and his wife were going to their nephew's school concert. He told her that when they got to the bridge and crossed over the old reservoir, he was thinking about the foliage on the trees around the pond. A blurry reflection of brilliant red and orange leaves stretched across the water, and he remembered thinking that it looked like a painting.

"I slowed down and opened the windows," he said. "I wanted to take it all in. And I noticed that it seemed very quiet. You couldn't even hear the bullfrogs that you usually do on the pond at that time of the evening. The stillness was so deep, and I could feel it vibrating under my skin. For some reason, I wondered if we were about to have an earthquake, and so I asked my wife if she noticed the same thing, and she said yes. She leaned forward then and pointed out the window, and she said, 'Do you see that?' I looked, and I said it was the first star on the horizon, and I thought it was beautiful ... We kept going. But we didn't talk much to each other, until a couple of miles from the school, when my wife suddenly yelled out my name and scared the shit out of me. I spun my head around so hard that I wrenched my neck. She said it wasn't a star, and it was following us ... 'Don't you see it?' she asked me. But I couldn't see it because I was driving, and I told her it had to be a plane or maybe a helicopter. Then she turned to look at it again and told me it was gone. She was so scared that she swore at me, which shocked me, because I never heard her swear. I didn't understand why she was so upset. I told her to calm down. I said it was probably a meteor ... A few minutes later, she told me it had come back again, and I told her it was just the moon, for God's sake. She said that it couldn't be, because it was flying above us and following us. I couldn't see the object out my mirrors, but I could see the light. I drove faster to get ahead of it. My wife was scared, and she was shaking ... On the last leg of the road into town, I went up the big hill. The thing had disappeared again, and we hoped it was gone for good. When we got to the top, at the point where you can look down and see the town, I slammed on the brakes. We slowed down, and then the engine died. It was as silent as a corpse when I tried to start it, and we were stranded. I looked out the windshield and saw the object hanging in the air in front of us, around a hundred and fifty feet from the ground. It was no plane. It was shaped like a disk with a pulsing light that burned our eyes. I felt like it was also burning my skin, and I almost couldn't stand it. But then it faded so that it was bearable ... My wife yelled something at me, but I couldn't hear her. When I tried to reach out to her, I realized that I couldn't move. I was paralyzed with fear, I think. But there was another force that was pinning me down and keeping me from getting away. I was totally conscious, hyper-conscious, but I couldn't bend a muscle in my face. All I could do was stare straight ahead at the light. It narrowed to a single beam shooting down from the bottom of the craft, and there were four beings in the center of the light, and they started to come toward us. I knew they were going to capture us. I thought, *Oh God, protect us from what's happening*. My wife said, 'Lock your door! Lock your door!' and this time I heard her ... I started to cry too, and tears were running down my face, but I couldn't wipe them off. The four of them came closer and closer, and then they were outside our doors, peering at us through the windows. They opened the doors and pulled us out. All of a sudden, I found that I could move again, and so I fought them. I fought them really hard. They were just little things, but they were incredibly strong, and they finally got the better of me and they carried us up a rising platform to their craft. I felt the tops of my shoes dragging on the platform. It scratched my shoes, and I still have them. That's all that I remembered at the time ... The next thing we knew, we were in our car, parked in the middle of the road with the engine running. I looked over at my wife, and she was slumped against the door, asleep. I put the car in gear and started to go forward, and when I did, she woke up and straightened herself. She didn't say anything to me, and I didn't say anything to her. We just went on our way, as if nothing had happened. We didn't know something had ... We drove on to the school to the concert, but when we got there, it was already the intermission. We didn't know why we were late, and we told our nephew that we got a flat tire, but the truth was that I couldn't explain it. During the concert, I couldn't sit still because I felt antsy and tense, like something was the matter but I didn't know what it was. And the whole time, my wife stared straight at the stage like I wasn't there ... After, we went home, we went to bed right away, and we slept late the next morning, and I never sleep late unless I'm sick. But it was also before we had kids. I think we were both confused because there was an hour of time that was just gone for us. We didn't tell anyone. She and I didn't even talk about it then. We've never talked about it."

"Your wife doesn't remember?" Gwen said.

"She's afraid of what she remembers, and so she acts like it didn't happen. She won't talk to me when I bring it up. I know she had dreams about it right afterward, like I did. She doesn't want it to be true. She pretends it isn't."

"Who can blame her?" Gwen said.

"I don't. Except that it makes me feel as if I'm all alone. I wish I could make myself pretend it never happened."

Gwen wished with all her heart that it'd never happened, so that no one would be harmed or need to pretend. Peter's story was life-altering. It upended the world as she knew it, blowing off the doors of the only reality that she recognized. People she loved were being hurt. It was tragic that Peter was disappointed in his wife, but Gwen asked herself honestly what she would do if she were Peter's wife, and it was possible she'd be in denial too. She couldn't bear the sadness of it all.

"This was the first time that you were abducted," she said. "But you said it happened more than once."

He bent his head and spoke softly, as if he felt ashamed. "Yeah, many times."

"Just you? What about your wife?"

"No, I don't have any reason to think it's ever happened to her again."

"And you? How often?"

"Like I said, it's different. You never know what they're planning. But I can tell when they're around or coming sometimes," he said softly, as if he was trying to keep them from overhearing him. "And also, the hair on the back of my neck stands up, and I have the feeling that I'm being watched. I run around and check on my kids because I'm afraid they'll take them too."

"What do they want?"

"I asked them once why they did this to me and other people," he said. "The answer I got was that there was no other way. They were doing what was necessary, and it couldn't be helped. So I don't hate them anymore. It didn't do any good when I hated them," he said. "They don't care. Hating made it worse for me not them."

She hated what he was saying. He identified with them, and he risked losing his humanity. "Jesus, don't give in, Peter. You can't do that."

"I haven't, but some things you can't fight. You've got to make the best out of it that you can, because you've got no other choice. I try to lock away my worries about the things I can't change in the back of my head, so I don't have to deal with them every day. That's what I try to do. But I haven't given in."

"Don't ever."

He smiled at her shyly. His shyness had to do with her. He wanted to say something else, but he was grappling with whether to. She distinctly felt what she'd suspected for a long time. He was attracted to her. His gaze made her uncomfortable, so she walked away from him. The distance made it feel less awkward. She pitied the loneliness that he wore like a second skin. Such deep loneliness. Did Vera feel that way too?

"In every other way but this, I'm an ordinary person—except for being abducted by aliens. I've got a wife and kids, a job, and a mortgage. I'm ordinary, but I'm not … What I said about how I survive, I told you for Vera's sake. That's what she has to do, and you have to help her, Gwen. When her memories break through and she knows, she'll need people who care about her to believe her," he said, pleading.

"I will."

"What about John?"

"I think you're wrong, Peter. I think John already knows, but he's forgotten or blocked it out." John had traced the phenomenon back to his wife. Maybe she hadn't left them of her free will. Maybe she was abducted. Peter had known her. She wanted to ask him about her. "How well did you know Suzy, John's wife?"

"Not that well, but I liked her. John was young when he met her. I think she helped to straighten him out."

"Straighten him out?"

"He was in his band, and he was kind of a party boy. Too much drinking, etc. and when he fell in love with Suzy, he changed to be with her. Luckily," he said.

"Do you know what happened to her?"

"I have some ideas."

"Do you think she's still alive?"

"I don't know. I hope so. It's Vera I'm worried about now. You'll help Vera?"

"Yes. I love her like she's my own daughter." She placed her hand on his. "But how can I help you?"

"You helped me. You believed me. Nobody else has. Especially not my psychiatrist."

Gwen turned her face toward the window. "The sun is coming up." She went and opened the curtains.

"Oh, yeah, I see it's getting light out."

The dawn brought Gwen comfort. The black cap of the sun was edging above the hills with a crown of golden light burning around it. She felt a sense of hope in the new day, despite everything. But she could never forget the grave information about Vera and Peter and so much more.

"Come look at this, Peter," she said, pointing at the sky.

He stooped so he could look from her vantage point. "Yes, it's beautiful."

"I'll make some coffee."

"Don't go to any trouble for me, Gwen."

"I need some. Are you hungry? I am."

She let Peter make breakfast for them, because he insisted. After they ate, he insisted on washing the dishes. She kept thinking that he had to go home to get some sleep and see his wife. By the time he was done, she was ready for him to leave. Not until he'd dried the last pan and put it away in the cupboard did he announce that he was leaving.

She waited at the door as he put on his jacket. "It's bitter cold this morning. I'll see you at work on Monday."

"Thank you, Gwen," he said, as he stepped out the door.

"Take care, Peter."

It was an empty phrase, take care, but there wasn't anything else that she could say. She hugged him, and he readily wrapped his arms around her. Then he left. She watched him from the doorway. Cold air blew freely into the house through the wide-open door, until he'd driven away. She was exhausted from talking and listening.

She drank another cup of coffee. Minutes passed when she forgot about the existence of time, and she only thought about the decision to tell John right away or to wait, or if she should even tell him at all. He might not believe her. If he believed her, she was afraid he'd get so outraged that it'd impact Vera. On the other hand, Vera was his child, and it seemed wrong to hide it from him. Also, she was afraid if she kept it from him that she'd lose his trust. They didn't always get along, but she thought she was right in thinking that they trusted each other, and she knew that his trust in her ran even deeper. She didn't know what to do—not yet.

She put her coffee cup in the sink and walked out of the kitchen and wandered around the first floor of her house without a destination, looking in the mirrors and outside the widows as she passed them. She noticed things like the dust on her bookshelves and on her television set. She felt indecisive and edgy, not knowing if she should stay up or go to bed. For the sake of making a decision, she decided to go to bed, and she went into her room and got into bed and pulled the blankets over her head. It amazed her that she was able to relax so fast. The blackout under the blankets and the weight of the covers helped her to let go, and her eyelids slipped closed. Her breath slowed and grew deeper, but it was agitated. "Stop hurting her," she mumbled, in the last thought she had before she fell asleep.

Chapter 11

In Vera's dream, the wind blew across the mountain in hard, cold gusts and swept away the snow from the tops of the boulders and sent it sailing down the slopes. The sky around the mountain range shone white and pale through huge bleak clouds. Vera stood on her skis in the gate at the top of the mountain, studying the clouds. They were complex formations of different shapes and shades of gray. As they moved in the wind, they overlapped with each other, forming giant masses that rolled across smaller clouds like a tsunami.

Some of the huge cloud banks were shaped like gyroscopes with dark eyes at their centers. When Vera saw them, she imagined that walking through the dark eyes would take her to other parts of the universe. Then she leaped, and began to fly down the mountain. The air whistled behind her skis, and the cheers from the crowd watching at the finish line rose faintly up the mountain as she raced, and she knew that she was the one to beat.

At first, the jackets of the people below looked like tiny blotches of primary colors to her, but as she went faster, they became a blurry rainbow spread across the snow. Ahead of her lay a sharp bank of snow. She made herself go faster. She was not afraid of falling, not today. She grazed the bank with her skis as she passed over it and used it as a launching pad to take off into the air. She took flight and waited to drift back down, but then she realized that she didn't feel the sensation of gravity dragging her to the ground as she should have. For a moment, she didn't believe what she was experiencing: the Earth under her skis was no longer there. She looked for the mountains in the east and the people at the bottom, but they were no longer there. It was like she was suspended inside one of the colossal clouds, because there was nothing but smoky-whiteness above and below her.

Then the clouds began to blow apart and float away in pieces like milkweed in the wind, revealing black space and strings of stars. To her fear and amazement, she began to shed her body; it faded away, like the clouds, and her molecules transmuted into an atomic version of herself. It occurred to her that she might be dead. She wanted to know the cause of her death. Then she remembered her last act on Earth while she was alive, and she suddenly re-experienced tumbling uncontrollably down the slope, like a ball of laundry tossing around inside a dryer, her arms and legs shattering as they dropped from the sky on ledges of frozen granite. Then she saw herself crashing into the mountain with a deadly force that broke her neck and killed her. Or maybe she wasn't dead? She needed a sign; she needed angels to appear.

There weren't any angels. She found herself floating in space. It was more colorful and much louder than she'd imagined it. She crossed over into other dimensions and traveled distances that were immense and ended up in other worlds. She traveled in time to the past and future over thousands of millennia and beyond. She experienced a strange new sense of identity, as one who belonged as much to the stars as to Earth. She didn't feel far away from home anymore. She saw herself living many different lives in far-off places simultaneously across the universe. Time had a different meaning in this mystical environment. She became used to being without her body and to being stardust.

Then everything changed, and she was moving much faster and transforming back into matter. She became aware of having five physical senses again. She smelled the earth. She heard the wind. The clouds faded away and revealed the crowd of people below; she realized she'd made it down the mountain and that she was almost upon them, and then she crossed the finish line and rode out her momentum until she stopped. She stood on her skis at the base of the mountain, utterly exhausted and gasping for breath, and her eyes were fixed on the sky.

The cheering stopped, and the atmosphere around her was cold and quiet, and the sea of people were staring at her in stunned silence. She stared back at them. She was equally stunned. A man stepped out of the crowd and walked toward her with a gait like he was in a hurry to get to her. He resembled her father, but when he stopped in front of her, she knew it wasn't him. He gave her an angry look that frightened her.

"Where were you?" he said.

She didn't have an answer. She couldn't explain where she'd been. It was impossible to, even to her father. She wondered who this was, this person yelling at her. She turned away from him to dodge his glaring eyes, and she saw a woman standing alone under a conclave of trees, and their eyes met. It seemed to Vera that she'd seen the woman's heartbroken face before. She had a faint impression of her smiling.

They watched each other closely from a distance, and finally, the woman began walking toward her. As she drew closer, Vera became more anxious, wishing that the woman would keep away, and then, with one more step, the woman disappeared in front of her eyes. One second, she was walking toward her, and the next second she was gone. That was when her dream ended, and she woke up right after it with her heart pounding, like she'd actually skied down the mountain.

There were loud bangs coming from outside. She sat straight up in bed. She felt only barely awake and half aware of where she was. Her disoriented state lingered for a while, before her mind could make sense of the reality that she was in. The first thing she remembered was that it was Monday, and she had to go to school.

In the driveway, below her bedroom window, John was getting his supplies to go to work. He rolled up the garage door and let it reel to the top with a slam. A minute or two later, he started throwing planks of wood into the back of his truck, creating a racket that made her react in anguish every time. Frustrated, she fell back down on her bed and tried to ignore the noise. She stared at the ceiling above her bed, and it unnerved her when she saw a giant nest of cobwebs dangling from the light. The crashing and bashing outside was shaking the cobwebs, and she was worried that they were going to collapse on top of her, any second.

She could hardly remember her dream anymore. The only thing left over from it was the feeling that it was an emotional and vivid dream. The noise that John was making was excruciating, and she covered her ears with her pillow and swore out loud at him. It was still very early in the morning, and, as usual, he was being thoughtless of her.

Finally, she made herself get out of bed. She sat up and put her feet on the floor. Her legs felt weary when she stood on them. Her whole body felt tired from all of the skiing she'd done the day before—and in her dream. To kickstart her body, she dropped down on the rug and did twenty-five pushups and then hopped up and did fifty jumping jacks. Her blood was flowing now, and she felt better. She left her room to go to the bathroom. She stopped in the hall and stood and warmed herself in the rays of sun that were pouring through the window. After a minute, she proceeded to the bathroom.

When she'd finished and gone back to her room, she looked out at John in the driveway. He was loading his truck, and she saw his mouth moving at the same time, and she knew he was singing. He tapped the beat of the song on the wood he was carrying, as he walked to his truck. He danced a shuffle both going to the workshop and on his way back with his tool bag. He whistled as he put the tool bag inside the front seat of the truck. As annoyed at him as she was, she felt glad that he felt happy. It was good.

When he was done, he walked toward the house, and a few seconds later, Vera heard the back door open and close as he came in.

"Vera?" he called.

"What?"

"Are you up?"

She wanted him to know she was mad at him. "Yes, of course. I couldn't sleep through all the noise you made."

"It's a work day and a school day, so it's allowed," he said without sympathy. "I'm going to make oatmeal."

"I'm going to take a shower."

She heard the scuff of his feet as he came halfway up the stairs.

"Hurry up," he called to her.

To respond, instead of answering, she slammed the bathroom door. "He thinks I'm stupid," she said, taking off her pajamas. She threw the top and the bottom pieces on the floor in different directions. "I'm sick of him telling me what to do."

She kicked the bathmat and yanked a towel off the shelf of the closet. Other towels tumbled out onto the floor in the process. She turned on the shower and stepped in while the water was still cold. She took her time in the shower and washed her hair luxuriously, wasting water in deliberate defiance of his rules.

When she looked in her closet, she had no idea what to wear. Half of her clothes lay dirty in the hamper. Her plan to do laundry over the weekend had failed. To her relief, she found one of her favorite skirts hanging there neat and clean and ready to wear, and she had a positive feeling about something for the first time since she woke up. She picked out a blouse, a sweater, and a pair of tights to go with it, and she got dressed.

She took out her scant bag of makeup and traced her eyelids and under her eyes with liner and coated her eyelashes with mascara. Lastly, she painted her lips with lipstick that was the color of pink geraniums. The girl that she saw in the mirror looked older than fifteen-going-on-sixteen, and not like such an ugly duckling. She didn't know this girl very well yet. She made a long inspection of her eyes. The sunlight sparkled in them, and she thought they were beautiful. But something about the girl disturbed her. She was pretty but wasn't carefree. Something precious was missing from her life, and she was hiding a secret. She walked away from her image in the mirror; she'd seen enough.

Before she went downstairs, she packed her bag for school, but her mind wasn't on her task, it was on RJ. She envisioned the night before last when they were alone at Lily Pond, standing on the ice with the wind bearing down on their backs, and she wasn't cold then, no, not at all. She worried about her attraction to RJ, because they'd been friends their whole lives, and she'd always loved him in that way. Her new feelings came out of nowhere and surprised her, and suddenly she couldn't stop thinking about him. It upset her that she daydreamed about kissing him. A relationship would be too complicated, but there was another reason she felt that way. She didn't know the reason, but it hung over everything.

She lifted her school bag and put the strap over her shoulder and went downstairs. John was standing at the kitchen sink.

"Hi," she said, coming into the kitchen. She sat down at her place in front of the bowl of oatmeal and banana John made for her.

He turned to greet her. "Good morning. How are you doing?"

"Good," she said, poking her oatmeal with a spoon.

"You're not hungry?"

Without answering him, she silently scooped up a slice of banana and put it in her mouth.

"It's probably cold by now," he said, and then he dunked the dirty oatmeal pan in the soapy dishwater.

"No, it's not cold," she said, lying.

"Do you want a glass of juice?"

"I can get it."

She opened the cabinet for a glass, and as she did, she had a memory of herself when she was young and little and needed to climb on a chair to reach the shelf for her Winnie the Pooh glass, and it seemed like only yesterday to her.

"Are you looking for your Pooh glass?"

"Any glass."

They're all in the dishwasher. They're clean. I asked you to unload the dishwasher last night, didn't I?"

"Yes."

"How come you never got around to it?"

"Sorry."

"Vera."

"I am. I'm sorry. I had homework and I was tired. I'll do it now," she said.

"Never mind, I don't want you to have to run to get to the bus."

"I said I'd do it."

"Okay, whatever you say. I made your lunch. It's in the refrigerator."

"Thanks."

"So, this might not be a good time to bring it up, since you seem a little grouchy."

"I'm not grouchy."

"Sorry, just teasing."

"Well, what now, Dad?"

"I don't understand why it takes you so long to take a shower. I don't get it."

It irritated her that he acted like it was the most serious problem in the world. "You always ask me that. I was only in there for ten minutes, as usual."

"Do I have to remind you that we have to be careful about our water usage? We're on well water, honey. And we had a drought last summer and—"

"Should I shave my head so I don't have to wash my hair?"

"Don't get sarcastic, Vera."

"I mean it. I don't know what your problem is."

"Calm down."

"I'll try not to waste water. I don't want to waste it."

"Okay. Are you going to eat your oatmeal, Vera?"

She ate another spoonful. "Yes. Yum."

"You make breakfast for us tomorrow."

"I will," she said. Then she changed the subject. "So, how'd I look on the mountain yesterday?"

"You looked really good, honey. You were fast and in control, and I think you've got a great chance of winning next week."

"I had a dream about the race last night," she said, suddenly thinking about it.

"Oh, yeah? What happened?"

"I was the one to beat."

He smiled. "I think you are. You know, you look so pretty today. You're pretty all the time, but you're a little more dressed up, and you put on makeup."

"I guess so," she said, as she scraped the last spoonful of oatmeal out of the bowl.

"Don't give me that look. I meant it as a compliment."

She couldn't keep herself from smiling. "I'm sorry. Thanks, Dad." He knew her tender spots as well as her sore spots. "I love you."

"I love you, Vera."

She went to get her coat, and she put her head on his shoulder for a second on her way past him.

"Any special reason that you felt like getting dressed up today?" he said.

"Not really."

"Oh, I just wondered if it was because of a—"

"No, it's not."

"I thought maybe it might be—"

"It's not anything. Stop it, Dad, please." If he didn't stop, there'd be an argument. He was making her tense.

"I was thinking of asking RJ to give me a hand in the workshop again. I haven't had him over to work for a while. I could use his help now. He's already a decent carpenter, and he takes direction well and he takes the initiative. He sees the things that need to be done and he does them."

"I hope you're not asking him over for my sake or something. You're not trying to set us up, are you?"

"What? Don't be ridiculous. I miss having him around. Why? Do you like him?"

"I like him as a friend."

"Does he like you?"

"As a friend."

"Really? I've just gotten the sense from both of you lately that you're more than friends now. I just want to tell you, Vera, that if you and RJ ever start dating, I wouldn't have a problem with that. I like RJ."

"We've never even talked about it."

"Thank you for telling me where you and RJ are at. But just so we're clear, I wouldn't mind if RJ was your boyfriend. I know that I can trust him. It's hard for me because you're growing up, but I accept it."

She walked away from him abruptly. "I'm going. I'll see you later, Dad." She didn't bother to zip her coat before she went out the door.

"Hold on. I'll drive you to school." He fetched his coat from the back of the kitchen chair.

She was tired of being pressured. There was no way she wanted to get a ride from him. "No, thanks. I'll take the bus, like I planned."

He looked disappointed. "Are you sure?"

"Yeah, I want a chance to be outside and walk around before I have to be inside all day. But thanks for offering."

"Okay. I'll see you tonight, honey. I love you."

"Love you too, Dad." She shifted her backpack so it rested more comfortably on her shoulder and closed the door.

She walked down the driveway and onto the road. It was another stormy-looking, melancholy winter day with a silver-white sun and charcoal clouds. She stopped and leaned her head back to see. The wind swept over her and left its icy fingerprints on her neck and bit through her mittens. She stuffed her hands in her pockets for warmth and kept pushing against the stiff breeze to the bus stop.

She wasn't surprised that there was no one else waiting when she got there, because there were only four other school-age kids that lived around her. They were younger, and they were usually driven to school by their parents. She babysat all of them. She thought that it would've been nice to have them with her today for company.

In a tree somewhere, she heard a cardinal's nervous whistle and saw a flash of brilliant red feathers flapping in a snowy mesh of tree branches. The little bird jittered around and never rested. *Because he doesn't trust the world enough to sit still*, she thought. It lived in continuous fear that something bad would happen, such as a hawk would swoop down and fly away with it, and have it for dinner. She felt like she understood the kind of fear the cardinal had when it was afraid for its life. But these morbid thoughts were too depressing, so she quickly put them out of her mind.

The cardinal suddenly flew away from the tree in a red blur. She tried to keep it in sight, but once it crossed into the woods it was gone. She was disappointed to see it go and felt sad in its absence. The empty bus stop felt even lonelier to her, and she was extremely conscious of being there all alone.

She heard a car approaching, and then saw it appear around the curve. It slowed down and stopped in front of her. The window came down little by little, and the driver leaned out. She quickly recognized her dad's friend Peter, Peter Cristopholos.

He opened the door and got out of the car. "Good morning, Vera. How are you doing?"

"Hi. I'm good. How are you?"

"Fine," he said. As he walked over to her, he pulled his jacket collar up so it covered his neck. "Waiting for the school bus?"

"Yes."

"When I saw you, I thought I'd stop and say hi and ask how you and your dad are doing."

"We're fine. I think my dad's still home, if you were going to stop by."

"No. He probably has to get to work, like I do. You look cold."

"No," she said.

"I heard you're racing on Saturday. Are you looking forward to it?" he asked.

She pictured herself shredding down the course. She could hardly wait to actually be in the moment, because all the fretting and worrying about competing would be behind her then. "I am, but I'm nervous," she said. "I'll be racing against some great skiers."

"You should feel confident about yourself. You'll do great. Maybe even win, right?"

"Yes," she said. She really did think it was possible, and she appreciated that Peter believed in her.

"Enjoy the experience and do your best. Those things are more important than we realize. They make us the happiest. They're more important than winning. They make you feel good to be alive."

She understood what he meant, but she didn't understand why he sounded so serious. Yet, she thought it was sweet that he expressed these things to her. They weren't just words when he said them. He meant them personally to her. "Yes, I'll remember that, Peter. Thank you."

"Good luck, in case I don't see you at the library this week. Okay? I really mean it, Vera. Good luck," he said.

"Thank you." She wondered what he was looking at when he scanned the area with his eyes.

"What time does the bus pick you up?" he asked.

"Seven thirty."

"Oh, so any minute now. Do you wait here by yourself every morning?"

She thought it was an odd question, but she answered him pleasantly. "Usually, unless my dad gives me a ride to school. It's quieter when no one else is here, and then I have a better chance of seeing wildlife. I try to stay quiet so they might show themselves."

"I imagine you'd get to see a lot of critters early in the morning like this."

"There's lots of kinds that show up. Deer, turkeys, fox, hawks, eagles."

"Animals are on the move this time of day."

"I've seen a moose twice," she said excitedly. "Once I saw a bear cub right over there at the bottom of that bank." She pointed across the road at the spot. "I watched it for a few minutes, but then it noticed me and cried and ran back up the bank to its mother. She must've been keeping an eye on it from there."

"I used to hunt deer, water fowl, and game birds. It helped to put food on the table. If people want to hunt, I don't have a problem with that. It's up to them, but I don't have the heart for it anymore."

Vera saw the bus coming toward them. The brakes sounded like an elephant trumpeting as the bus slowed down to stop. "Here's the bus." The door opened for her to get on. "Bye, Mr Cristopholos. It was nice talking to you."

"Good luck in the race. Please say hello to your dad for me."

"I will."

She waved goodbye as she boarded the bus. She crossed down the aisle and picked a seat by herself. The bus was half-empty, so there were plenty to choose from. After she sat down, she looked out the window at Peter walking to his car. He got in and sat behind the steering wheel, and he watched the bus, like he was guarding it. She didn't understand why he was just sitting there and why he hadn't driven away. She thought that something might be wrong with him. He might be sick. She would've gone back to see, but the bus was already moving, and his car soon disappeared out of sight in the rearview window.

She turned around and sat back quietly in the seat. She folded her hands in her lap and watched the trees go by, and she had a sensation like the bus was going in slow motion. The branches protruded out above the road and entwined with the electric utility wires. There was a screeching noise every time one of the low-lying ones scraped against the bus. She glanced up at the gaps between the bundles of branches where the sunlight shined down into the trees. There was something soothing about it that made her want to close her eyes and let herself fall asleep. She tried, but she kept thinking about Peter. After a few minutes, she began thinking about RJ, and to control it, she began playing with her phone.

There was a message from Louisa, but before she had a chance to check it, the phone rang.

"Where are you?" Louisa said loudly. Behind her voice was a cacophony of kids' laughter.

"I'm on the bus."

"How long until you get here?"

"Five minutes."

"I'll see you outside. Oh, wait! Can you help me with geometry today again after school?"

"Yes, but I'm not that great at it either, Louisa."

"But you got an A on the last test. I got a C."

"I studied hard," she said, slightly insinuatingly.

"I don't seem to get it, no matter what. Last year I did great in algebra. I actually like algebra. Oh, Michael's walking over. I've got to go."

"Bye, Lou."

She hung up, and soon she was back to thinking about RJ against her will. She felt nervous about seeing him at school, and she felt stupid for feeling that way. She kept telling herself that it was just RJ, who was her friend, not somebody she didn't know who she wanted to get to know. At her most tortured moment, she literally hated herself for being obsessed with him. She was feeling more like herself when the bus got to the school. She whispered "Finally" and threw her backpack over her shoulder so she would be ready to get off as soon as it stopped.

"Bye, Carol. Thanks," she said as she rushed to the steps, but she was stopped by the kindly voice of the driver asking her a question.

"How are you doing today, Vera?" the driver asked.

Time seemed to have stopped as she stood gazing at Carol's familiar round face, with its soft smile and halo of gray hair, and she felt like she was a little girl again. "I said good morning to you when you got on, but you didn't seem to hear."

"I'm sorry."

"It's okay. I wondered if maybe you weren't feeling well, or if there was something that was bothering you."

"No, everything's okay," Vera answered without looking Carol in the eye. Her voice sounded so deliberately cheerful that it seemed clear she was exaggerating it, and she believed Carol knew that.

Carol paused, and then she smiled. "Okay," she said. "You have a good day. See you this afternoon."

"See you this afternoon."

Vera stepped down onto the sidewalk and stood and listened to the gears grinding on Carol's bus as it pulled away. Carol's kindness somehow made her think of her mother, and for a second, she wanted to cry. She pulled herself together so she wouldn't walk into the school in tears.

She looked across the parking lot and scanned among the many different coveys of students standing around in front of the school until she was able to locate Louisa and her beau. As usual with Louisa, when she was in love, she became oblivious to everything else, but when Vera saw them together, she realized that Michael looked equally enthralled. He was a handsome exchange student from Great Britain, with a sexy English accent that Louisa adored. She loved to watch Louisa in action, and she laughed at her friend's ability to charm him into submission. She almost didn't want to intrude on them. She was invisible to them when she first walked over, and she said hello, but they didn't hear her.

A minute or so went by, and Louisa finally noticed her. A smile burst onto her face like a sunbeam. "Where'd you come from?" She rushed over with Michael in tow and locked arms with him and Vera, and they went into the school.

Vera parted with her friends in the lobby to go to her locker. She looked out for RJ along the way, in order to avoid him. She managed to navigate to her locker through the crowd of students without seeing him. She put away her coat and other things and kept her eyes looking straight ahead, so she wouldn't make eye contact with him if he suddenly appeared. When she was done, she closed her locker, thinking how she would like to shut herself inside it too, and walked to the stairs to go to her classroom on the second floor.

At the landing, she happened to glance down at the hallway, and among the students milling around and going to their classrooms, she saw RJ. He was laughing, and he looked very pleased with himself for something. Next, she realized that he was talking to a beautiful senior girl named Kendall, or she was talking to him while he gawked at her. Kendall flipped her hair and then flipped it again, and RJ just stared stupidly at her. Vera tried not to let it bother her, but unsuccessfully. She couldn't stand to watch them, and she was exposed in the open, where he could easily see her.

She tried to rush up the stairs, but she was pinned against the railing by students coming up the stairs, and so she couldn't escape. Then he saw her, and he looked surprised, maybe even embarrassed. Kendall was still talking his ear off.

Doesn't that girl ever shut up? Vera thought.

It was torture to be stuck there and have to pretend that she didn't see him. She felt hurt and disappointed, but that didn't make any sense, because she knew that technically he wasn't her boyfriend. She thought it was ridiculous, she berated herself, but it was the way she felt. She thought that he liked her romantically, and he showed all the signs, and despite all of her hesitations and doubts, she liked him romantically too. Her faith that she could let herself fall in love with him was crushed, because now Kendall was interested in him, and as far as Vera could tell, he certainly seemed interested in her.

RJ wasn't listening to Kendall anymore. His eyes were on Vera. Kendall finally caught on that she no longer commanded his attention, and she stared in the direction that he was looking.

Great, Vera thought. Now Kendall was staring at her too. She rushed up the stairs and got away from them as fast as she could without running.

***

At the end of her last morning class, Vera left the room to go to lunch. She heard a commotion in the stairwell that sounded like an angry mob. There was a cackle of laughter, followed by taunting and insulting words and profanity, and one of the voices stood out loudly among the rest, and Vera thought she knew who the voice belonged to—a bully in the school. She also picked out a single frightened voice demanding weakly to be left alone.

Vera leaned over the railing to get a clearer look at what was happening. A bunch of girls encircled another girl, who they'd backed up against the wall. She was trembling. Vera had seen the girl around school, but she didn't know her name. Vera's impression of the girl was that she was very quiet and self-conscious, but Vera had never made an effort to get to know her. She decided that she couldn't allow them to taunt the girl any longer, and she went down the stairs and walked up behind them.

"She's got blood smeared all over the back of her skirt!" one of the girls yelled to a couple of kids walking by.

Vera recognized her voice: the chief bully.

The girl continued with her cruelty. "She didn't know she got her period. Turn around so I can take a picture of your bloody skirt." She laughed a self-satisfied laugh, egging on her crew. They congratulated her for being funny.

Vera felt a surge of loathing that was too big for her entire body to hold. She seethed with revulsion for the bully and her friends. Their injustice incited rage in Vera that she didn't know she was capable of feeling.

Every little thing that Vera noticed about the bully made her seem more repulsive to her. In Vera's unchecked judgment, even the girl's body looked deformed, made deformed by her nasty character—a big, clumsy, ugly barrel of a body. She shoved past the barrel-shaped girl and her friends to the girl who was cornered. Her face was tear-stained and distorted with fear and shame.

Vera tried to act normal and nonchalant. "Hi, I'm Vera."

"I know your name," the girl said. Then she saved Vera embarrassment by stating her name. "I'm Suzanne."

Vera stumbled an apology. "I'm sorry, Suzanne." Then it dawned on her that the name was the same as her mother's, and her breathing stopped for a moment as she absorbed that revelation. But it wasn't the girl's fault that her name was painful to Vera. She wanted to help her and put her at ease, so she said, "Do you mind if I call you Suzy?"

"Suzy? No."

Vera whispered to her so her tormentors couldn't hear. "Suzy, can I walk with you to the girls' room?"

"Everyone will see my skirt," Suzy said, looking panic stricken.

"Put on your coat or tie it around your waist. I'll walk right behind you as close as I can."

"Everyone's going to know," the girl said, as she put on her coat.

"No, they won't. Don't worry."

"They're laughing again."

Vera stared at the barrel-shaped girl and the rest of them with righteous indignation, for in her mind they were terrorists. Somehow, she knew what it felt like to be hunted and cornered. But how did she know that when she'd never lived it? She thought it must be from a dream.

"Fuck them," she said, loudly and emphatically.

The girls shifted their feet nervously, like a chorus line of clumsy dancers.

Vera could see that she intimidated them, and she was glad. She saw Suzy trying to suppress a laugh. "Come on, Suzy. Let's go." And they walked away.

At the door to the restroom, Suzy turned to her. "This is my first time. I didn't know it was coming. It just happened."

"That's usually how it happens, I think. It did to me."

Fortunately, the bathroom was empty. Vera led Suzy over to the sink. She opened her school bag.

"Here's a tampon," she said, handing it to Suzy.

"Thank you."

Suzy went into a stall, and when she came out Vera said, "I'll wash off your skirt. It's not so bad. I think we can get it all out." She took a handful of paper towels from the dispenser, wet them under the faucet, and lathered them with hand soap. Then she knelt and lifted the hem of Suzy's skirt and dabbed the bold red smudges of menstrual blood with the soapy paper towels. She paused when she felt Suzy put her hand on her shoulder.

"Thank you for helping me."

"Those girls are vicious. I couldn't let them do that to you."

"I wish I could've handled it myself."

"It was scary. There were eight of them and one of you."

Vera cleaned Suzy's skirt until it was spotless, and then Suzy stood in front of the radiator to dry it. Vera asked her if she wanted to eat lunch together. The expression on Suzy's face was full of gratitude, which stirred poignant feelings in Vera of joy and gratification. She thought it was the most generous thing that she'd ever done for someone.

After she parted with Suzy, she had time before her first class in the afternoon to go outside for air. She walked around the baseball field, staring at the ground and thinking about Suzy. She couldn't think of anything worse than being held against your will under someone else's complete control and turned to stone by fear.

Her thoughts preoccupied her for quite a while, and she realized that she'd lost track of the time and her class had started. She ran to the door and power-walked down the hall to her classroom. The teacher stopped talking in the middle of a sentence when she came in.

He raised his eyebrows at her. "We've started already, Vera. Please take your seat."

"I'm sorry, Mr Dubicki."

A couple of students made a joke and snickered at her as she passed them. She ignored them and went directly to her desk by the window, and right after she sat down, it started snowing.

Chapter 12

At two forty-five that afternoon, Vera came out of the school and waited for Louisa on the sidewalk. The character of the weather had changed since morning, when it'd been gray and gloomy out. The sky was much brighter with a suggestion of blue and more sun. Vera felt better than she had all day. Louisa and Michael came along holding hands and stepped up on the curb where Vera was standing.

"Hey, you're finally here," Louisa said.

Vera felt even more rejuvenated when she heard her friend's cheery voice, like she was a dry plant that needed to be watered. "Hi, Louisa. Hi, Michael. How's everything going?"

Louisa looked into Michael's eyes and smiled. "Very nice," she said. "Michael, can we give Vera a ride home?"

"I'd be happy to," he said.

Vera didn't want him to go out of his way for her. "But my house is way out of town in the opposite direction. You don't have to bother."

"No worries. It's my pleasure. And it'll give me an opportunity to bop around the back roads and get to know my way around."

"All right."

As they walked to the car, Louisa whispered in Vera's ear. "Michael goes to Eton back home in England."

"I know. You've told me that ten times already."

"Eton's what we call in America a private school, but in Britain they call it a public school. Isn't that weird?"

Vera got into the backseat while Louisa and Michael talked with a friend, and she started thinking about Louisa telling her about wanting to go to college in England. She decided that it sounded like a good idea and that she should look into going to college there too. Louisa wanted to be near Michael, but Vera was interested in changing herself. Maybe the only way to do that was to go somewhere far away and completely different. And it wouldn't hurt if Michael had a brother.

Michael started the car, but then he got out again. Leaning on the door, he cupped his hand to his mouth.

"RJ, hey, mate," he called, waving his arms to get RJ's attention.

Vera slunk down in the seat when RJ started to walk toward them. She heard Michael ask him if he wanted a ride.

"I've got my car, but thanks, man. I appreciate it, though. So, what's going on?" Then he saw Vera in the backseat, and he tapped on the window. She rolled it down. "Hi."

"Hi," she said coldly.

"Do you have a minute to talk?"

"Not now. We're about to leave."

"We can wait. We can wait, can't we, Michael?" Louisa said.

"No bother. Take your time."

At first, Vera wanted to say no, but in a few seconds, she had a change of heart, and after that she wasn't sure what she wanted to do. However, it felt satisfying in a vengeful kind of way to keep RJ in suspense as long as she could. There was a strong urge in her to tell him to go away and leave her alone.

"All right." As she got out of the car, she turned and spoke to Louisa and Michael. "You don't have to wait for me. I'll take the bus. It hasn't left yet."

"I can give you a ride home, Vera," RJ said.

Vera let his offer go in one ear and out the other. "I'll call you later," she said to Louisa.

"Okay. Talk to you then," Louisa said, and she and Michael drove away.

Vera started walking fast, and RJ had to jog to catch up to her. He fell into step beside her.

"So, Michael has a driver's license?"

"Yes."

"How did he get one? He's only been here three weeks."

"It's a British driver's license."

"And he can drive with that here?"

"Yes," she said, impatiently. A sheepish look crossed his face, and she felt bad that she'd snapped at him.

"I didn't know you could do that here," he said.

"I didn't either, but you can. What did you want to talk about?"

"Nothing. It's just that, well, that girl today."

"Kendall?"

"Kendall? No, no not her. I mean the freshman girl who you helped. I don't know her name."

"Her name's Suzy. The whole school knows about that."

"Everyone felt sorry for her and thought those girls were horrible."

"Not everyone did."

"Most everyone. But it was impressive how you stood up to them and helped Suzy."

"I thought you were too busy with Kendall to see that."

"Are you mad at me because I was talking to Kendall?"

"I don't care about that."

"Then why are you mad?"

"I'm not mad. Just forget it. It doesn't matter."

"What doesn't matter?"

"Just leave me alone."

He shoved his hands into his pockets and nodded his head, and his manner and body language toward her changed, and she knew that he was fed up with her.

"Okay, I'm going. And you'd better go too. The bus is leaving," he said. He turned around and marched to his car.

As soon as he was gone, she started having regrets about how she'd handled things, which had been like a spoiled brat. The bus was boarding, but she remained to watch his hair tossing in the wind, but he never turned and looked back at her. He hadn't ever been this mad at her before, and she didn't blame him, because he hadn't done anything wrong. He could flirt with as many girls as he wanted. Rationally, she knew it wasn't any of her business, but it didn't stop her from feeling hurt. When she'd seen him with Kendall, she'd reacted like he'd broken a bond of faith with her.

A few toots of the horn from the school bus got Vera's attention, and she knew she had to hurry. She jogged from the baseball field and got on the bus.

Carol greeted her with her angelic smile. "Hi, Vera, how was your day?"

Vera told her it was fine, and she smiled just enough to be polite, and she went down the aisle to the back of the bus and sat down. From her seat, she could look directly out the back window, and the first thing she saw was RJ and Kendall talking together by his car. Kendall said something she probably thought was funny, but was probably stupid, and he laughed. Vera was glad when the bus got way ahead and she couldn't see them anymore.

The bus rolled on, taking forever to get her home because there was a slow-moving snowplow in front of it. When they finally reached her stop, the bus pulled over and came to a halt, and the snowplow continued on its jangling way. Vera got up and went to the front. She tried to be cheerful when she said goodbye, but she had the feeling that Carol saw through her façade.

"You have a good night, Vera," Carol said, gently. "See you tomorrow."

Then she was gone, and Vera began the short walk home. She distracted herself by looking at nature as she tried to put the day behind her. There was a tussle going on in the sky between giant gray clouds smashing together, like ancient continents colliding to form the super continents. The limbs of the trees swayed up and down in the wind as she walked beneath them. She heard a sharp crack of a branch breaking off an old oak tree and a *whack* when it hit the ground.

These were the last sounds she heard before the wind died and the landscape became eerily still. A deadly quiet rolled in like a thick fog, engulfing and silencing every living creature and earthly sound. In the absence of ordinary, natural things, the environment was alien to her.

Then she saw the huge craft. It was so big that it blocked her view of the sky. It was about a thousand feet in the air, casting a looming shadow over her. At least a dozen smaller flying objects hovered around it. She realized that she was being watched, watched from above and also from somewhere closer. Yes. Four skinny, little humanoid beings appeared from behind the trees and came at her, and she screamed. When they grabbed her arms to make her go with them, she fought them with kicks and punches, exhausting herself.

Beyond them, she saw a man standing in the middle of the road, who looked normal—not like them, and she stopped screaming. She couldn't see the face of the man at first. His tall, broad frame reminded her of a sturdy oak tree. The man came closer and nodded at the four beings, as if they knew each other, and their reaction suggested that he was familiar to them. When she was able to see his entire face, she recognized that he was Peter Cristopholos. She couldn't hear what he was saying, until he started raising his voice at them. The first word she heard clearly was her name, Vera, and everything he said next was audible.

"She's too young. She's not ready. I'm not going to let you take her."

The faces of the beings expressed emotions of surprise and confusion. They leaned their heads in, like they were conspiring together about their next steps.

"Take me instead," Peter yelled. "I won't struggle with you this time. I'll go willingly. You know I'm still useful to you. Let her go and take me."

There was no reaction from them.

"Hey, guys, come on, do we have a deal?"

The beings broke up their circle and moved toward him in unison and clasped their hands on his arms and shoulders. Vera realized at that moment that she could move her feet and legs again and that she was free to run from them.

"Get out of here, Vera," Peter yelled.

She shook her head vehemently. "No." How could she leave him? He'd saved her, and she had to try to help him.

"I said go home. Go home, Vera," he pleaded to her.

She shook all over with fear.

"There's nothing you can do, Vera. Run."

She realized he was right. She wasn't brave or powerful enough to prevent them from taking him, and she had no choice but to get out of there before they took her too. It was shameful to turn and run, but she did. She glanced back once to look at Peter. It was surreal, like a sinister fairy tale that'd come to life, seeing them drag him away. In this story, he was a good giant, and they were his subjugators, the evil gnomes. They walked in unified step, and the next moment, they slipped through an invisible slot in the air and they disappeared.

Vera turned and fled. She ran all the way to her house and up the porch steps, and skidded to a halt at the door with her key in her hand. Trying to unlock the door, she fumbled with the key and dropped it. Her bulky gloves were in the way, so she tore them off, but her hands were shaking. She had to concentrate hard to get the key into the lock. Finally, she got the door open and went inside and slammed and locked it.

She walked backward away from the door, her heart pounding. Spark awakened and came over to her. She ran up the stairs to her bedroom, and he followed her.

She threw herself down on the bed, and she lay there a long time shivering. The room was freezing, but there was heat in the house and the windows in her bedroom were shut. She felt disoriented, and she couldn't remember anything between the time she'd gotten off at the bus stop and gotten home. There were too many missing pieces, and nothing made sense to her.

She slid closer to the edge of the bed and gazed lovingly at Spark lying on the floor. He was a comfort to her. She said his name softly, and one of his eyes opened to peek at her. He got up stiffly and put his head on her hand and wagged his tail. Sadly, he was too old to get on the bed by himself, so she gave him a boost up, and they got comfortable together. She put her arm across his body and petted him gently, and before she fell asleep, she thought how lucky she was that he was there with her.

When she woke up about an hour later, she wondered what time it was. She guessed by the meager amount of daylight in her room that it was about five o'clock. A quartet of birds jetted past the window, creating a disturbance of noise and motion, and she sat up abruptly. Her blanket fell on the floor, and she saw that she hadn't taken off her jacket or her boots before she had lain down. There were pools of dirty slush on the bedspread where her boot soles had been. She couldn't explain this to herself either. Why hadn't she taken them off? It wasn't like her at all.

Vera heard her phone ringing in the distance, which was downstairs in her bag. She felt dizzy when she got up too fast, but it passed quickly.

"Hello?" she said, answering it.

"Hi, Vera. It's Dad."

"Hi."

"How was school?"

"Good."

"Good. I'm just calling to let you know I'm running late."

She glanced around at the empty rooms. "How late do you think?"

"Maybe an hour or a little more. Is there a problem, honey?"

"No."

"If you're hungry, go ahead and eat without me."

"No, Dad. I'll wait to eat with you."

"That sounds good. I'll see you later then. Bye."

"Bye."

She held onto the phone for a minute before she put it down. She almost fell into a trance wishing that she wasn't alone, but she pulled herself out of it and went back to her room to change her clothes.

She looked in her drawer for her most comfortable baggy flannel pants and long-sleeved T-shirt. After she put them on, she went downstairs again to start making dinner. On the middle shelf of the refrigerator, she found a brown paper bag with a note on it that was signed by her Aunt Bonnie. Inside the bag there was a large container of her aunt's homemade lobster stew. Uncle Tony, her Aunt Bonnie's husband, was the captain of his own small fleet of lobster boats. Vera thought it was a nice surprise, because now she didn't have to think about what they'd eat for dinner.

She got out a pot with a lid and put it on top of the stove for later, and then started to chop vegetables for a salad. She concentrated on cutting the tomatoes and radishes into relatively even sizes, like she was performing an important task. This way she was able to free her mind briefly from her cares.

About fifteen minutes before her dad was supposed to be home, she poured the lobster stew into the pot and put it on the burner to simmer. She came back to it every few minutes to stir it. Every stir released more of the stew's fragrance into the air. She had made biscuits, and they were in the oven now, and she'd just begun to be able to smell them baking. The heat from the oven saturated the oven door, and it felt good to lean against that great warmth.

As she waited for the biscuits to be done, she hummed and sang softly to herself. She sang a little more loudly, and it pleased her that she liked what she heard, and she gradually got over her shyness, which always gripped her when she sang, even when no one was around to hear her. She felt like she was discovering that she had a nice voice for the first time, so she turned up the volume once more and also added some sassy style to her interpretation, and then without any self-consciousness at all, she belted it out with abandon, which was how John always belted out a song.

Through the window, she saw headlights in the driveway. Realizing that her dad was home, she stopped singing. Her confidence faltered. She didn't feel ready for him to hear her sing yet.

He came in and scraped the dirt off his boots on the floor mat. "Hello," he said. Spark came over to him. "Hi, buddy. Where are you, Vera?"

"In here."

"Something smells good," he said, coming into the kitchen. "What's in the pot? It's not lobster stew, is it?"

"That's right."

"Did Aunt Bonnie bring that over?"

"Yes, it was in the refrigerator with a note. It's ready, if you are?"

"Definitely," he said, as he washed his hands at the kitchen sink.

Vera ladled the stew into bowls and put the salad and biscuits on the table, and they sat down to dinner.

"It's delicious, as usual," John said, after tasting his first spoonful of the stew.

"It's really good. It was nice of Aunt Bonnie to give us some."

"I guess that means I have to call and thank her tonight," John said, chuckling.

"She's your sister. You should call her anyway."

"You're right, but you know how we drive each other nuts sometimes."

"You think that Aunt Bonnie is bossy, but she just wants you to be happy."

"I know she does, but she'd run my life for me, if I let her. Anyway, how was school?"

She wanted to forget about the entire day, not be reminded of it. "It was fine. But you asked me that already on the phone."

"What's the matter, Vera?"

"I'm just nervous about my history test, that's all. It's tomorrow."

"Oh. Are you prepared for it?"

"I will be. I have more studying to do tonight."

"So that's it? Your test is the only thing that's bothering you?"

"Yes."

"I don't know, Vera. I can never seem to get a straight answer from you about anything."

He looked hurt, and she supposed it was because he was sorry that she didn't confide in him like he was her best friend. "I guess I'm more private than I used to be."

"I understand," he said. "But there are things I need to know about, and we need to talk about, because I'm your father. Okay?"

"I know."

"It's hard to believe you're as old as you are now. You've always been independent, but now you really help take care of us." He reached for another biscuit. "You made these from scratch, right? They're delicious."

"Thank you."

John chatted to her about his day at work. She listened but said very little. When they were done eating, she carried their plates to the sink.

"I'll do the dishes, honey," he said, rising from the chair.

"No, I'll do them. I don't mind."

"We'll do them together."

She rolled her eyes at that suggestion, but she was careful that he didn't notice it. If it was up to her, she'd do the dishes by herself. Whenever they did the dishes or cooked together, the kitchen didn't seem big enough for the both of them.

The note from her aunt that had come with the stew lay on the counter. Vera knew what it said.

"Dad, did you read the note from Aunt Bonnie?"

"What note?"

"There on the counter. She taped it to the bag."

"No. Should I?"

"She's talking to you, so yeah."

He leaned his elbows on the counter and began to read the note, and Vera waited for his reaction. A few lines into it, he picked it up and held it closer to his face. He put his hand under his chin, and a serious expression materialized on his face. Vera was certain he read it two or three times, but possibly more, and he grew sadder each time, which pained her. When he was finished with it, he put it down and walked away.

Vera picked it up and read it aloud: "Hi, John and Vera. Here's a container of lobster stew I made last night. Enjoy! Hey, John, guess who I ran into at a concert last week? Gwen with her date. I didn't know she had a new man. Did you? And he is hot! Gwen seemed really into him. I just thought you'd be interested. Love you!" She put the note down. "Well, Dad?"

"Your aunt has a sharp wit."

"Doesn't it bother you?"

"That Gwen is seeing some guy? That's her business."

"Oh, come on."

"Vera, that's enough. I'm going to play my guitar. I'll be in the music room."

But she felt emboldened, and she wasn't willing to back down. "You love Gwen. Why don't you admit it?"

"You don't know what you're talking about."

"That's not true. I think you should—"

"Enough," he demanded.

She wasn't going to let him off the hook that easily. "What are you afraid of? You should pay attention to your feelings. Mom's been gone a long time." She didn't mean to mention her mother. It'd slipped out in the most natural way, even though she wasn't supposed to talk about her.

"I said that's enough, Vera."

She fell quiet and stared at him resentfully. Why was it so wrong for her to mention her mother? "I'm sorry," she said. It was what he expected her to say, but she didn't mean it.

"I'm sorry, too," he said.

She looked up at him, surprised by his apology.

"I'll see you in a while," he said, as he left the kitchen.

She heard him begin tuning his guitar, and she shut out the kitchen lights and started to go upstairs. She stopped on the second step and leaned back against the wall. Her hands were shaking. "Oh, God, I'm so scared."

"Vera?" John said, from the door of the music room. "Why did you say you were scared?"

"No, I didn't say that." He'd startled her. She thought she'd whispered softly enough so he couldn't hear.

"No, it was clear what you said. What's happened? Why are you scared?"

"I don't know."

"What do you mean? Something either happened or it didn't."

"Please, don't get impatient, Dad."

"I just want you to explain. I need to know."

"Lately, I've been having nightmares. It makes me scared to go to sleep."

"I'm sorry. That's awful. Do you want to tell me about them?"

"No. I'd rather not talk about them. I'm going to my room to study. Good night."

"Wait a minute. Vera, I can't leave you like this."

"I feel better now." She did feel better. His caring made her feel loved. His protectiveness made her feel safer. She kissed him. "I love you, Dad."

"I love you. I'll check in later."

She managed to smile, and then she turned and went up the stairs. In her bedroom, she sat down in the chair by the window and gazed at the sky. The moon glowed warmly in an ocean of black sky. She sat there thinking about her mother, and she wished she hadn't brought her up, because now she couldn't get her out of her mind. She wondered if they'd ever see each other again. Her mother knew where to find her, and if she really wanted to see her, then she'd show up someday. If that ever happened, Vera wasn't sure how she'd react to her, whether she'd stand aloof from her or throw her arms around her. Either way, she knew it would be terribly emotional.

She studied for a while, until the material for her history test seemed to have stuck. By then, it was late, she was tired, and it was time to go to bed. She took her clothes off and left them in a pile on the floor and changed into her pajamas. She lay down on the bed and positioned herself so that the moonlight would shine on her. Tonight, the moon seemed like it was the real moon, with its soft, tender light.

"Good night, moon," she said.

Chapter 13

On Saturday evening, coming home from Vera's ski race, John was stuck for a while behind a state truck that was spraying road salt across the lanes to make the ice melt. When the truck finally moved aside and he could pass it, he sped up, but he paid attention to the road and continued to drive with caution. As he drove, he thought about Vera's race and the day on the mountain. Vera had come in second, which to him was great. Considering the competition, both he and Vera felt it was a triumph. He was proud of her, and she also seemed proud of herself, and of course, that made him happy.

Despite feeling happy about Vera's accomplishment, he had a different issue that gnawed at him. He was trying to decide on which of the two exits for Pangea he should take to go home. If he took the first one, he'd go straight home, and that'd be the easiest thing for him to do, if he wanted to play it safe. The second exit was the difficult one. It represented a big chance he'd be taking. He didn't think it was an exaggeration to feel like it was one of those critical, pivotal decisions that people make in life—or not.

He checked the time. It was five minutes past six o'clock. Vera was spending the night with her team and coaches at a lodge at the mountain. They were going to ski all day the next day and come back in the late afternoon. So now he was driving home alone, and he had a decision to make. He turned up the volume of the jazz music that he was listening to, and if he'd been home, he would've also picked up his guitar and played along and improvised with the tune. Instead, he fingered the chords that he heard with his right hand and noodled around on the fretboard of his air guitar. He hoped the music would stop him from thinking about Gwen and the guy that she was apparently involved with, but it wasn't working.

After the competition, he'd taken Vera to lunch, and they'd skied together for several hours in the afternoon. He and Vera had been eating at the restaurant when Gwen and her date, along with Louisa, had shown up for lunch. Louisa had walked over to their table and chatted with them for a few minutes. He and Gwen had exchanged waves before she sat down. The guy had looked over at them too and said hello to them. It wasn't lost on him when the guy placed himself up against Gwen, so they were touching, and when he put his arm around her. *That guy's the possessive type*, he thought.

Then he'd had to put up with the sight of Gwen and the guy holding hands during the race and romping around on their skis on the slopes for the whole damn day. His admitted jealousy aside, he thought the guy didn't know how to ski worth shit. In a perfect universe, he wouldn't care about any of it, but he found himself in the sorry position of caring a hell of a lot. Before his mind was made up, he found himself coming up on the first exit. He let the first exit go by and drove on to the next one.

The road sign after the exit ramp said three miles to Pangea center. He had just three miles to prepare a speech—a confession rather—telling Gwen how he felt about her. He realized there was a chance that she wouldn't be alone, and so he told himself that if the guy's car was parked outside her house, he'd just keep going. He turned down Gwen's street, which was a long corridor of old mill houses that he'd helped to renovate into condominiums and single-family homes. He drove to where the road looped into a cul-de-sac, where her house was. There were a few cars parked on the street, and he looked to see if any of them belonged to the guy. Vera said that he drove a new BMW, but all of the vehicles he saw were on the older, pedestrian side, not fancy, high-end, high-priced German luxury cars. He thought he was safe, and he coasted slowly around the cul-de-sac and parked on the street.

The wind was fierce when he got out of the car and walked to Gwen's front door. He knocked twice and stepped back and waited for her to answer. At first, she seemed glad to see him, so he thought. The expression on her face suggested joy and warmth, but that didn't last. When he smiled at her, she frowned at him.

He had cold drops of water dropping on him from the porch and dripping down his head. "Hi," he said.

"What are you doing here?"

He stepped closer to her. "Sorry for coming by like this unannounced. Are you busy?"

"Yes, I'm kind of busy. Is Vera—are the girls all right? Did something happen?"

"No, they're fine. It's not about them. Can you spare a minute to talk?"

"You should've called."

"I know. But can I come in?"

"Okay, but I don't have much time."

He came through the door when she stepped aside. "Thanks. It's cold out there."

"I thought you liked the cold."

"Yeah, true," he said, smiling. "We really do know each other well, you know. Gwen?"

"I might as well get you a beer," she said.

"Thanks."

They turned the corner on the way to her living room, and he saw the boyfriend there posed on the couch with a glass of wine in his hand. The boyfriend stood up and walked over to him holding his wine glass.

They stood together in a triangle with Gwen as the triangle's vertex. "John, this is—"

"Alex," the guy said and stuck his hand out for John to shake.

"And Alex, this is—"

"John. Nice to meet you, Alex. I'm a friend of Gwen's."

"It's a pleasure to meet you too, John," Alex said. "We saw you at the mountain today, didn't we?"

"John is Vera's dad," Gwen said. "I'll get you your beer, John."

"Actually, Gwen," John said, stopping her. "I'll take a glass of wine, if that's okay."

Gwen nodded and left. John saw how Alex kept his gaze on her until she left the room. Though he hated admitting it, he realized that Alex was a pretty fit and rugged guy, what some people—like his sister—would call hot. He had good hair, with no bald spots, and he wore nice clothes, and he drove a beautiful car. He could almost see why his sister thought he was so great, but he couldn't for the life of him understand why Gwen was attracted to him.

"Vera, yes of course," Alex said, as if he'd forgotten that she existed. "We were watching and rooting for her today. She's an incredible skier. I was impressed. Too bad she didn't win, though. I'm sure she will next time."

John's impression of Alex was that he was a guy who thought he knew everything about certain things that he knew nothing about. "Second place in a race like that is nothing to snivel at. Vera knows it," John said.

Gwen came back into the room. "Here's your wine."

"Thanks."

"We were just leaving to go to dinner," Alex said.

"Oh, sorry to delay your plans."

"No, no problem," Alex said. "Please join us, if you like."

"Oh, no, but thanks. Here's to you. Salud." John raised his glass. "Salud is an old Italian toast for good health for a hundred years."

"Salud," Alex said.

"So, Alex. You drive a BMW, don't you?"

"I do."

"I didn't see it when I drove up."

"I dropped it off to be detailed. Gwen's going to drive me to pick it up in the morning."

John took a short sip of his wine. "In the morning?"

"That's right," Alex said, putting his arm around her.

John turned to her. "Can we talk now, Gwen?"

"Okay, yes. What is it?"

"In private?"

She gaped at him in surprise. "I'll be right back, Alex. It's something about our daughters. They're best friends," she said.

Alex looked at his Cartier watch. "Our dinner reservations are for seven o'clock."

"I know."

"All right, honey bear. I'll be here waiting for you."

As they walked away, John thought he saw Gwen wince as Alex called her honey bear.

They went into the kitchen, and she turned on the light.

"Honey bear?" he said, as he closed the door.

"I know, I know. So, what do you want to talk to me about, John?"

He turned off the lights that she'd just turned on and walked toward her.

"Why did you do that?" she said.

"There's plenty of light coming from the street. We can still see each other."

"Barely. I'm turning them back on. You're being weird."

"Wait."

She stood with her back against the refrigerator door. His hands trembled as he put them around her waist ever so gently. He leaned in and kissed her mouth. "Oh, Gwen."

She grabbed his hands and pulled them off of her. "Don't. What are you doing?"

He looked back at her with his arms dangling at his sides, speechless and dejected.

"Go home," she said.

"I love you," he said.

"What?"

"I love you. I do. I wish I'd told you a long time ago, but I couldn't. I wasn't ready."

"No, I don't believe you. This is crazy. You came here and walked in on me and Alex to say that?"

"Yes, I had to. I didn't know how you'd react, but I had to tell you, before it was too late."

"John, please just go."

"I will. In a minute. I know you're probably shocked."

"Shocked? Oh, God."

"I know. But you always knew it, didn't you?"

"No, I didn't. I never ever believed that."

"Well, I've loved you for a long time, almost since we met. But I've been in denial. I love you. I love how you love Vera. You're beautiful in every way. I'm happy when I'm around you. Even when we squabble, I'm content to be around you. And, man, just knowing you has opened my eyes."

"Look, John, first, you embarrassed me in front of Alex, and then, you do this. It's not fair to me, and it makes me angry. Go, just go."

"All right, I guess I said my piece," he said, stumbling out the words. But he couldn't make himself leave yet. He put his arms around her, and this time she didn't stop him. A rush of joy washed over him as he kissed her. He touched her breasts, a moment that he'd dreamed about for so long. Her skin was soft as satin, the way he knew it'd feel. She moaned. He whispered in her ear. "I've been a gentleman for ten years, but I just couldn't wait anymore."

"What am I supposed to say, John?"

He put his hand under her skirt and touched her leg. "I hoped you'd say you felt the same about me."

She broke away from him and turned on the lights. "Alex is waiting for me," she said. She walked out before he could say anything to stop her.

He stayed for several minutes after she left, and that was longer than he should've stayed, and he knew that, but he could barely breathe as he tried to absorb the surges of hurt that swept over and over him, like a cold ocean tide, and the pain depleted him of all of his strength. He knew that every time he saw her that he'd feel the same pain as he did now. He wondered if it'd been worth it. If he hadn't done it, he'd never have known, and now he knew. He supposed that was something.

If there'd been a door in the kitchen to the outside, he would've left through it so he didn't have to face Gwen or lay eyes on Alex again. He heard Alex from the living room asking Gwen, "Where's John?" She replied that he'd gone to the bathroom. To support her story, he waited a few more minutes before he came out into the open. When he returned to the living room, Gwen was sitting close to Alex on the couch, and when they saw him, they stood up.

"I guess I'll head out," he said, picking up his jacket. "Thanks, Gwen. Good to meet you, Alex."

"Same here," Alex said.

John went to the door to let himself out, but Gwen followed him. Before he left, they looked at each other quietly, and he leaned over her and rested his forehead against hers.

"I love you. Remember that. Good night," he whispered.

"Good night."

He didn't want to leave. He didn't want to take his eyes off her. He waited there until she'd shut the door, and then he walked to his car.

He drove home by instinct, without paying constant attention to the journey. He thought about what he'd done and what had happened as a result of it. His awakening of his feelings had come, and the reckoning with it amounted to a simple equation: his jealousy and his fear of losing her. *What does it say about me as a man?* he thought. Perhaps he was the product of his past experiences. Or maybe the issues were larger than that and universal. Maybe it was just that it was common in human nature to take precious things for granted, or to be afraid of loving another person so desperately.

The usual ten-minute drive took fifteen minutes. He saw his house in view coming around the bend in the road. As he pulled into the driveway, he thought about making a drink and sitting in the hot tub, because he felt like he needed soothing. He went up the porch steps to a pitch-black house, and on the other side of the door, Spark was whining and barking.

"Hey, boy, I'll be right in." He inserted his key into the lock, but before he turned it, the door swung open on its own. "What the hell?"

He was alarmed at first, before he remembered that his neighbor, who'd taken care of Spark for the day, must've accidentally left the door open. Spark put his nose around the door and pulled it open far enough so he could get out, and rushed past John and squatted in the snow.

Standing in the doorway, he felt for the switch on the wall to turn on the front hall overhead light. When he went in, he decided to do a sweep of the house to make sure everything was all right. He checked all around downstairs, and then he went upstairs and looked from room to room. In Vera's bedroom, there was a cold breeze coming in through the windows. He went over to close them, and he ended up slamming them shut to vent his frustration with her for leaving them open. A feeling came over him that he had to make sure of something before he decided that all was well. He got a flashlight from a box in her closet and shined it down on the ground under her window, looking for footprints and tracks in the snow. The only thing he saw was his own set of footprints, where he'd walked around.

He'd checked the entire house and the cellar, but he wasn't sure that he felt quite at ease yet. He put the flashlight away and went downstairs to start a fire in the woodstove. He pulled the hassock in front of the stove and sat down to stir the bed of tiny red coals that remained from that morning's fire. He added paper and kindling to spark flames and kept adding bigger logs until there was a warm, steady blaze. Spark came over and sat down and stared at the flames with his filmy old eyes.

"The fire feels nice, eh, buddy?"

He left Spark by the fire and went and made a drink and walked with it outside to the backyard. He undressed and climbed into the hot tub and sipped his drink and watched the stars. The drink and the bath began to relax him. He lifted his arm in the air and pointed at Cassiopeia in the north and Orion in the south and exclaimed at the sight of a shooting star. How velvety black and glittering the night sky was, and its glory and beauty filled his senses. He felt like he'd be content to stay just as he was forever.

Eventually, the time came when he had to get out of the hot tub or he'd fall asleep there. It wasn't easy for him to leave the comfort of the warm, bubbling water. He reluctantly got out and walked naked to the house carrying his clothes and empty glass, took a quick shower, and went to bed. He lay awake for a long time thinking about Gwen and remembering when he blurted out that he loved her. Even though it hadn't done any good, he was glad he said it.

He'd managed to get in a few well-deserved digs at Alex, when Alex provoked them. He grinned at his own audaciousness when he'd confessed his love to Gwen and come on to her physically hot and heavy while Alex sipped his wine in the next room. When he thought about it objectively, it seemed totally irrational. He'd done it out of pent-up passion and longing that came from his history of friendship and attraction with Gwen. In some ways, it felt to him like they already were lovers.

Sometime after midnight, he was awakened by the phone ringing. He groped for it in the dark.

"Hello?" he said.

"Hi."

"Gwen?"

"Yeah. I'm at your door."

He ran down the stairs two at a time and opened the door. Gwen had a crown of freshly fallen snowflakes in her hair.

"Were you asleep?" she said.

"Not for long. Come in."

"Thanks."

She remained very still and quiet standing by the door. Her cheeks were puffy from being pinched by the cold wind.

"Do you want to take off your coat?" he said.

"Yeah," she said. But she didn't move.

He held her hands and took off her mittens, and he pulled her coat off her shoulders like he was unpacking a child from a snowsuit, and it made her laugh. She looked up at him and slipped her hands inside his shirt and placed them on his chest. Then she kissed him, and they fell on their knees by the fire. They slowly undressed each other, and he pulled the comforter from the couch and wrapped it around them. He lovingly touched her body and trembled at her touch. He climbed on top of her. *At last*, he thought.

"I love you," he said, as he entered her.

"I love you too."

Part 3

Chapter 14

When you exist in a no-man's-land between two different realities, you might feel an intuition that there's a mystery that involves you, that makes you unlike everyone else in the world but for other chosen people. You go to war with the shadow half that you didn't know existed, but that has disquieted each day of your life since it all started. If you knew the secrets that were hidden for years, it'd tear apart the reality that characterizes you to yourself and turn the truth that you believe into a lie. You could spend your life without the security of knowing where you belong. Only to Earth? Or to other worlds, too? Someday it all will come out.

The greatest fear you have is that one day you'll think of yourself only as stardust instead of flesh and blood. On the other hand, if you look at your experiences from the perspective that they serve a higher cause, it helps you justify your misery. You may learn how you fit in the universe—that you're both insignificant and important. It's a burden to be one of the few human beings who can say for certain that we're not alone, and no one believes you. Unless you find a way to deal with the load of it, there may be no hope for you.

***

In the predawn hours of Monday morning, Peter Cristopholos guided his car along the winding road that led to Blue Jobe Mountain. On most Monday mornings, he left for work early before the sun rose, but today, instead of going to work, he'd turned left at the crossroads and headed in the direction of the mountain. In the distance, he could see the shadowy outline of the tip of the summit pitched against a hint of morning light. A trail of steam swirled from the opening of his coffee cup, like the genie of faint clouds that hugged the mountain. He took comfort in holding the hot coffee cup, and the satisfaction he got from the flavor, and how it put him in touch with his humanity.

He started driving faster so he'd arrive at the top of the mountain for sunrise. The road was as dark as a cave except for the narrow path of light the headlights gave. The turn lay ahead of him. He took it and started to ascend the mountain road, driving past the trailheads as he continued up the hill. Finally, he drove through the gray misty fog and came to the gravel parking lot. There was a pavilion with a rustic beam roof and a stone chimney and a small building that was the ranger's office, now closed.

He realized he really had to go to the bathroom. He checked the restroom door outside the ranger's office, and he wasn't surprised to find that it was locked. He went and stood a couple of dozen feet off into the woods to commune with nature.

Afterward, when he wasn't distracted by his bladder anymore, he looked around at his dark surroundings. There were sounds of animal activity in the woods, footsteps and scampering on the ground and in the trees. He sat down on a stone bench that overlooked the valley, but the darkness and the mist still obscured the view for now. He shifted his position on the bench a few times trying to find a level of comfort, but a stone slab wasn't a forgiving place to park one's ass on a frigid morning. That was for sure.

He sipped his coffee and thought about his reasons for being there. He had his own private reasons, but not because he was waiting for the aliens to come for him. No, he didn't sense them at all. At times, when he sensed them coming, they showed up as expected, but he felt nothing like that now. He couldn't ever be certain about what would happen, and there was a chance that he was wrong now, because they were the ones that governed his life, not he.

He felt the icy cold of the bench soaking into his lower back through his clothes, and when he couldn't take any more of it, he stood up and walked down the trail through the woods. After about a hundred yards, he saw the silhouette of a moose on the path, and he turned into a statue to watch without startling it. As an outdoorsman, he'd had encounters with moose before. So he knew that they could be dangerous if you startled them or got in their way, like they might trample you to death. The bullwinkle swiveled its big head with its imposing antlers back and forth and sniffed the air. Peter stared at it with wonder. He thought how lucky he was on this morning to cross paths with a moose at dawn. Then the stately wild creature picked up its heavy feet and departed into the woods. And just like that, he was alone again with his thoughts.

He never got used to being lonely. For him, it wasn't a feeling, it was a continuation of a permanent state of being. All the years of therapy he'd gone through, and the doctors had tried, but in the end, they'd written him off as delusional. He didn't blame them for that, because even he could hardly believe himself. His worst disappointment was his wife's refusal to accept it or talk about it, even though she knew about the abduction they'd experienced together twenty-five years ago. She was too scared to remember, and so she pretended to forget. He felt sorry for her, but he felt sorrier for himself, because it'd been her only abduction but his had continued from that day onward. Sometimes he found it hard to forgive her for all of that.

He thought about his friends, all of the people who knew him well but didn't know him at all. Then he thought about Gwen, the one friend who believed him, and it cheered him and lightened his burden to remember that. Almost two weeks had passed since his visit in the middle of the night. Before he left early in the morning, he'd hugged Gwen at the door. All of this time, he hadn't stopped thinking about her because he was so attracted to her, but he felt ashamed because of his wife. He still loved her. She loved him. He knew that she'd mourn for him deeply when he was gone.

All around him in the trees, the birds were waking up and starting to sing their morning songs. There was a shadow that came into view just over his shoulder, and he looked up in time to see an owl soaring through the dimly lit forest with a skill that was honed to perfection. Owls, hawks, falcons, eagles, he loved all the noble birds of prey. A tree branch swung up and down, flinging off snow, as the owl came in for a forceful landing. Peter could see the great bird as it rode out the wave by clutching onto the branch with its talons and artfully holding on. There was a small gap at the top of the tree, which allowed the owl to be bathed in a beam of light from the rising sun.

Peter began walking fast to match the speed of dawn. The emerging sound of cars in the distance broke the illusion of remoteness for him. Suddenly, he remembered that this small sovereignty of wilderness was abutted by roads and civilization, and he thought of his crew who would be leaving to go to work soon and expecting to see him there. He felt pride in thinking about them, because they were an excellent group of people and workers. They were his employees, but he also considered them his friends. Despite that, none of them would have the faith in him that it'd require to believe his story, if he told it to them. It was far too unbelievable and outside the paradigm of human acceptance. He noticed how in his deep contemplation he'd slowed down to a snail's pace, and he started walking fast again.

Up ahead, he saw the opening in the trees that led to where he intended to go. He turned there and stepped onto a narrow footpath that cut through a dense thicket of evergreen trees, the scruffy, low-lying kind that grew near the sides of cliffs. The branches lashed at his body and their needles struck him in the face as he followed the tight path to its endpoint.

Finally, he walked into the open, onto a cliff that protruded over the valley. The sun was growing stronger every second, and far off in the distance, he could already faintly see the ocean. It was a smudgy, ethereal line of blue across the horizon, forty miles to the east. He'd always lived that close to it, and now he regretted more than ever that he'd missed so many chances to go there more often. What could he do about that now except let go of his regrets? The past was the past, and he couldn't change anything.

The rocks on the side of the cliff were slick with ice, but that was okay with him. He stepped down onto the first icy boulder and then the next and another and another. On the third rock, he slipped, so to make it easier, he wrapped his arms and legs around it and slithered down. Strangely, he felt calm and invincible, like he was a kid again, climbing on the cliffs of the rocky coast of Maine with no fear of falling. His shirt was soaked with sweat under his jacket, and his hands were hot inside his gloves. He used his teeth to pull off his gloves, and he threw them over his shoulder into the abyss and watched them sail away in the wind. Soon the incline became more vertical and too steep for even a goat to climb, except for one more small ledge, and he realized he'd gotten to the place where he couldn't go any further.

He hopped down onto the final ledge, and it was a big step, even for his long legs. Weathered in the stone was a tall depression that was just the right shape and size to lean back in, and he compressed himself into it, and it fit him like a coffin. He took in the panorama that lay before him. At the top of a tree along the bank, he noticed there was a hawk, and it was watching him, and then in the next instant, it swooped into the sky. Peter took one step forward and stood with his feet pointing over the ledge, where the forces of nature converged on him, reminding him of his smallness. The wind nearly knocked him off his feet as he stood there looking out in awe.

His mind took him back in time to another landscape that had so mesmerized him that he'd never forgotten the experience of seeing it for the first time. One summer, he and his family spent two weeks on vacation in Provincetown, Massachusetts. Sometimes with his family and sometimes by himself, he explored the dunes and the beach for hours. It impressed him that Provincetown, just a little patch of sand on the fist of the arm of Cape Cod, jutted defiantly into the Atlantic Ocean, as if it were tempting Mother Nature to pummel it with storms. When he closed his eyes, it felt as if he were walking along the quaint streets of downtown Provincetown again, past the rows of Cape-style and Victorian houses bunched together. Stonewalls wrapped around these tiny properties, and the yards were speckled with flower gardens and flower pots bursting with rainbows of blooms.

One of the days there, he'd taken a tour of the historic dune shacks, where a generation of artists and writers had lived and worked in the summers many decades ago. Some of them were authors whose books he'd forced himself to read in high school, but after visiting the shacks where they'd created some of their masterpieces, he'd read them again—this time with a fresh attitude and an open mind. In his imagination, he pictured those great artists sitting by campfires on the beach, as they'd done all those years ago, passing around bottles of booze and having drunken, passionate conversations about art, politics, and philosophy under the stars, and he could almost hear the ocean as they'd heard it, roaring in the blackness on those long, magical summer nights, and he thought that was what it was like to live.

In the two weeks he spent in Provincetown, he took long walks every day in the shadows of the dunes of the National Seashore. He often stopped to marvel at the way the tops of the dunes curled down at the tips, like waves, and leaned out toward the kingdom of the ocean, and he wondered what it'd be like to be in Provincetown—on the edge of a continent—during a ferocious storm. Now as he stood on the ledge and looked across the mountain valley, he felt the same love for God's creation that he felt then. It was true that he hated life, but he'd always loved the world, and he believed that there was a better life awaiting him that would never end. It was time for him to move on.

He started trembling, thinking of God and the consequences of going against His law, and he said a prayer for forgiveness. But he had to free himself.

Quickly, he slipped his hand in his pocket and took out his pistol. It felt heavy in his hand. He pointed it at his head and fired. His body fell forward and dropped two hundred feet onto a field of rocks. His last thought was a hope that his body would be scavenged by animals and recycled into the earth, and there'd be no trace left to find of his physical form.

Chapter 15

Peter Cristopholos had been missing for ten days when his broken body was found by two hikers at the bottom of a cliff on Blue Jobe Mountain. Neither the police nor any of the other searchers had thought to look for him there in the middle of winter. The news sent shock and sadness throughout the town, where Peter had been a familiar member of the community. Before people found out the cause of his death, there was speculation that he could've been murdered.

During the search, his wife didn't seem surprised about his absence, which some people said was odd. She told everyone it was just a matter of time before he was back. Then the police came and told her he was dead, and she was inconsolable.

On the morning Gwen heard, she was barely awake when a colleague called and broke the news to her. After she hung up, she stood paralyzed, absorbing the tragedy. In the car on her way to work, she barely heard the sounds of civilization around her and arrived there barely remembering anything about the ride. For a week, she'd been home sick with the flu. Until the phone call came, she'd felt well enough to go back to work, but now she wasn't sure she'd be able to climb the stairs to her office on the second floor.

Halfway up the stairs she stopped and bent over the railing to wait for a dizzy feeling to pass. "Fucking flu," she cursed, and then in a self-conscious check on herself, she looked around to see if anyone had heard. Her body wanted to be dragged home, but her heart and mind said not today. Peter was dead, and it seemed unreal to her. *Poor man, my poor friend*, she thought.

At the top of the stairs, she saw a group of her colleagues standing together. They were talking in quiet voices about Peter, and when they saw her, they opened up their circle to her. No one knew much about what'd happened to him, only that some hikers had found him on Blue Jobe. Gwen listened, but she was afraid she'd break down if she said anything. She touched her sweaty face; she was suddenly very hot, and someone asked her how she was feeling and said that she didn't look well. She responded that she was still a little weak from getting over the flu, excused herself, and went to her office.

The slant in the old floor made the door to her office swing back and crash against the wall when she unlocked it. The violence of it sent a jolt of fright through her, and she had to take deep breaths in order to calm down. As she turned to hang up her coat, she noticed a vase of tulips sitting in the middle of her desk with a card attached. She gasped at the dazzling colors of the arrangement of flowers: pink, yellow, red, white, and orange. The orange ones stood out most to her. They were like flames. All the colors bundled in the vase were beautiful, but they looked too selfishly bright to be there on this day of blacks and grays.

She took the card and read it: *Gwen, to bring you joy. Love, John.* She sat down at her desk. Everything had changed in just a few days. Peter had died. She'd learned that Vera was in constant danger, and she and John had become lovers.

She'd let the weeks pass without telling John what Peter had told her about Vera. Sometimes she thought that she was doing the wrong thing and wished that she'd told him right away. By omitting the truth, she put their relationship in jeopardy, but she was too afraid to have that conversation with him. She held back because she wanted to spare him pain and anguish, and she was worried for Vera. If John knew about it, things might be worse for Vera. Every time her father looked at her, he'd be unable to think of anything else, and neither would she. What would the consequences of neglecting to tell him be? She'd tell him at some point, and then she'd find out what they were.

Next to the vase with her tulips from John there was a week's worth of mail stacked on her desk. She picked it up to go through it. Among the junk mail, she saw a handwritten envelope without a return address. There was a handwritten letter inside it that she began to read.

Gwen,

Please don't be sad for me. I'm at peace, and it's what I wanted. The abductions were never going to end, and I couldn't keep that up for the rest of my life. I didn't want to die a raving lunatic, and that's where I was headed. It was killing my soul to live like that. I was losing my humanity, like you said.

I want to make it clear that what happened to me won't happen to Vera. What I did doesn't predict what her life will be like. With support from people who love her, she'll find a way to handle it. She'll have a good life. I hope she can find the purpose for things and be at peace with herself.

I never found it, but that could be my fault—didn't look hard enough—but I think it exists. For Vera things are going to be different—happier. She won't be so alone. It's very important that she's not alone, but you'll watch out for her like she needs. Goodbye. Thank you for believing me and for being my friend.

Bless you,

Peter

Gwen looked up from the letter. There was the sound of someone's footsteps in the hallway. They shuffled down the floor and faded away and it was instantly silent again, and she wondered if she'd only imagined them. She carefully laid the letter on the desk. It held his voice, words, feelings, intentions, and hopes, and so it had to be treated with the utmost reverence. It proved that Peter had killed himself. Ever since the night he told her about the aliens, she dreaded he might do that.

She stepped away from the desk and looked out the window that faced the front of the building. Down in the yard, one of Peter's crew of maintenance technicians, Gary, was spreading sand on the ice on the walkway. Her eyes followed the top of his navy-blue hat as he went about his work, as if it was just another ordinary day, and that was exactly what Peter would've wanted everybody to do.

"Poor Peter," she whispered.

Looking down through the bare branches of the trees, she saw Gary put the bucket on the ground and sit on the stone wall. He slumped over and put his head in his hands and began to sob. For several minutes he poured out his grief, until a woman and two children appeared and walked toward the library. When he realized there were people coming, he stood and picked up his bucket and crossed to the other side of the building. Just then, the phone rang in her office, and Gwen wiped the tears from her eyes and slowly pulled herself away to answer it.

***

That same afternoon, Vera walked rigidly through the crowd of students leaving the building after school. She passed the buses that were parked in a line along the curb and didn't slow down at her own bus, and her driver, Carol, who was standing outside talking to one of the other drivers, saw her.

"Basketball practice today, Vera?" Carol said.

Vera waved at her as she went by. "Yes, see you tomorrow."

When she got to the other side of the school and out of the sightlines of everyone, she started walking faster, as if she might break into a run. As she pushed herself into the wind, her hat slipped off her head and clung to the back of her hair. She was trying to escape, and it didn't matter to her which direction she went in, if only she could change her life back to the way it was before the moment that she heard Peter was dead.

At that instant, her buried memories of her abductions were cracked open and spilled out into her conscious mind, as if a cork had been released from a bottle, and the contents had flowed unstoppably over the side. She knew with certainty that her dreams and hallucinations were memories of real, lived events, and without warning, the earth shifted beneath her feet. Who could she tell about it? No one. They'd think she was crazy. But Peter had known. He'd been like her. He'd tried to protect her. And now he was dead, and she thought she knew why he'd taken his own life.

She heard someone call her name from a distance, and she turned and saw Louisa running toward her.

"Hey, where are you going?" Louisa said.

Vera shook her head. "I don't know. Somewhere."

"What do you mean? We have basketball practice."

"No, I can't."

"What? Why not?"

"I just heard about Mr Cristopholos. They found him dead."

"I know. It's awful. He killed himself. Why would he do that? He was such a nice man. I liked having him as our basketball coach in elementary school, remember?"

"Yes."

"His son is a babe. I'm sorry. I know that sounds so bad. It just came out. I really do care about Mr Cristopholos and his family. I feel very sorry for them. It's terrible."

Vera felt faint and started to fall, but Louisa caught her by the arm and kept her from going down to the ground. She was too weak to stand, even with Louisa's support, and she started to sink on her knees onto the wet curb.

"Come over to the bench," Louisa said.

"I feel sick," Vera said clutching her stomach.

Louisa took out her water bottle from her school bag and gave it to her. "Drink some of this water."

"Thanks, Lou."

"How do you feel now?" Louisa said, after Vera had taken a long drink.

"All right."

"What going on, Vera? What's the matter with you?"

"I've got to go." Vera said, and she stood up.

"Go where?"

"Someplace. It's near here. Something happened to me there a long time ago."

"What happened to you?" Louisa said. Her concern turned her face into a future, more mature version of herself that one day she would become.

"It's a long walk. I've got to go, Louisa."

"I'm going with you."

"No, you don't have to. You shouldn't be involved."

"What are you talking about? God. You're really scaring me. I'll go with you. I think you need me to. Let's go."

Vera paused as she tried to make a decision. "All right. It's this way." She led with Louisa right behind her.

"We've got to trudge through all that snow? I wish I'd worn my big boots," Louisa said.

The march was exhausting. They spoke just twice, and both times, Louisa asked Vera how much farther they had to go, and Vera's answer was they were almost there. She'd answered evasively because she didn't remember how far she'd walked to get there the first time. It was so long ago. Vera gained fresh strength from having Louisa for company. Because of her, she felt braver and safer than she would've alone. She gazed at their surroundings, seeing the landmarks that she remembered that pointed her toward the spot where she'd been abducted on the day that she'd run away from school. She could see the place in her mind, and it was just beyond the next hillcrest of snow.

They climbed the slope of the snow ridge, and they could see up ahead of them a band of trees where there was a wide opening at the edge of a forest. The opening among the trees had a stump in the center of it. It was the place that Vera was searching for, and she gasped.

"What's the matter?" Louisa said.

"This is it."

Not much had changed there, except the branches had grown almost all the way across the clearing so that they touched and made a bridge, but it was the place she remembered. She would've been petrified going to that anomalous inlet if Louisa hadn't been there with her.

But was she putting Louisa in danger?

"Over there?" Louisa said, pointing to it.

"Yes."

They walked through the final part of the marshland to the edge of the woods. Vera felt disoriented when she entered the clearing, and her dark secrets came alive to torture her. All of her memories of the abductions ran together in her mind. It'd take a long time before she could make sense of all the jagged pieces.

She wanted to scream for help. She had the feeling they were coming for her, and she looked up to search for them in the sky.

Louisa kneeled on the ground next to her. "What are you looking at Vera?"

"You won't believe me."

"I promise I'll believe you."

"No, you couldn't."

"Vera, I'm your friend. You can tell me anything."

"This . . . this is where it happened."

"What happened?"

"Oh, God, Lou. I'm so sorry. It's too dangerous for you to be here."

"Dangerous?"

"Yes. I found out some things about myself that I didn't know, and they're horrible things that I can't imagine happening to anybody. And I've had nightmares about them my whole life, but they're not nightmares."

"I remember your nightmares, and you waking up screaming in the middle of the night. You tried to tell me about them, but I got too freaked out."

"Yes, but they're real. They're real experiences that've happened to me."

Louisa moved closer to her and looked into her eyes. "You've got to tell me about them. I'm not freaked out now. Well, maybe a little, but please, Vera."

"Do you remember the day I left the soccer game and ran away from school? This is where I came, and this is where they took me."

"Who took you?"

"The little people, that's what I call them."

"Like from your dreams."

"It was very quiet and peaceful here that day for a while, and I liked being alone. I watched some chipmunks running around and listened to the birds." She put her hands over her face. "And then, oh, God. They captured me and made me go with them on their ship. They come from another planet or another dimension. I don't know."

"Vera—"

"I know I sound crazy."

"I believe you, Vera. No, you don't sound crazy. I believe you."

"You do?"

"I remember once, when I slept at your house, I saw them taking you out through the ceiling, and I felt so bad because I couldn't help you. They made me so I couldn't talk or move. I thought I was dreaming. Oh, Vera." She put her arms around her.

"This is my life, and it's never going to stop. And I don't know who or what I am. I really don't."

"It'll be okay."

"How do you know? They kidnapped Mr Cristopholos, and he killed himself."

"That's not going to happen to you, Vera."

"But I keep thinking—"

"Don't think. Let's just get out of here. Come on."

"Okay."

"Now," Louisa said.

Louisa set a quick pace for them to walk at. Before they got too far to see, Vera turned to look at the clearing that they'd come from, and a shiver went up and down her body. Nothing could make her go back to that dark and terrible place ever again.

"Vera, come on," Louisa said.

Vera pulled her eyes away and followed her friend.

They hurried to get back before dark. Vera tired easily, and at one point, she leaned on Louisa's shoulder as they walked. But little by little, she began reconnecting with the world, and she felt a sense of peace because she was so grateful for that. She looked mindfully at every corner of the landscape, and her heart leaped at the beautiful pink reflection of the setting sun on the white snow. Her hands and feet were numb with the cold, and she curled her fingers against her palms to warm them. She didn't mind the pain of being cold because it reminded her that she was human, and she hoped it meant there was hope for her, after all.

Except her positive frame of mind was ephemeral, like a snowflake, and it didn't take long for it to melt inside her. She had more fears than hopes. Would she end up like Peter? Why them? How was she supposed to live this way? Her ideas about time and place and what was or wasn't real were shattered, and the foundation of her life was ripped out from under her. When she tried to see her future, she saw nothing, only a black wall.

Chapter 16

Gwen left work that afternoon and drove to see John. He was expecting her, and when she pulled up in her car, he was watching out the window for her. By the time she walked to the front porch, he was already standing at the door, holding it open for her.

"Hi," he said, and he kissed her. "Come on in."

She took off her coat. "Hi. It's nice and warm in here."

"I'm glad you like it."

She grabbed him around his stomach and pulled him up to her and kissed him long and fully.

"Hey, now" he said, with a big flirty grin. "Give me a minute."

He knelt in front of the woodstove and stirred the coals and replenished the fire with some logs. Gwen sat down on the couch and watched him. Much to her chagrin, she literally couldn't take her eyes off him. His self-assured movements and the easygoing masculinity that he projected mesmerized her. In her entire life, no other man had attracted her like he did.

He seemed to know it when he looked over his shoulder and smiled at her. "Do you want a glass of wine?" He wiped some soot off his hands over the hearth.

"Sure."

He sat down next to her and poured them some wine.

"Thank you for the tulips. They're absolutely beautiful," she said.

"I'm glad you like them. How's the flu?"

"All right. Better."

"You must be thinking about Peter. You look so sad. I'm sad."

Now was the time for her to tell him what Peter had said about Vera, but she was reaching for the right words, which didn't even exist. There wasn't any way to go around it or to make it sound less terrible or incredible beyond anybody's imagination. The explanation she had to give him was horrific. She took a deep breath. "Yes, poor Peter. It's so tragic."

"Yeah, it is. He was a good man."

"I'll miss him. I always saw him two or three times a week at the library or at meetings."

"I don't think I ever told you, Gwen, but when I was a kid, our dads were close friends, and Peter was kind of like an older brother to me. I actually learned a lot of outdoor skills from him. He was the one who really taught me how to fish."

"I didn't know that."

"Yeah. I've been thinking about the friendship that we had when we were kids. I think he was a lot different then, a lot less serious. He was more lighthearted. He could actually be kind of a practical joker."

"I can imagine that."

"Yeah. And he also had a big heart, like he did as a man, but I think he was happier then. Maybe it had to do with his marriage. I really don't know." He took a long drink of his wine.

As Gwen listened, she stared at the pool of red wine in her glass and the way it shimmered in the firelight like a lake under a full moon, and she remembered the faint look of suffering that would come over Peter sometimes, when he thought no one could see. She knew the reason. No wonder he was unhappy.

He put his arms around her, and they leaned back against the couch. "I'm sorry you're still not feeling well. You didn't have to come, you know. I'd have understood if you wanted to go home."

"I have an important reason."

"Oh, yeah?" he said, suggestively.

"I have to talk to you."

"What is it?"

"This isn't easy."

"What's wrong?"

"A couple of weeks before Peter died, he came to see me at my house."

"Yes?"

"He told me something about Vera."

"What? What did he say?"

"From what I've seen with Vera, I believe it's all true."

"Be blunt with me, Gwen."

"What happened to her mom is happening to Vera. They're both victims, John."

"Victims? What do you mean?"

"Vera has been abducted multiple times, like her mother. She's—"

"Abducted? What are you talking about?"

"Meaning . . . she's been abducted by beings not from this planet, like her mother was . . . like you alluded to the time you told me about your wife."

"No."

"But, John—"

"That's not happening. Not to Vera."

"According to Peter, it is."

"What the hell was wrong with him? What did he know? I don't understand why he'd say something like that. If it wasn't so disturbing it'd be funny."

"Oh, John, it breaks my heart, but it's the truth. He had the same experiences. He saw Vera there."

"And where the hell was that?"

"On their ships."

"Yeah, right. And you really believe that?"

"Yes, I do. Peter finally convinced me. What he told me brought back memories of strange things I witnessed that happened to Vera over the years. She's suffering through the same experiences, as he did. I think that's why he killed himself."

"Killed himself?" he said, and his eyes grew wide.

"He sent me a letter before that, and I read it today at work. He wrote that he was going to commit suicide. Here it is. You can read it."

He read it and handed it back to her. "He killed himself, and it makes his death even sadder. But it doesn't prove he was right about Vera. It proves he wasn't in his right mind."

"And the reason he wasn't is because of the abductions. Vera's are real too. Maybe you don't remember, or you blocked it out, but I think that on some level you know what's been happening, because you alluded to it."

"No, I didn't. That's bullshit."

"John, a long time ago, you told me about your wife." She took his hand and spoke to him in the gentlest voice she could. "You told me that she suffered from hallucinations and she had psychological problems. You said she believed she'd been abducted by people who were aliens or extraterrestrials, and they took her to a ship—"

He stood up quickly, and she had to move to get out of the way. "I don't remember that."

"You remember, but you're choosing to deny it. We were talking one evening outside in your front yard, under Vera's window, and you told me your wife tried to tell you that she was a victim of these abductions, and she claimed the beings came and took her anytime they wanted. And you told me that sometimes you're sorry that you didn't believe her."

His face lost color. "I'm sorry for a lot of things."

"But you thought that she could be telling the truth."

He ran his hands through his hair. "Sometimes I wondered."

"Vera is her daughter, and I've heard that the phenomenon may involve other family members, and even generations of people from the same family. Oh, John, don't you even think it's possible? After what you've experienced with Vera."

"Jesus Christ. There was the thing I saw in her neck."

"What thing?"

"A tiny triangular shaped object I felt under her skin after I found her unconscious in the woods and carried her home."

"And just a few weeks ago, Vera vanished from the library."

"She was with RJ."

"RJ brought her home, and he was trying to protect her. He made up that story about asking her to leave with him, which wasn't true. I think she was abducted that day."

"I don't know. But if Peter thought Vera was in trouble, why didn't he come to me?"

"He was going to, but he was afraid you wouldn't believe him. He came to me instead that night, and he was in absolute despair."

"And that's why he killed himself? Because he thought he was being abducted by aliens."

"He was all alone with his experiences. He couldn't talk about it with anyone. His wife wouldn't believe him. Without anyone to support him, he couldn't bear the trauma by himself anymore. But it's different for Vera. She has you, me and Louisa and your family. We can try to help her and understand her and make her happy, if we can. Peter came to me because he wanted me to know that when Vera is no longer in the dark about this and she remembers things, she'll need us to believe her and help her deal. I know it's not easy, but you've got to accept the truth."

He leaned against the wall with his forehead touching it, panting. She went to him and made him turn around. She held his head in her hands, and his hair fell across her fingers and slipped between them, and she looked into his furious eyes.

"I want to kill them," he said.

"I don't blame you."

"When did he tell you about this?"

She hesitated. She was afraid of what he would say when she admitted it. "It was a few weeks ago."

"Why didn't you tell me right away?"

"John," she said kissing him.

He lifted her hands off his face. "No, I want to know."

"I wasn't sure how I'd tell you because it's so awful. I could hardly face it, and I was afraid."

"Afraid of how I'd react or something?"

"Yes, to be honest, that was part of it."

"Well, Vera's my kid."

"Of course, she is."

"So, no matter what, I should've been the first one to know."

"Yes, you're right."

"And since I wasn't, you should've told me right away."

"I know. I'm sorry."

"I actually think you've made things worse, Gwen."

"How?"

"You said you were afraid to tell me. Why? Because I'm too erratic and impulsive? You think I might go off the deep end and do something that might hurt Vera."

"No. That's not true. I know you love her. I also didn't want to hurt you, John. I hated that it would anguish you."

"Strange. That's what you've done."

"John, come on, please."

He put his hands on her waist impulsively and drew her near to him. "It's up to me to keep Vera safe," he said, his voice breaking.

He kissed her, and she kissed him back with equal parts of sorrow and passion, until he stepped aside and walked away from her. His rejection felt like getting kicked in the gut, and she stood there, stunned. She became aware of a draft from the hallway, and she started to tremble.

"Don't be angry at me, John. Please try to understand."

"Vera will be home soon."

She knew what he meant. "All right, I'll go."

"You underestimated me, Gwen."

She cringed when he said it. "You're right. But, please, that's not what's important here. Don't let it matter to you now."

There was nothing more she could say, so she put on her coat and readied to leave. "I love you," she said. She kissed him on his cheek.

"I love you," he said. Then he opened the door. "Be careful driving. The roads will be slick."

"I'll call you later?"

"Yeah, whatever."

From her car, she saw John's porch light go on. It cut a bright slice out of the twilight sky. *So much loss*, she thought. Her head throbbed. She was hot and flushed, and her fever had returned. She hated leaving him like this.

Chapter 17

In March, the first flock of Canada geese returned to Pangea on a buoyant wind from the south to nest on Mill Pond. In the weeks that followed, the pond became more populated, as many more geese arrived, and also a pair of swans, who were a huge local attraction because they came back every spring. The people in the town had given them the names Hamilton and Alexandra. When the swans returned to the pond, the people liked to think of it as a sign of spring.

There was still snow around the pond, and trenches of dirt and ice. There were still dead stalks and brittle brush in the marshlands and fields. Many weeks would have to pass before any green popped out. It was the time when the pussy willows were in bloom, around Louisa's birthday. She'd soon be sixteen. And in May was Vera's sixteenth birthday, when the lilacs were in bloom.

On the morning of her birthday, Vera took a walk with Spark. The lilacs' thick scent hung in the moist air, dampening her skin like perfume. She stopped to plunge her face into the purple blossoms, to binge on their fragrance.

"So beautiful," she said. She ran her fingers across them as she started walking away. Spring overwhelmed her with its exquisiteness, but in her heart, she felt like a stranger to her senses, as if she was on Earth as a visitor for the first time.

"I belong here," she yelled. Her voice echoed. Spark turned his head and looked at her.

They walked slowly the rest of the way home, while Vera wondered what she could expect from the future. Since Peter's death, the trigger that had ignited her memories of her abductions, she'd grown increasingly aware of the times and places that they had happened. Then, finally, the day had come when she could remember everything, leaving her with new, uncharted questions and fears. Did she have anything to look forward to in life? Could she dream of having a career and a family? Would she have any freedom whatsoever over her destiny? The uncertainty was too hard to bear. All she wanted to do was sit under a tree for the rest of the day and listen to the birds. She wanted to be around something peaceful and beautiful to overcome the dread that she felt.

She needed a pep talk, so she gave one to herself. "I refuse to be upset on my birthday," she declared.

John was waiting by the truck when they got back, and Spark trotted over to him, wagging his tail.

"Where'd you go, Vera?"

"Not far. Down the road a bit."

"You were gone a long time."

"It didn't seem it."

"I'm glad you're home."

She wasn't sure that he was all that happy behind the smile he had on his face. The feeling she got from him was that he had a secret worry that he was hiding from her. What was it? Did he know? He had dark circles under his eyes, which made him look older, but that didn't diminish his handsomeness. She placed her hand on his shoulder and kissed his cheek, soothingly. In return, he flashed another smile—a more convincing one this time—and kissed her forehead.

"Are you ready to leave for your birthday day out?" he said.

"Yeah, as soon as I use the bathroom. Come on, Spark."

She absentmindedly slammed the storm door as she went in the house. She froze, expecting him to yell at her to "take it easy on the door." But he didn't, which was different for him. Spark went over to his bed to lie down, and she used the bathroom. After that, she went to get her wallet. She took it from her dresser and turned to leave, and there was a ball of light that was floating in the middle of the doorway, and she'd have to go through it to leave the room. She hesitated, even though she told herself that it was a only a reflection.

As she watched it, it began to move and to change shape. It flashed and changed colors, and she felt like it wanted her to see it and was attempting to communicate with her. She didn't know or care about what it was doing. She wished it would disappear. She looked out the window for John, but she couldn't see him. She tried to call for help, and she couldn't utter a sound. The orb blinked in a steady progression of different colors, from pink to red to blue to green to yellow to white.

Suddenly, it flew directly toward her and hovered near her like a hornet, and she jumped out of the way, and when she did that, she smashed her head on a hook on the closet door. The orb dangled in the air at eye level with her, almost touching her. She launched herself off the balls of her feet and fled from it. Her body turned into a mist of energy, and when she got to the wall in her room, she didn't stop, and she passed through the solid wall and came out the other side, and she was astounded to be standing in the hallway.

She ran down the stairs and outside and slumped against the wall of the front porch. She was gasping for breath. "Oh, God," she mumbled. Then she heard her dad call to her.

"Are you coming?" John said.

"Yes." She put on her sunglasses and went to meet him.

"All set?"

"Yes."

He looked at her skeptically. "Is anything wrong?"

She wanted to say she thought it was a stupid question, since she'd just walked through a fucking wall, but in her heart, she didn't want to be nasty and hurt his feelings, either. "Yeah, I'm fine," she said. "My friend Marissa called while I was in the house. She was upset because her boyfriend just broke up with her."

"You mean Marissa from the ski team?"

"Yes."

"That's too bad. It's good she has you to talk to."

"Nothing I said helped."

"It'll hurt for a while, but she'll get over it. There's other fish in the sea."

"That's pretty lame advice, Dad. Is that what you'd say to me?"

"Yeah, probably. Are you mad at me?"

"No, I'm fine," she said and started to go to the truck.

"Wait a second," he said taking her arm. "What's wrong?"

"It's PMS. Okay, Dad? I'm about to get my fucking period."

"Watch your mouth, Vera."

"I'm sorry. But I don't like it when you don't believe me."

"Okay, okay. My God, it's your birthday, and we're supposed to go out for the day to have fun, for God's sakes. I don't want to waste this beautiful day fighting. Do you?"

"No."

"Good. Then let's go."

"Can I drive?"

"No, not right now."

"But I need more practice before I take my driving test."

"Maybe on the way home," he said, slipping the keys into the ignition. "Come on, get in the truck."

"I'm not sure I want to go."

"What are you talking about? We planned this. You wanted to take a walk along the coast and get fried clams."

"What's the point? All we do is fight."

"That's not true. You're exaggerating."

"Yes, we do."

"And you think it's all my fault, don't you?"

"No, I don't think so. But—"

"Let's drop the subject," he said. "Come on, get in the truck and let's go."

"I don't want to go."

"Vera, stop being moody and get in the truck," he said angrily.

"No."

"Let's not ruin your sixteenth birthday," he pleaded. "If we do, we'll both be disappointed. Let's go have fun."

"All right. If that's what you want."

"It's your birthday. It's about what you want, but I think we should do what we planned."

She thought about it for a moment, and finally it was the fear of being alone after what'd happened to her that made her relent and agree to go with him. "Okay," she said.

She got in the truck and buckled her seat belt. She leaned back in the seat and fell into a broodiness that set the tone of the drive. As John drove away, she said to him, "The neighbors probably heard you yelling at me."

His face reddened. "They probably did."

"Where did you go when I was in the house?" she said.

"Nowhere. I was standing by the truck like I was."

"But I looked out the window, and I could see the truck, but I didn't see you."

"I was right here, Vera. I don't know why you didn't see me. Were you looking for me?"

She fell quiet and looked away.

"Vera?"

"Dad, let's not talk about anything now, all right?"

"You were fine before you went inside, and suddenly now you're mad. Why can't you be honest with me and tell me what's the matter?"

"How can I be honest with you? You're like a dictator."

"A dictator? Well, I guess it's my job to be a benevolent dictator sometimes."

She turned her back on him with a cold shrug, and they rode in silence for miles traveling to Ogunquit, Maine. John focused on driving and Vera withdrew into her own thoughts. The route they took was buttressed by forested lands and fields. Cool air flowed through Vera's open window, bringing with it the scent of apple blossoms. Framed by the window, the landscapes they passed looked like painted canvases of spring. Soon, Vera began to feel calmer, and as she viewed the beautiful scenery, she was reminded that spring never failed to reassert itself when the time came. Spring was the season of misty air and new growth, when the northeast woods became like a rainforest.

The road was hilly like the back of a snake. The last hill was the biggest one, and they started to go up it. Vera felt the sensation of the g-forces in her stomach, something that'd thrilled her when she was young, because it was like riding on a roller coaster, and it felt that way again now. She remembered she and her dad would drive up and down the hill just for fun a hundred times.

"Do you remember what we used to call this sort of tall steep hill?" John turned and asked her.

"A grandfather hill."

He looked happy that she did remember. "That's right. Okay, we just reached the top, and now we'll go down."

For a fraction of a second, Vera was weightlessly suspended in the cab of the truck, but this time she didn't like the feeling she got. In no way did it remind her of the grandfather hill from her childhood. It brought out the memories she had of when she was ensnared by an excruciating light that lifted her to a waiting ship in the sky and an alternate reality. She shut her eyes to block a barrage of images.

She couldn't help fidgeting because she felt like she was in a cage, but John didn't notice how anxious she was. He was too absorbed in his own thoughts to pay that much attention to her. She leaned back against the strap of the seatbelt. It made the perfect cradle for her head. She tried to think about something else. *Today's my birthday*, she thought. *I'm sixteen.*

She pictured the number sixteen in her mind. Sixteen was a good age. She fell into daydreaming about who she wanted to be and what she wanted to do in her lifetime. She felt a haughty sense of satisfaction about being young and having her whole life ahead of her, and she forgot that she wasn't wholly in control of her own fate.

She had a dream of becoming a professional musician, of course, because of her dad. She believed she could be good at it if she could learn to play the guitar and sing. When she was younger, she was interested in becoming an astronomer. She knew all about the constellations and how to read every part of the night sky. She had wanted to be an astronomer ever since the first time she saw the stars and understood what they were. She didn't know then that she was so personally involved with the universe, and it seemed ironic to her looking back on it. But now a switch in her head was turned on, lighting her brain with information that she couldn't forget.

Several months had passed since she'd begun remembering, and she still had no idea what the alien visitors wanted with her. She didn't know why, but she sensed that turning sixteen was a significant milestone to them. It even felt as if they were on their way then to abduct her again.

Their truck went over a big bump in the road, and it jolted her back to this reality, the one of being with her father on her birthday and going to the Maine coast with him.

"We're almost there," John said, as he touched her on the shoulder.

"Yeah, I see."

She stared at herself in the sideview mirror. She thought she looked young for her age, but she felt much older. In her reflection, she saw a girl who was desperate to be safe and searching for answers. During the ride, it got to a point that she burned inside to share her secret with him, and she thought about blurting it out. She saw the sign that said, "Welcome to Ogunquit" just ahead on the road.

"What a beautiful day to do this," John said.

They parked in the village and walked down the shady lane to Perkins Cove, passing tall oak trees and quaint cedar-shake buildings of shops and art galleries on both sides of the street. The view of the harbor in Perkins Cove unfolded before their eyes as they got closer. Vera glimpsed sailboats with shining, pillow-white sails on the horizon. The air smelled savory of flowers and sea. She promised herself that she would remember that fragrance forever.

They walked to the water's edge and looked out at the ocean.

"I had a sailboat once, when I was a kid," John said.

"You know how to sail? Will you teach me?"

"We don't have a boat," he said.

"You should buy one, or build one," she said.

He laughed. "Maybe someday." His attention was drawn to something splashing in the water. He pointed toward the spot. "Vera, look. It's a seal."

"I don't see it."

"By the channel marker. Do you see it now?"

"No," she said, frustrated.

"I wish I'd brought the binoculars. Here." He took her hand and pointed it in the direction where the seal was bobbing on its back in the water.

"Oh, yeah, there it is. There are two of them," she said in delight. She ran down the shore for a better view.

He came up beside her and cupped his hand above his eyes to block the sun's glare. "Very cool."

"Look how they're playing together. The only thing they care about is having fun doing their thing. I'm jealous," she said.

"Do you really feel that careworn, Vera?"

"No, I didn't mean it that way."

"I'm hungry. Let's go get some lunch."

They strolled to Barnacle Billy's at the edge of the water and sat down at a table on the outside deck.

"It's not too chilly to sit out here, is it?"

"No, I like it," she said.

He handed her a menu. "What do you want to eat?"

"You already know what I want, Dad."

He ordered two fried clam dinners, cups of chowder, and a large side of onion rings, and when it came, they ate slowly to make the most out of every bite and to savor the pretty scenery and each other's company.

"Wow, I haven't been this full in a long time," he said.

The food tasted so good that she didn't want to stop eating until it was gone. "I haven't either."

"I'm glad you're enjoying it."

She nodded very slightly at him and picked up the last fried clam on her plate and put it in her mouth.

The waitress came and cleared their dishes, and John paid their bill. On the way out, he suggested they get ice cream cones.

"Sure," Vera said.

John got pistachio and Vera got chocolate from a stand that sold homemade ice cream. They walked over to a makeshift plywood art gallery, where an artist was working on a painting of lobster traps. There were at least a dozen more paintings of charming coastal scenes displayed for sale all over his kiosk, hanging on the plywood walls and standing up on metal folding chairs and on the ground.

They joined the crowd of people watching the artist paint. Vera realized he was the same artist who'd painted at Perkins Cove since she was a kid. She felt excited to see him again, and somehow, it was reassuring to know that he was still there. He was almost exactly the same as she remembered him, and she was just as intrigued by him as ever.

His business sign was a piece of driftwood with his name painted on it in fancy capital letters. His hair was still long and curly, but it was white instead of blond, and he still kept his tan face a little unshaven. His thick eyebrows loomed over the bridge of his prominent nose. Even his clothes were the same: a faded denim shirt, unbuttoned and with the sleeves rolled up to his elbows, cut-off denim shorts, and a cotton handkerchief tied around his neck. When Vera was very young, she was a little bit intimidated by his intensity and self-important air. She was too scared to talk to him or to look at him eye to eye. He was a man who'd spent his life with his blue eyes fixed on the sea, and for a long time, he represented passion and freedom to her, and she was in awe of him.

From her older perspective, she saw him a bit differently. She noticed something about him that she couldn't see then. His chin raised in the air looked overly intentional and his tight-lipped expression looked exaggerated. It occurred to her that part of it was an act to make himself appear very artistic and unapproachable to people and to be seen as someone who answered a higher calling than everyone else. She wasn't put off by the new impression she had of him, and she didn't think less of him because of it. It endeared him more to her, and in her heart, he remained a great artist.

As she weighed these thoughts, a man in the crowd said to the woman beside him, "You call that art? It's nothing but cheap, tacky crap."

Vera and John turned around and looked at him, along with most of the other people.

"The guy is a hack," the man said aggressively. This time he seemed to want everyone, including the artist, to hear him. Then he and the woman left and walked away abruptly.

Vera stared as the man and his girlfriend crossed the lane toward one of the fine art galleries. The clothes that the couple were wearing were chic and expensive. Vera noticed with disgust that they didn't slow down their stylish, lean bodies even once to let anyone by them. She wanted vengeance for the artist and for anyone else that the man had offended, for that matter. She had a good pitching arm. She could barely stop herself from chucking a rock at his head. She knew that she could hit him dead-on. As the man and the woman entered the art gallery, the hanging wind chimes on the door clattered discordantly, like the man's vicious remark.

"What's the matter, Vera?"?" John whispered.

"I hate that man."

John stared at her, eyebrows raised, and asked, "You hate him? Why?"

"He's mean. The things he said about the artist were terrible. I don't like it when people are mean."

"I don't either. If it makes you feel any better, he just made himself look stupid in front of a lot of people. He's a snob. Forget about him." John put his arm around Vera's shoulders. "Come on, let's take our walk along the coast."

It was only a short walk to the entrance of the Marginal Way, the trail that ran along the ocean above a series of beaches and cliffs. The wind off the ocean blew on them unabatedly as they started down the trail, but Vera liked feeling the rough touch of the wind on her face. To experience the effects of nature made her feel like she was an indelible part of it. Suddenly, she could breathe again. About five minutes down the trail, they stopped and looked below at the waves pummeling the cliffs. The surf splashed over a ring of rocks and formed a foaming pool. In the churning water, she saw a crab clinging to a rock. Inch by inch, it was attempting to climb to safety before the next wave dragged it out to sea.

"You can do it, little crab," she called, like it was the little engine that could.

Her encouragement seemed to inspire the crab to try harder, and it surged to the top of the rock and scurried away. Watching it escape and scramble to safety gave Vera hope, as if her life depended on the crab surviving.

They continued on their journey and reached a spot where the trail narrowed and it was necessary to walk in single file. There was a family heading toward them from the other direction. John and Vera stepped aside to let them pass. One of them was a boy roughly the same age as Vera. His athletic body reminded her of RJ. He smiled brightly at her as he went by, and she smiled back at him. After he'd passed, she turned around and saw him looking over his shoulder at her. They exchanged a few more parting looks before she lost sight of him.

"That boy reminded me of RJ," John said, as they started walking again.

"A little bit, I guess."

"What's RJ been doing lately? I haven't seen him for a long time."

"I'm not sure. I guess he must be busy." she said, hoping that would end the conversation.

"You're still friends, aren't you?"

She decided to be honest with him for once. "No, actually we're not, Dad."

"Oh, no, what happened?"

"I got mad at him, and since then we stopped being friends."

"What did he do to make you mad at him?"

She frowned at him to indicate that she didn't want to talk about it. She was too embarrassed to admit she was jealous because RJ flirted with a girl. She didn't want to confess that she thought she was stupid to get upset about it, because her life was too volatile for her to fall in love, anyway. The more she considered it, the more hopeless it sounded to her.

"You don't have to explain," John said breaking the silence. "It's just too bad that it turned out that way, and I'm sad. I bet you'll be friends again. Don't count out the possibility."

"I haven't."

"I'm glad," he said. Then a faraway look appeared in his eyes. "I remember when the two of you were little and you used to have wrestling matches to settle your arguments. But your relationship is different now. Of course, it's not as simple as that."

"I don't understand what you're talking about, Dad."

"You're not little kids anymore." A huge wave smashed against the rocks and sprayed salty water on them. "Wow, that's cold."

"It felt good," she said.

"Vera, I know you don't want to talk about it, but as I said, I hope you and RJ will talk things over and be friends again. I know he really cares about you. I can see it in his eyes. It's the same way that you look at him."

"Please, Dad," she said, entreating him to leave her alone.

"I just think it's a shame. You like each other so much that—"

She erupted. "Quit, Dad. What about you and Gwen? Why can't the two of you ever get it together? Why don't we talk about that."

"I've told you before that I don't think that is any of your business."

"You always say that, but I think it is. Gwen's like my mom. Aren't you ever going to tell her how you feel?"

"I did."

"What? You did? When was that? What did she say?"

"It doesn't matter. Let's get back to talking about you."

"Gwen was seeing someone for a while, but then she suddenly broke up with him. Louisa didn't know why. Did she do that because of you?"

"Lower your voice. We're in a public place," he said, looking around to see if anyone could hear them.

"Oh, Dad, that's so wonderful. So why aren't you together now?"

"That's enough. Let's go back. There's no point in talking about it, because now we're not together anymore."

"What? Did you get scared and back out? Oh, Dad, Mom's been gone a long time. You can love someone else."

"It's not about that. Oh, Vera, I'm so sorry you had to grow up without her."

"So why did I have to grow up without her? God, we hardly ever talk about her. I don't know why she left or anything about her. Didn't you love her?"

"Yes, I loved her. We both loved each other."

"Tell me something about her, just one thing. How did you meet?"

"It was when I had my band," he said.

His eyes shone as he told her the story, proof for Vera that he'd loved her.

"I'd never been in love before I met your mom."

"Did you have a lot of girlfriends?"

"Well, yeah. I was in a band. I thought I was in love a couple of times, briefly, but not really. When I fell for your mom, she gave me a real sense of purpose that I'd never had before." He laughed. "I didn't even know I was missing one, until I met her."

"But why did she leave us?"

His face grew sad. "I don't know why, Vera. But it certainly didn't have anything to do with you. She had some mental illness and emotional problems for a while leading up to it. It's been hard for me to forgive myself for letting it happen."

"You never tried to find her?"

"Of course I did. I tried for a long time. I'm sorry I couldn't. I may try to find her again. She loved us, honey, but she was troubled."

"What do you mean?"

"It's strange and complicated."

"Was she troubled like me?"

"Are you troubled?" he said. There was a look of pained concern on his face.

"Yes," she said, looking down at the cliffs. They didn't look so steep that she couldn't climb down them. "Troubled like my mom."

Then, without another thought, she threw her right leg over the gate, and then her left leg, and started to descend the cliff. John yelled for her to come back and went after her.

The lower she went down the face of the cliff, the louder the roar of the waves grew in her ears, and soon she could hear nothing but that. The spray from the water blew up her nose as she maneuvered herself down the rocks, stepping and sliding. She was not scared at all. The thought of falling excited her, as the barriers between time and space and the earth and the universe melted away. She sped up her climb down, but rushing made it difficult to keep her footing on the slick rocks. She lost her balance and slipped a few more feet.

"Vera, that's far enough! Wait for me," John jumped and wriggled down to her. He was soaked and dirty, and his arms were covered with scratches and scrapes. "What the hell are you doing? You could've gotten killed," he said trembling with emotion and fatigue.

"I've got to escape," she said.

"Escape from what?" he said, grabbing her arm to stop her.

Desperately, she uttered, "I have to tell you something,"

"What is it? You can tell me," he said. The anger had drained out of his voice.

She wondered if she should bother to tell him. She felt as if the story of her life was plain to see written all over her; aside from that, where would she even start?

"I think I know. No, I'll say it. I know," he said, embracing her. "You remember, Vera. I remember now too."

She began to cry. "What do you remember?"

"About the beings who take you, who steal you from me."

"How do you know?"

"I had a revelation suddenly, like you did. But I've always had dreams about the things that happen to you. Now I see there were physical signs, but I ignored them and chalked them up to anything I could think of to explain them to myself, and then I forget about them. They were just gone from my mind, and I'm ashamed of that. I guess I was scared to know the truth, or maybe they erased my memory too.

"But now I remember nights when I woke up to a blinding light shining over the house, and I tried to get out of bed to check on you, but I couldn't move. I could hear what was happening, but I was paralyzed. The morning after, you'd come downstairs or I'd find you in bed with your pajamas on backward, or inside-out. All of that was like a haze for years, but these past few months, things started to come out that made me believe that this was happening to you. I thought about your mother and how she tried to tell me about the experiences she went through. I didn't believe her. I should've."

She'd never seen him cry, but tears ran down his face.

"When I heard about Peter being dead and that he'd committed suicide, that's when it all came out and I couldn't stop it."

He rocked her in his arms like she was a baby. "I love you."

"Why do they do this to me?"

"I don't know."

"I hate them. Someday, they may not let me go. But what also scares me —"

"What, Vera?"

"What if someday I don't want to leave them? I don't want that to happen. Why did they pick me? Is there something about me that makes them do this to me? Or maybe there's something they want to teach me or make me understand, and that's why they take me."

"It's my job to protect you, and I can't," John said sorrowfully.

"It's not your fault. Nobody can stop them. They always say they try not to hurt me and I shouldn't be afraid."

But they did hurt her, even when they didn't mean to, and she could hear them saying to her, "Don't resist, and when we're done, we'll return you." Her encounters with them were terrifying, but she was curious about them; there was a piece of her soul that was in awe of them, and she wanted them to help her to understand the essence of the universe.

"Don't trust them, Vera," John said, as if he'd read her thoughts. "They torment you the way they did to your mom."

"What?"

"Your mom would try to tell me stories about what they did to her, but I didn't believe her. Ever since she left, I felt if I'd believed her that she'd still be here. I didn't help her the way I should've, but I can help you, Vera."

"You can't stop it, Dad."

"Jesus, that's too hard for me to accept. I want you to understand something. I'm going to always be here for you as long as I live, which is going to be a long, long time. Right? And by then you'll have a family of your own who loves you, and you'll be able to rely on them. Cling to us. We'll remind you where you belong. The people who love you matter more than the aliens or whatever the fuck it is they're up to."

"I hear what you're saying, but I'm so confused."

"You're my child and I'm your dad. Your home is with me. That's the greatest significance, understand? You can have a good life, a great life. I know it."

"How do you know that?"

He took her by the shoulders and looked directly at her. "Vera, you have the right to live your life, and you will. You're a sensitive and caring girl." He stopped and corrected himself. "I mean—young woman. You know that life is precious and you shouldn't waste it, and you won't. You haven't got a shallow bone in your whole body. The things that are part of you are permanent, like your brave heart and deep soul. I'm proud of you, and I know you have the courage in you to face this and to live a good life."

He made it sound easy. She knew it wouldn't be. "I'll try."

"I love you so much, Vera. Please never forget where your home is, your real home. You can't ever forget it."

She nodded and kissed him, and they climbed back up to the top of the cliff and the trail. They got soaked on their way to the truck in a rainstorm that fell from a lone formation of dark clouds in an otherwise bright blue sky. Vera wished that the rain could magically rinse out the memories down to the residue and set back time and make her ignorant again.

You're always supposed to keep going no matter how bad things are, she thought.

It was one thing to say that, but she was afraid she didn't possess the inner strength to keep fighting. There were only two alternatives, either to fight or give up, and she wasn't ready to give up. She prayed for the faith and strength to deal with the peculiar suffering that fate had put on her.

On the way home, they took the scenic road that wound along the coast. They made one stop at a peninsula of rocks that went out a few hundred feet into the ocean, which Vera said looked like paradise. The evening sun draped them in a blanket of warm-colored light as they stood at the edge of the point and looked out to sea. A flock of shrieking gulls flew by them, disrupting the quiet.

It was nine o'clock when they got home. The porch light was off, but they could see the front door in the moonlight. As soon as they went into the house, Spark tottered outside to do his business, and Vera waited for him and then brought him inside.

"I'll take care of him," she said about Spark as she pointed at his empty food bowl. She filled it and put it back on the floor.

"I still have to give you your birthday present," John said.

"Oh, yeah?"

"Come this way."

She followed him to the living room.

"I'll be right back," he said, as he was leaving.

She sat down and crossed her arms and looked at the objects in the room, and to her relief, everything felt normal. She didn't detect any sense of menace or foreboding in the house. She looked over at Spark. He was sleeping peacefully and contentedly again, and she thought she should also feel that way, and she promised herself she'd try.

John called from the other room to her to shut her eyes. "Are they shut?" he said, before he came in.

"Yes."

"Hold out your arms in front of you. Don't open your eyes until I tell you to."

He laid something gently in them and stepped back. It made a tonal ring when he transferred it into her hands. The object had a smooth, curved bottom and sides.

"Wow," she said.

"Okay, go ahead."

She opened her eyes to behold her gift, a beautiful guitar. She looked it over in amazement. The amber color and the soft shine that emanated from the wood was something to marvel. The weight of it felt just right in her hands. It was perfection, except she didn't know how to play it, at least not yet.

"It's beautiful."

"You always wanted one."

"Yeah," she said, looking at it from the neck to the stem.

"I made it for you."

"Really? It's a work of art, Dad."

"Did you notice what I put on the neck?"

Along the length of the neck, he'd inscribed her name in flowing calligraphy letters in mother of pearl. At first glance, she thought it was just a pretty decorative scroll. Even if she never learned to play the instrument, she thought it was worthy to display as art. A feeling of joy at the prospect of learning to play came over her. It would give her a goal, a purpose, to tether her to the world.

"Wow, it's magnificent. Does this mean you'll teach me?"

"That's the plan," he said, as he sat down in a chair.

"I don't understand. You used to think it wasn't a good idea, because all we did was fight."

"It doesn't have to be that way. You're older, and I'm a bit mellower than I used to be. So do you want to?"

Before she answered, he took the guitar from her hands and snapped on the shoulder strap and handed it back to her. "You know a few chords already, don't you?"

"Yes," she said, putting her fingers on the frets.

"Good," he said, leaning back in a comfortable position. "Start playing them."

Chapter 18

The lilacs and the apple blossoms came and went, and within a month of Vera's birthday, it was summer, and the long days rolled on into July and August.

On a hot day in early August, Vera was outside in her yard, waiting for Gwen and Louisa to pick her up for a hike along the river. She could hear tree frogs croaking from a tiny nearby pond on their property, and she couldn't help laughing about the endless, screeching racket that those spirited little guys could make. They sent their voices reverberating far and wide. It was so loud that it pained her ears, but she loved it. She thought how hearty and lively they sounded. They gave her a taste of what it felt like to be free and wild. They even brought out the optimist in her.

The afternoon heat was beginning to bother her. She could feel the skin on her shoulders getting sunburned. She moved under the big oak tree by the driveway. Under the tree cover, it was still possible for her to appreciate the day, and she felt content, which she didn't take for granted, because peaceful emotions didn't come easily to her.

John came out of the house. The door slamming startled the tree frogs into silence, but that only lasted a few seconds and they picked up their croaking again where they left off.

"Are they late?" he said.

She stood and wiped off the seat of her shorts. "No, but any minute, though."

He gazed at the road. "Oh."

They saw Gwen's car approaching the driveway. Vera went to meet them as Gwen parked. The passenger door flew open, and Louisa got out.

"Hi," Louisa said, waving in her exuberant way. "Are you coming with us, John?"

"No, Louisa. Not this afternoon. Thanks, though."

"Why not?" Louisa said, looking at Vera for support.

"Come on, Dad."

"Well, Gwen, what do you think? Do you mind if I come along?"

"If you want to," Gwen said.

"Okay, I will. But can I meet you there in a little while? I need to put some tools away."

"Yeah, that's fine," Gwen said.

"I think I'll bring my fly rod and do a little fishing while I'm there. It's been a while," he said. "You'll be able to see me from the trail."

"Okay, we'll see you there. Let's go, girls," Gwen said.

John watched them drive away, until he couldn't see them any longer, and then he went to his workshop. Ten minutes later, he was loading his fishing gear when another car drove up behind his truck in the driveway.

"RJ!" he called, when he realized who was in the driver's seat.

RJ leaned out of the window. "Sorry. I didn't notice you were leaving. I'll back up so you can get out," he said.

"No, that's okay," John said. "How are you doing?"

"Good. I didn't know you were going somewhere."

"I'm glad to see you. It's been a while," John said. "I missed you."

A bashful smile crossed RJ's face. "It's good to see you too."

He put his hand on RJ's shoulder. "How's everything going?"

"Everything's okay. How about you?"

"I'm good. Did you stop by to see Vera?"

"Is she home?"

"She just left with Gwen and Louisa to walk the river trail. I'm going down with my fishing rod to meet them. Come with me."

"I don't have my gear with me."

"No problem. I have another fly rod you can use."

"Oh, yeah? Okay, I'll go with you."

"Good. I bet Vera will be glad to see you."

"I'm not so sure."

"Don't worry about it. But I bet she will be. Let me get my extra rod."

He went back to his workshop, and RJ moved his car and parked it out of the way.

"I know a lot of good secret spots on the river to cast a line," John said, as he got in the driver's seat of the truck.

"Me too. The ones you showed me a long time ago, John, and a few that I found on my own."

John turned the truck onto the road, and they drove to the river, parked, and took their fishing gear out of the back. John felt glad to have RJ's company. They walked down the trail carrying their rods over their shoulders, chatting casually as they went along. After they'd gone a couple of hundred yards, John stopped and pointed at a slab of rocks on the shoreline that was visible through the woods.

"Let's throw our lines in over there. Gwen and the girls will be able to see us when they come that way on the path," John said.

They got off the trail to take a shortcut through the woods and entered a forest of white birch trees. Green vegetation carpeted the forest floor, and they were up to their ankles in it. When they were halfway down, the land dropped off at a steep incline, and they picked up momentum and were running down the hill, barreling toward the water's edge. At the riverbank they went out onto the rocks and took their individual spots and began to fish.

Twenty minutes passed, and John hadn't even had a bite on his line. He hadn't even seen fish splashing in the water. He wondered how RJ was doing, if he'd had any luck. John glanced over to where RJ was and watched him cast a line. It'd been about two months since he'd seen him, and in just that short time RJ had gotten taller, and his shoulders were broader. From the back, he almost looked like a grown man.

"Any nibbles? Not the best time fishing today, is it?" John called over to him.

"No," RJ said glancing at the sky. "It might be it's too windy for them to bite."

"You're right. Who taught you all this stuff about fishing, anyway?"

"You did," RJ said with a grin.

"You want to give it a few more minutes and then we'll look for Gwen and the girls?"

"Okay."

They went back to fishing quietly. RJ's gaze was focused on the end of his line, and he didn't see John looking at him covertly from the corner of his eye.

"I heard that you and Vera had an argument a while back, and now you're no longer friends," John said, voicing what he'd been thinking.

It took a second for RJ to look him in the eye and answer. "That's right."

"That explains why we haven't seen you in a while."

"Yes."

"Can I ask what happened?"

"It's not a big deal."

"Nobody wants to tell me anything."

"No, it's not that. I get why you asked."

"You know, it's not my business anyway."

"No, I'll tell you. I think Vera got mad at me because she was jealous. She saw me talking to a girl at school, and the girl was kind of, you know."

"Flirting with you."

"Yeah, and Vera just got really upset, and she didn't want anything to do with me, and when she wouldn't talk to me, I got mad and walked away from her. I didn't even think she'd care if a girl flirted with me."

"Obviously, she does."

"I don't know what's going on. Anyway, I came over because I wanted to try one more time before I gave up."

"Well, Vera can hold a grudge. But I don't think it'll last forever."

"Except it's been months."

John shrugged. "Yeah, sometimes she lets it go on too long."

"I didn't mean to hurt her. If I thought she liked me, I wouldn't have flirted with anyone."

"You didn't do anything wrong."

"I like Vera. I really like her."

"So, when you say you really like her, does that mean you like her romantically?"

RJ blushed. "I like her romantically, but also as a friend."

"I like you, RJ, and I trust you. I don't have a problem if you and Vera start dating. But keep in mind, I can be pretty protective."

A nervous expression appeared on RJ's face. "I will. I know."

"Relax, I'm just teasing you. But we understand each other?"

RJ laughed. "Yeah, we do. But she's not talking to me anyway."

"I don't think she's stopped liking you after all these years."

"I haven't stopped liking her."

RJ spoke with real feeling about Vera. It was clear by his words and also by his voice and the expression of open tenderness on his face that he cared for her. It comforted John that Vera was loved by a lot of people. Love was a powerful force to attach her to home.

"I wish I could talk her out of being mad at me," RJ said. "Vera and I aren't even going out."

"She's awfully sensitive sometimes, too sensitive. But she's special. You know?"

"Yeah, I think she's special."

"She's an ordinary teenager, but she has special insight and experience of things none of us do. Do you know what I mean?"

RJ looked at him stunned, but gaining an understanding of what he meant, he nodded. "I think so."

"I think that someday Vera is going to be very wise. She has that in her," John continued softly. "But she's very vulnerable, and she needs people in her life who care about her."

"She has a hard time trusting. She always has," RJ said.

"There are reasons for that."

"I know."

"She's strong-minded, and that's a good thing to help her get through. Except she needs a special kind of looking after."

"No matter what happens, she's still my friend. I won't let her down."

John looked at the sky and gazed from horizon to horizon. It'd suddenly gotten very quiet, and that got his attention. He sensed something, a presence hiding behind the baby blue sky.

"John?" RJ said.

"What?"

"You were lost in your head."

"Sorry."

"What's going on?"

"Did you notice how quiet it got?"

"Yeah, I did. But wait, do you hear that? That buzzing noise?"

"It sounded like a power line humming. And now it's gone."

It grew quiet again for a minute or two, and then they heard a hard splash in the water at the end of RJ's line.

"I've hooked one," he said.

"I'm going to try again," John said. He cast, and seconds later he had one on the line too.

The witching hour, and the fish were biting. By the time they'd finished fishing, they each had three fish. They put their catches down on a rock to inspect them.

"Those are some big trout," John said. He picked up one of the fish and held it in the air where the light of the late afternoon sun shone on it and made its iridescent scales glimmer like a rainbow of mother of pearl. "Pretty," he said, mesmerized. He wished Vera was there to see it. "Can you come for dinner, RJ? We can cook these on the grill."

"I have to call my mom, but she probably won't mind."

They gathered their gear, and John saw three bright colored flashes between the trees about a hundred yards away, and pointed them out to RJ. "There they are."

Louisa saw them before Gwen and Vera did. She waved and called to them. "Hi! Hey, RJ, when did you decide to come?" Her voice echoed in the breeze, as she came toward them.

Vera walked in the middle of their single-file line, between Gwen and Louisa. She was more surprised than Louisa to see RJ with her father. At first sight, she was glad to see him, but she was also embarrassed to be in close company with him, after their long estrangement. There was a current of nervous energy between them. She glanced at him every few seconds, and she saw him constantly stealing looks at her.

John sensed the awkwardness between Vera and RJ too. As RJ hiked by his side, John saw that he had the jitters, and he kept running his hand through his hair. He also knew by observing her body language that Vera was approaching RJ tentatively as well.

Vera slowed down and dropped back to walk side by side with Louisa, which brought John's attention toward Gwen. His heart started to ache, and he could already feel the tension between them. In their time apart, he came to accept that Gwen had meant well, and he didn't hold a grudge against her, though he could see how she might think he did. He regretted that he'd been quick to judge her and get angry.

When Vera and RJ finally met up on the trail, John was watching them. *They'll make up now*, he thought.

***

The bright sun in her eyes made it difficult for Vera to see RJ, but she could hear his footsteps. Before she knew how close he was to her, he was standing in front of her.

"Hi," he said.

She hoped that they could restart their friendship, but she thought they should let the idea of being in love just fade away. She wasn't quite reconciled with this decision, though it was the logical one. She couldn't deny that her emotions were torn. "Hi," she said. "What are you doing here?

"I went to your house, and your dad asked me to come along."

"Why did you go to the house?"

He took a deep breath and proceeded. "To talk you out of being mad at me."

"I'm not mad at you, RJ."

"You're not? I thought you were upset—because of Kendall."

She was embarrassed that he'd brought it up. "I overreacted, and it was stupid."

"We were just talking. I didn't mean to hurt your feelings. I'm sorry."

"You don't have to apologize. As I said, I was dumb to get mad. It's none of my business, RJ. If I felt hurt, it was my fault."

"Just for the record. I never went out with her, you know. And I never wanted to."

Vera felt a tinge of satisfaction at the news, but what she'd said about it not being her business still applied. "RJ, you can date whoever you want."

He reached for her hand. She looked down at their joined fingers and she was surprised by the urge she had to kiss him.

"I don't want to go out with anybody except you," he said.

She couldn't help it, and she laughed. It was an authentic reaction to her happiness at him saying this.

"If you don't feel the same way, that's all right," he said, misunderstanding what she meant.

"No, that's not it. You just surprised me. I wasn't expecting what you said."

"Oh, okay. Then what is it?"

She started walking, and he came along with her. She took his hand and gaily swung their arms back and forth. Everyone waiting for them saw them.

"Hi, Vera, did you enjoy the hike?" John said grinning.

"Yeah, it was great. Is something funny, Dad?"

"Funny? No."

"I bet he's thinking how cute you and RJ are together," Louisa said.

Everyone laughed, except Vera. "Cut it out, Lou. You're embarrassing us."

"Mom and I were talking," Louisa said, ignoring Vera's complaining. "Do you want to keep hiking a while longer?"

"Yeah, sure, for a while."

"I asked Gwen and Louisa to come over for dinner," John said.

Vera looked at John and then at Gwen. "Can you make it?"

"Yes, we can," Gwen said.

"I invited RJ too. RJ, don't forget to call your mom and ask if you can eat with us."

"I will, John."

"Okay, come on, girls. Let's do this," Gwen said, ushering Vera and Louisa along.

John went up to Gwen and put himself near her without touching her. "See you in a couple of hours or so?"

"Yeah, about that. Bye."

Before Vera left, she put her arms around RJ and kissed him on the mouth. She heard Louisa gasp and say, "Oh, my God."

"Bye, RJ. See you tonight?"

"Yeah, bye," he said dreamily.

Then they parted until later on. Louisa slapped Vera's shoulder jokingly. "You just kissed, RJ. That's historic." Gwen had already started up the trail on their second hike, and they hurried to catch up with her.

"Well, well," John muttered, as he picked up his fly rod and tackle box from the ground.

"What?"

"Nothing."

"Okay."

"Before we head back, RJ, I want to see if I can catch a couple more. That all right?"

"Sounds like you want my help."

"Oh, no, I don't need your help to catch fish. I need you to help me cook them."

"Absolutely. I know a good recipe from my mom for grilled trout."

"Great. I can't wait to try it."

Chapter 19

At dusk that evening, an unidentified flying object appeared on the violet horizon along with the first star. The object dangled there, hidden as a planet in a shimmering halo of light. It blinked every so often, giving off clues to its true nature.

Anyone who happened to be watching eventually saw it rise higher in the sky and drift across the moon in a steady motion. Onlookers might've mistaken it for a satellite or a plane, until they saw it shoot up into the sky in a zigzag, quickly reverse course, and fall back toward the earth. The object halted in midair and righted itself by ninety degrees and floated down, like a magic carpet. Red lights twinkled on the tips of the right and left sides of the craft and then twinkled out.

***

On the way home from the hike, Gwen, Louisa, and Vera had stopped at the grocery store to buy a loaf of bread and vegetables for a salad for dinner. Vera was sitting in the backseat of the car with the bags of groceries, and she smelled the freshly baked bread wafting from the bag, and it made her hungry. She could feel her stomach growling, but the noise was drowned out by the loud crooning of a collective of tree frogs. She wondered how many of them it took to make such a symphony, but it sounded like thousands. They created a vibration like a Buddhist chant that stirred a pleasant feeling from her head to her heart. She wanted to tap Louisa on the shoulder and draw her attention to them, but Louisa was engrossed in listening to music through her headset.

Gwen glanced at Vera in the rearview mirror. "Wow. Those tree frogs," she said.

"I know. They're amazing," Vera said.

Up ahead on the right lay a tiny convenience store that in addition to everything also sold worms and firewood. Gwen put on the blinker and turned into the parking lot.

"I forgot to get beer for your dad," she said getting out of the car. "I'll be right back."

Louisa sat up and looked around. "Why did we stop? Where's my mom?"

"She went in there to get beer."

"We were just at the grocery store."

"She forgot it."

Louisa took off her headset and tossed it on the seat. "Uh, I'm starving. They'll probably eat without us."

"No, they won't."

Louisa swiveled around and threw her arm over the top of the seat. "I can't believe you kissed RJ."

"I can't believe it either."

"I could see it coming. It was inevitable."

"Stop, Louisa."

"What's the matter? Obviously, you like RJ."

"Just don't start making a big deal about it. I'm still not sure what to do."

"Why?" Louisa said. Then she seemed to understand. "Oh, Vera," she said in a voice that was soft and sad, the opposite of her normal effusive one. "Don't be afraid. It's natural to fall in love. They can't stop you. It's your life. You're human."

"It's pointless," Vera said.

"No."

"I never know when they'll take me or what's going to happen to me. I never know if they'll bring me back."

"You always come back, so don't say that."

"There's no way to be sure I will."

"No, I guess not. But lots of people care about you, Vera. And that includes me, of course."

"I know. But it's hard. Here comes your mom."

They stopped talking just before Gwen got back in the car.

Night had fallen. They rode in silence while Vera looked at the stars, but they couldn't hold her attention. She felt anxious. It seemed to be taking forever to get home.

"How are you doing back there?" Gwen asked over her shoulder.

"Fine."

"It was great seeing RJ today. I hadn't seen him in a couple of months. He seems good. Don't you think?"

"Yes," Vera said, smiling to herself in the dark.

"They've always had crushes on each other," Louisa said, pulling off her headset.

"You're exaggerating."

"No, I'm not exaggerating. But you both just had to grow up, Vera."

"What a sensitive observation, honey," Gwen said.

"Well, it's true."

Vera sank her head back against the seat. "We'll see."

"Yeah, we'll see," Louisa said laughing. Suddenly, she leaned forward and pressed her hands on the windshield. "Did you see that?"

"What?" Gwen said.

"I think it was a shooting star. I saw it over there. That's east, isn't it?"

"Yes, that's east."

"I didn't see it. Did you see it?" Gwen said to Vera.

"I saw something."

"Wait, look at that," Louisa said. She rolled down the window and pointed at a glittering streak of light that was moving laterally in the sky, until it stopped in one place and sat there and flashed like a blue globe.

"I see it," Vera said, and she turned her eyes away.

"Was it another shooting star?" Gwen said.

Vera twisted in her seat.

"No, I don't think it's a shooting star," Louisa said.

The mood in the car became hushed. Vera waited. The air felt heavy, and slowly but surely, it was closing in on her, foreboding about what was to come. She closed her eyes and withdrew inside herself. But in her mind's eye, she had a vision of a large oblong craft lingering hundreds of feet above them, and there was no doubt that they were there.

"We're almost home, Vera," Gwen said.

She took a deep breath. It didn't make any difference, because they always knew where to find her. But they were almost home, and she would feel better being there with the people she loved.

A flash of light pierced the dark and blurred the sky. Vera turned and looked out the window, and she saw the object hovering above the river, drenched in its own vicious light, like an erupting star.

Louisa screamed.

Gwen put her foot on the gas, but the object stayed with them. "Oh, God," she cried out.

The car was awash with the light, making it impossible for them to see each other. Louisa slid away from Gwen's side and crept across the seat and stood on her knees and thrust her body out the window up to her waist.

"It's so close," she yelled.

"Louisa, get back in the car," Gwen said.

"I need to see it. It's following us. You, assholes! Leave us alone."

"Louisa!"

"I'm giving them the finger. Get away from us!"

Gwen grabbed her by her shorts and yanked her inside the car. "Stay in your seat."

Vera realized that one of her worst fears had come to life, and Gwen and Louisa were caught up in her ordeal, in the bullseye of an alien abduction. In the front seat, Gwen tried to clutch her daughter tightly.

"Gwen," Vera said too softly for her to hear her, and she repeated herself. "Gwen, stop and let me out, please."

"Stop? Absolutely not."

"You've got to."

"No. You stay in your seat too."

"You have to. I'm putting you and Louisa in danger."

"No, I won't do that, Vera."

Gwen steered the car around a sharp curve, and the object kept pace with them. Then they realized that they couldn't see it anymore.

"Is it gone?" Louisa said.

Vera wouldn't voice her thoughts, but she didn't think it was gone. As the road became straight again, they saw the UFO floating about twenty feet off of the ground. The craft didn't make a sound, and the vicinity around it was silent as stone. Vera felt an expectant presence emitting from it, as if it was waiting for her.

Gwen slammed on the brakes, shifted the car into reverse, and hit the gas. Simultaneously, the dashboard lights flickered and went out and the engine died. The car rolled down a slight incline and halted in the middle of the road in front of the UFO.

Gwen hit the dashboard with her fist. "Where are the other cars? There are always cars on this road."

"We have to hide," Louisa cried hysterically. "We can hide in the woods."

"No, that won't help," Vera said, knowing that escape was impossible and her capture was inevitable. The alien beings were omnipotent. She could only wait for what she knew was coming. As she waited, time had no beginning or ending. Whatever the beings wanted to do with time, they could do—pause, slow, or speed it up at their will to suit their purpose. "It's over."

Gwen grasped for Vera's hand and gathered Louisa against her.

As she clung to them, Vera said goodbye to them in her mind, and she prayed for courage to break away and go willingly, so that her friends wouldn't be in harm's way. She thought about how Gwen was like a mother to her. Louisa wasn't just her best friend, but like a sister to her.

She put her hand on the door handle, not only to save her friends, but because she was being drawn to the craft, like a moth to a flame.

"No, Vera," Louisa cried.

"I don't have a choice, Louisa. It's the way things are."

"Don't open that door, Vera," Gwen shouted.

"Look, they're coming," Vera said.

Four thin impish figures came out of the light and approached the car.

Vera began to cry. "I love you. Tell my dad he shouldn't worry. They always bring me back."

She got out and ran toward the light and rushed into the middle of it. The four spindly little men swarmed around her, and then she was gone.

Chapter 20

John and RJ waited at the house for Gwen, Vera, and Louisa. As time went on, John found it difficult to suppress his growing concern.

"Why are they taking so long?" RJ said.

"They had to stop at the store," John said. "But they should be here any minute. Why don't you put the fish on to cook."

RJ dropped the trout on the grill, and a circle of smoke and steam encircled them as they sizzled. When they were cooked on one side, he came back and flipped them over.

"They smell so good," John said.

Where are they? What's keeping them? he wondered. Every time he heard a car, he turned to see if it was them coming down the road, and he tried to will it to be. He imagined Vera coming home any second now and gracefully walking toward him with that light-footed gait of hers.

Twenty minutes later, the fish were done, but Gwen, Vera, and Louisa weren't back yet, and John's thoughts about what could've happened to them were increasingly morbid.

RJ stood close by, swaying slightly back and forth on the balls of his feet. They hadn't spoken about it, but John knew he was worried.

"Nobody's answering their phones. What should we do?" RJ said.

John pulled his keys out of his pocket. "We have to find them. Keep trying to call."

They ran to the truck, threw open the doors, and leaped in.

Through a corner of the windshield, John saw a vivid multicolored light above the horizon. "Look at that," he said.

"I see it. What the heck is it?"

"I don't know."

In a rush, John forgot to see if there was a car coming before he turned out of the driveway.

"Jesus Christ," he said, as he slammed on the brakes, barely avoiding an accident.

The driver of the other vehicle yelled at him and then gunned the engine and drove away. John took off fast down the road, and they watched for the object as they drove. They finally saw it again, and it was changing from a cylinder to a crescent to a circle to a flat line. The thought crossed John's mind that it was only an optical illusion on the windshield and that all of this was just another nightmare, even though every cell in his body told him that the object was real, and he knew what it meant.

No more lying to myself, he thought. For many months, he'd fooled himself into believing that Vera's abductions had ended with the last one, and clearly, he'd been wrong. *Where are you, Vera? Tell me so I can save you.*

Then he saw a large white orb, about thirty feet in diameter, appear below the craft. It crossed above the truck. By the way it was flying, it looked like it was tethered to the craft by an invisible wire.

"RJ, look at that."

"I see it."

"We've got to find Vera."

There was another car in front of them, but John couldn't pass it. The driver of the car slammed on the brakes and made a frantic U-turn in the middle of the road and sped away in the other direction from the phenomenal sight.

John and RJ didn't take their eyes off the orb or the craft until they came to a thick bank of trees on a hill that obliterated their view. When they came around the other side of the hill, they saw the craft and the orb again. Seconds later, the orb vanished, as if it'd been sucked into the blackness of space or absorbed into the craft from which it came.

About an eighth of a mile in the distance, they saw Gwen's car. It sat cockeyed in the middle of the road with its headlights pointed at the woods.

"There they are," RJ yelled.

John went faster to get to them.

Gwen's car was badly damaged. The windshield was cracked and bowed inward. There was a series of black indentations across the hood; they were hot to the touch, and they looked like they'd been caused by extreme pressure that'd come down on the car from above.

John got out and opened the driver's door of Gwen's car. He found Gwen and Louisa both unconscious and curled together in a ball with their backs arched toward the roof of the car.

"Gwen," he said.

"Louisa, wake up," RJ said, reaching for her.

Gwen opened her eyes. "John."

"Are you all right? Can you move?"

She looked at him in confusion, her eyes wide with terror. "Vera? Where is she?"

"They took her," Louisa screamed.

"You saw it? You saw it happen?" John said.

"Vera jumped out of the car. We couldn't stop her. She ran into the light, and they took her."

"I'm sorry. Oh, my God, John, I'm sorry," Gwen wailed.

He held her in his arms. "It's not your fault. It's mine. I believed it wasn't ever going to happen again."

Then he let Gwen go and stood up and cupped his hands around his mouth and called Vera's name, over and over in painful mouthfuls. He wore out his voice. He was dripping with sweat.

"John, John, stop, it's no use," Gwen said. She embraced him.

He let his head fall on her shoulder, and he broke down and sobbed. She caressed his hair. Was it the end of the beginning or the beginning of the end? He didn't know.

"We'll get her back," she said.

"Yes," he said.

"We will," she said.

He raised his head and stared into her eyes. She was so beautiful. His love for her was so enormous, but how close he'd come to losing her. He stepped back from her. "Where did it happen?" he said.

She pointed to the place in the road where Vera had been abducted. "There."

"I love you," he told her.

"I love you."

He walked a hundred feet and looked up at the dark sky. In his mind was something that someone wrote a long time ago about reality being a sliding door. He was looking for that door now. But even if he found it, he didn't know how to pass through it to help Vera.

"Vera, do you hear me?" he said. "I love you. I'll be there when you get home." He couldn't take his eyes off the sky. "Please, almighty God, bring her home safe and sound."

***

John's voice reached her, softly but distinctly, on the tail of the cosmic wind.

"I hear you, Dad. I'm here," Vera said.

He asked her if she was afraid.

For his sake, she lied. "No, I'm not afraid. Keep talking to me, Dad. Please. Keep talking until I can't hear you anymore."

He did, and for much longer. But then his voice began to fade in her ears, and eventually, she could no longer hear it, and then, the only sounds that she could hear were the vibrations emanating from space and the aliens' buzz-like voices inside the spacecraft.

She looked down at her planet from space. The earth swelled in front of her eyes. At first, she could see all of Earth's intimate details and massive features: the mountains, trees, and skyscrapers looming over their surrounding areas. Soon, she was seeing it from a vaster, higher distance, and everything that had looked so enormous now looked minuscule. She had a broad view of the oceans and the landmasses, but soon she could only see the glowing curvature of the Earth. The spacecraft flew faster and faster, and the world grew smaller and smaller, and soon, she could no longer see it at all.

Panic descended on her, and she cried out to her captors to let her go, even though it was in vain. It never mattered how unwilling or terrified she was, because nothing ever stopped them. Desperate for comfort, she remembered what John had told her. Hold on to your humanity. Don't forget where you belong

"I will," she promised him.

She looked out at space. Its beauty captivated her. She felt the mystery of it. It pulled at her, like it always did. She didn't want her life to straddle two different realities, but she was, slowly, becoming less certain about where she belonged.

"Vera."

"Dad?"

"Don't forget where your home is."

"No, Dad, I won't ever forget it."

She heard noises behind her, and turned around and saw them. "They're coming for me."

"Vera, what's happening?"

Her last words must be ones to give them both hope. "Don't worry. They've always brought me back, so far."

- End -

Acknowledgments

Writers spend many solitary hours writing their books. But they also need support from other people in order to achieve success. I'd like to thank the following shining stars who, in their own special ways, contributed to my efforts to write and revise this book and to get it published. With your help and encouragement, I became a published novelist.

Thomas Payne. As my faculty adviser, you helped me during the early stages of writing my book. One of the best pieces of advice you gave me was about developing a vivid sense of place. I also appreciated that you were enthusiastic about my story. At one point you said to me, "Somehow, somewhere, someday, it's a publishable book." After that, I became more determined than ever to complete my book. Thank you for helping and encouraging me.

Mark Malatesta. I was thrilled when you took me on as your client, because I knew it meant that you thought that my manuscript was worthy and that I was ready to pursue publication. As my author coach, you taught me what I needed to know about book publishing and pitching to agents and publishers. You made me realize that persistence was the key; you were right, though I never doubted you for a moment.

Patricia Haendler. Thank you for creating a true work of art for the cover of my book. I love how the drawing reflects the atmosphere in the story and how stunningly beautiful it is. Thank you for your dedication to getting it just right. I couldn't be happier with the way the cover art turned out.

Diana Dexter. We've been colleagues and friends for many years, so I already knew what a good editor you were when I asked you to proofread my book. Thank you for going through it so thoroughly and quickly. The changes you made and the revisions you recommended made it much better.

Angela Smith; Cynthia Miller; and Karen Reinauer. Thank you for reading the latest revision of my book and calling out missteps and giving suggestions. Each of you is a talented writer and editor. I love the small, intimate writing group that we've built. I love that we can trust each other to give thoughtful feedback about our work. I love that we nurture each other's craft.

Catherine DeNunzio. You read my book and gave me suggestions for tightening parts of it, and I was able to improve the pacing and flow of the story where it needed it. Also, you let me bounce ideas off of you, which was an enormous help. You and I are family, but our bond of blood is all the more special because we both are writers—you're a poet and I'm a fiction writer.

Eddie Langlois. Your artistic accomplishments are many, both in the visual arts and in the theater. So I felt confident turning to you for help with visualizing the cover art for my book. The paintings and sculptures you create, the plays you direct, and the costumes and sets you design are unique, beautiful, and evocative. You know how to thrill an audience and stir their emotions. There's no one else quite like you. For your inspiration and friendship, thank you. "Mz A."

Finally, I want to express my gratitude to God; my parents Fran and Don Masi; my brothers Chuck, Steve, DJ, and Chris Masi; my husband John Layton; and my aunt Susan DesRochers. Behind all of the good things that happen to me in my life, there is always you.

ROUNDFIRE
BOOKS

FICTION

Put simply, we publish great stories. Whether it's literary or popular, a gentle tale or a pulsating thriller, the connecting theme in all Roundfire fiction titles is that once you pick them up you won't want to put them down.
If you have enjoyed this book, why not tell other readers by posting a review on your preferred book site.

Recent bestsellers from Roundfire are:

The Bookseller's Sonnets
Andi Rosenthal
The Bookseller's Sonnets intertwines three love stories
with a tale of religious identity and mystery spanning
five hundred years and three countries.
Paperback: 978-1-84694-342-3 ebook: 978-184694-626-4

Birds of the Nile
An Egyptian Adventure
N.E. David
Ex-diplomat Michael Blake wanted a quiet birding trip
up the Nile – he wasn't expecting a revolution.
Paperback: 978-1-78279-158-4 ebook: 978-1-78279-157-7

Blood Profit$
The Lithium Conspiracy
J. Victor Tomaszek, James N. Patrick, Sr.
The blood of the many for the profits of the few... *Blood Profit$*
will take you into the cigar-smoke-filled room where American
policy and laws are really made.
Paperback: 978-1-78279-483-7 ebook: 978-1-78279-277-2

The Burden
A Family Saga
N.E. David
Frank will do anything to keep his mother and father
apart. But he's carrying baggage – and it might
just weigh him down ...
Paperback: 978-1-78279-936-8 ebook: 978-1-78279-937-5

The Cause
Roderick Vincent
The second American Revolution will be a
fire lit from an internal spark.
Paperback: 978-1-78279-763-0 ebook: 978-1-78279-762-3

Don't Drink and Fly
The Story of Bernice O'Hanlon: Part One
Cathie Devitt
Bernice is a witch living in Glasgow. She loses her way
in her life and wanders off the beaten track looking for the
garden of enlightenment.
Paperback: 978-1-78279-016-7 ebook: 978-1-78279-015-0

Gag
Melissa Unger
One rainy afternoon in a Brooklyn diner, Peter Howland
punctures an egg with his fork. Repulsed, Peter pushes
the plate away and never eats again.
Paperback: 978-1-78279-564-3 ebook: 978-1-78279-563-6

The Master Yeshua
The Undiscovered Gospel of Joseph
Joyce Luck
Jesus is not who you think he is. The year is 75 CE. Joseph
ben Jude is frail and ailing, but he has a prophecy to fulfil ...
Paperback: 978-1-78279-974-0 ebook: 978-1-78279-975-7

On the Far Side, There's a Boy
Paula Coston

Martine Haslett, a thirty-something 1980s woman, plays hard on the fringes of the London drag club scene until one night which prompts her to sign up to a charity. She writes to a young Sri Lankan boy, with consequences far and long.
Paperback: 978-1-78279-574-2 ebook: 978-1-78279-573-5

Tuareg
Alberto Vazquez-Figueroa

With over 5 million copies sold worldwide, *Tuareg* is a classic adventure story from best-selling author Alberto Vazquez-Figueroa, about honour, revenge and a clash of cultures.
Paperback: 978-1-84694-192-4

Readers of ebooks can buy or view any of these bestsellers by clicking on the live link in the title. Most titles are published in paperback and as an ebook. Paperbacks are available in traditional bookshops. Both print and ebook formats are available online.

Find more titles and sign up to our readers' newsletter at www.collectiveinkbooks.com/fiction